THE UN-FAMILY

THE UN-FAMILY

LINDA HUBER

This edition produced in Great Britain in 2022

by Hobeck Books Limited, Unit 14, Sugnall Business Centre, Sugnall, Stafford, Staffordshire, ST21 6NF

www.hobeck.net

A CIP catalogue for this book is available from the British Library.

ISBN 978-1-913-793-93-7 (pbk)

ISBN 978-1-913-793-92-0 (ebook)

Cover design by Jayne Mapp Design

Printed and bound in Great Britain

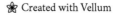 Created with Vellum

PRAISE FOR THE UN-FAMILY

'*The Un-Family* is an utterly compelling psychological suspense. Linda Huber is an expert in the genre and I knew I'd be hooked from page one ... tense, tense, tense and highly recommended.'
Claire Chase

'Read it in one sitting – I could NOT stop reading – I loved it!'
Philippa Evans

'I have read several books by Linda Huber and I really enjoyed them. I knew I wouldn't be disappointed with this one, and I certainly wasn't.'
Sarah Leck

ARE YOU A THRILLER SEEKER?

Hobeck Books is an independent publisher of crime, thrillers and suspense fiction and we have one aim – to bring you the books you want to read.

For more details about our books, our authors and our plans, plus the chance to download free novellas, sign up for our newsletter at **www.hobeck.net**.

You can also find us on Twitter **@hobeckbooks** or on Facebook **www.facebook.com/hobeckbooks10**.

For Matthias and Pascal

PROLOGUE

THE BODY TUMBLED DOWN THE SWOLLEN RIVER, CARRIED BY THE current and the mass of wood and debris freed by Saturday's storm. A head was nowhere to be seen, but one trainer-clad foot kicked ineffectively against a blue plastic drum, and a sleeve was caught in a branch, raising the arm in a grotesque salute to the first streaks of dawn in the east. The only sound was the rush of water as the river crashed along, spilling over its banks in places as it surged through the countryside sweeping up lost or forgotten articles. By the time the sun blinked over the horizon, the body was already several miles downstream.

The teenage boy on the riverbank turned to his companion. 'Did you remember the matches?'

She patted the inside pocket of her rain jacket. 'I've got a lighter. This is flowing pretty fast, though. I don't think we should go out today.'

The boy dropped his end of the double-seater kayak they were carrying and tightened the straps of his rucksack. 'Don't worry, babes – I'll look after you. Ten minutes' ride and we'll be on the island having that champagne brekkie you wanted.' He slung an arm around her, kissing the top of her head when she leaned against him.

Together, they lowered the red-and-yellow kayak into the river, the pull of the current strong even at the bank. The boy's wrists trembled as he held the boat steady while his girlfriend clambered into the front seat, then he dropped into the rear and pushed off from the bank. Seconds later, the river was in full control, whipping the kayak this way and that as it floundered through the turbulence.

The girl's voice rose in panic. 'Shit, no, this is crazy! Back – we have to go back!'

The boy behind her was struggling to keep them upright. 'It won't last. Paddle for the island.'

His words were drowned in the roar of the river as the kayak swung round and shot downstream. The girl shrieked as they fought against the powerful surge, their paddles making no impact in the swirling water.

'It's okay – look, it's carrying us to the island!' The boy leaned perilously to the right to keep the kayak afloat.

The girl's eyes closed as they hurtled into the middle of the river amid the mess of wood and junk being carried downstream. The island – a small, oval-shaped bump of land at the widest point between the banks – swooped up, and the boy tossed his paddle on land to grab hold of a bush. The kayak jerked, then swerved into a bobbing pile of driftwood at the mouth of a tiny inlet.

The boy grabbed another bush and hauled, his expression agonised. 'Pull – you have to help!'

The girl obeyed, seizing branches, straining as hard as she could then letting go to grab the next branch. The kayak inched to safety, grating on rocks below the water. The girl scrambled up and onto dry land.

'Quick, we need to get it right up the beach!'

She grabbed the kayak then glared at the boy, now motionless in the back seat, his face aghast. He was clutching a white, bloodless wrist emerging from a sodden denim sleeve that was caught on a jagged piece of wood floating beside the kayak. The strap of a soaked canvas rucksack was twisted around the lifeless arm, and just underwater, dark hair floated gently around a face with staring eyes.

'It – oh fuck no, it—'

He vomited into the water.

Recognition filled the girl's eyes as she stared at the body. She shrieked again.

PART I
FOR BETTER, FOR WORSE

A few weeks beforehand

CHAPTER 1

MONDAY, 10TH MAY

A CRASH CAME FROM THE KITCHEN BELOW, AND HOLLY JERKED out of the doze she'd fallen into after Dylan sneaked out of bed. She rolled on her side and focussed bleary eyes on the alarm. Half past five – even for Dylan, this was an early start. The tinkle of broken crockery being swept up and dumped in the bin floated up the stairs, and glory, that was his third breakage in four days. They'd have nothing left to put food on if he went on like this. Holly pushed the duvet to the side. She'd get up and say goodbye, then bring a cup of tea back to bed for a snooze. It was her day off; no need to start it before the birds were up.

She joined him in the kitchen end of the living area. 'Okay?'

Dylan didn't look at her. 'Perfectly. The orange mug is no more. Have you seen my grey folder?'

Holly pointed down the room. 'On the sofa. Do you—?'

'Sorry, I don't have time, Holly. We have an early meeting with the new IT person who's starting today, and I have to do the introductory tour and everything. As if I didn't have enough on my plate.' He detached his mobile from the charger and stuffed it into his jacket pocket.

Holly rubbed his back. 'I'll be driving home with you, if that's okay? I'm meeting Valerie for lunch in town.'

'Fine, yes. Text me.' He aimed a kiss at the top of her head, missed, and strode off without a second glance, grabbing his folder on the way. His car engine roared, then faded into the distance. Holly breathed out through pursed lips. He needed to calm down, and an hour-long commute up the A22 to Croydon wasn't the best time to do that.

Fred, Holly's German pointer cross, was sniffing around hopefully, and she spooned smelly dog food into his bowl before making tea and toast. She was wide awake now; no point going back to bed. Thanks, Dyl. On the upside, she had more day to do things in, but the niggle in her head was jabbing harder every day. Dylan's new job wasn't great for either of them. He'd been as nervous as a kitten since the beginning of April and his promotion to distribution manager in the medical supplies company he worked at. It was a huge step up his career ladder and it meant they had a lot more cash to splash; the downside was that it needed every last nerve in her body as well as his to cope with the stress. Was any job worth losing your work-life balance for? To say they didn't have enough free time together was an understatement; Dylan practically lived at work these days. Mind you, her hours were irregular too. It was par for the course when you were a vet.

She stood for a moment gazing out of the kitchen window, where green was the predominant colour no matter which way you looked. East Sussex was a fabulous place to live, with bustling market towns and quaint villages dotted around in a mixture of forest and farmland. Resignation pulled at Holly's gut as she slid her mug into the dishwasher. A fabulous place to live, yes, and the lovely home box was ticked too. She and Dylan had pooled resources and bought the house as an investment not long after they'd met two years ago, then instead of selling it on after the renovation, they'd moved in. Those had been heady days, falling in love and setting up home, but now her job and Dylan's were conspiring against them as a couple and Dylan was showing no signs of acknowledging the problem, never mind trying to fix it. Holly stuck her chin in the air. Women were better at this kind of thing, weren't they? The new job stress couldn't last forever. She would fix their relationship.

———

A MORNING AT THE SHOPS, lunch on the Embankment with her best friend and an afternoon at the Tate Gallery did a lot to make up for the early start, and Holly sat down on the train to Croydon afterwards feeling compensated for her weekend on call. Now to have another go at improving relations with her husband. Surely she'd manage something before they were back in Market Basing.

Dylan's company was in a modern block around fifteen minutes' walk from the station, and as usual, she texted him just before the train pulled in. His answer came promptly: *Meet you at the car. It's in UG2 beside the lift.* Holly pulled a face. Pity... Before his promotion, she'd always gone up to Dylan's office and said hello to the team. He had a different office now, and it would have been nice to meet the new team. Maybe he wasn't in the office this afternoon, of course.

He was waiting by the Audi when she arrived, and Holly went to kiss him. 'Good day after your early start?'

He nodded. 'The new assistant's going to make a difference. You? How was Valerie?'

Holly settled down in the front, slipping her shoes off as he reversed out of the parking space. Ah, that was better. 'She's good. They're going to – oh!'

Something had rolled out from under her seat and brushed

against her foot, and she bent to pick it up. It was a lipstick, in a black-and-gold case bearing the name of one of those brands that charged you a month's rent for a bit of lip colour.

Dylan squinted across, frowning as he negotiated the spiral ramp up to street level. 'Yours?'

'In my dreams.' Holly opened the lipstick. Bright and shiny red lips, hm. Not quite her style, was it? Imagine wearing this to work then having a spaniel slobber all over you... Which led straight to the question: 'Who's been losing lipsticks in your car, Dyl? Do I have a rival for your affections?'

He wasn't looking at her, but while making a joke of it was her automatic reaction, part of Holly was holding her breath for his answer. A grumpy stressed-out husband was one thing, finding a posh lipstick in the love of your life's car was quite another.

He snorted. 'Chance would be a fine thing. When am I supposed to have time to meet anyone else?' He accelerated to beat the lights.

Holly waited until they were past the junction. 'Whose is it, then?'

'Huh? Oh – it must be Emily's. She was taking a load of stuff to the station at lunchtime, and I gave her a lift. Her bag was on the floor there.'

Emily was one of the secretaries. She didn't seem the type to have this lipstick, but then you never knew. Holly blinked unhappily – her fix-our-relationship talk with Dylan hadn't exactly got off to a brilliant start, had it? It was hard to know what to say after this.

Dylan started for her. 'Hey, I was wondering about a holiday this autumn? We'd need to book soon.'

Holly put the lipstick down on the tray between the two front seats. He was making an effort; that was good. Chill, woman. Soon they were batting ideas about autumn holidays back and forth, in between Dylan moaning about the other road-users, and Holly relaxed. You didn't need to have deep and weighty conversations all the time; a nice chat could improve an atmosphere no end too.

Home again, she turned to Dylan as he locked the car. 'Why don't we go to the pub for dinner, as you're home early? We didn't go all weekend.'

'That's because you were working. Nice idea, but I have to prepare for a meeting tomorrow and I don't know how long I'll need. But if you make sure you're not on call next weekend, we'll go then.'

Gee, thanks, Dylan. Holly pulled a face as she followed him back to the house, her moment of optimism fading. Okay, he was tired, and in one way he was right, because she'd spent all Saturday evening with a dalmatian who'd eventually needed a caesarean section. Friday had been down to him, though – he'd been to someone's leaving do at work.

He winked at her. 'I'll leave you to make dinner, shall I? Don't want to annihilate any more crockery.' He jogged upstairs to the study.

Holly took a quiche from the freezer and bunged it into the oven, then fed a clamouring Fred. This boy was due a long walk in the woods after dinner, and Dylan had stopped coming on dog walks when the new job started. Holly made a lettuce salad and laid the table, listening to the murmur of Dylan's voice on the phone upstairs.

Was it really Emily's lipstick?

CHAPTER 2

TUESDAY, 11TH MAY

TUESDAY MORNING, BACK TO THE DAILY GRIND. HOLLY PULLED ON the jeans she wore at the practice and topped them with a red shirt while Fred danced around at her feet, keen to get going. Poor pooch – he didn't know it yet, but he was out of luck today. She was at the surgery from eight until five, which meant he'd be spending the day in the staffroom. It was better for him when she had rounds on the farms and he could come with her, though Holly's own favourite times were the two half days a week she spent at the nearby wildlife centre. As newest vet in the practice, it was her job to help out in the centre when their main vet wasn't around, and her visits there – well, they'd turned into the best bits of the week. Working with wild creatures was definitely the direction she wanted her career to go in. Next job, zoo vet?

She ran downstairs. Dylan had left already, almost as early and grumpy as yesterday. Her mission to improve their relationship was getting off to a sticky start, and to be honest, that lipstick was still rankling. He'd been very quick to start a conversation about holidays afterwards. As a distraction? But no, that was unfair; he had a new job and was stressed and crabby, that was all.

Her phone rang when she was packing her bag for work. Help, surely not an emergency already... Holly dived to answer it, her eyebrows shooting up when she saw 'Megan' on the screen. Dylan's sixteen-year-old niece had lived with her grandmother in nearby Linton Keynes since her mother's death four years ago, and shouldn't she be on her way to school right now?

'Hi, Meg. Everything okay?'

Megan's voice was higher than usual. 'I don't know. I'm worried about Grandma. She's not up yet, and she always gets up before I leave for school. She was a bit dithery yesterday, too. Do you think I should wake her?'

Holly thought quickly. 'Dithery' didn't sound like her mother-in-law. Elaine was seventy-five and very fit, and while there was no reason she shouldn't have a lie in, it did seem odd. She put her heart and soul into taking care of Megan. On the other hand, looking after a teenager could be hard work, and Meg wasn't always all sweetness and light, especially now with GCSE exams looming. Maybe Elaine needed the extra sleep.

'Have you looked in on her? I would knock on her door, stick your head round and say goodbye.'

Steady breathing sounded in Holly's ear while Megan went upstairs, then came a quick knock and, 'I'm off, Grandma. See you after school.'

Elaine's response was almost inaudible, but a moment later Megan was back on the phone.

'She said, 'Lord, have I overslept?' She's getting up, but she sounded a bit woozy, and she's not usually a woozy in the morning person.'

'Well, she's just woken up – but tell you what, I'll give her a call in an hour or so, and if I'm not happy, I'll get Seth to go round.'

Megan sniffed. 'Good luck with that. Thanks, Holly.'

'I'll text you later.' Holly ended the call. Touch wood Elaine was okay, because Megan was right; it wouldn't be easy to get hold of Seth. Dylan's twin brother lived at the other end of Linton Keynes to his mother and Megan, but his job as music events manager at various venues across the county meant evening work, and he was rarely up before lunchtime. He wasn't big on answering his phone, either. Holly tapped to connect to Dylan – she'd better fill him in on what was happening with his mother. He should be prepared, in case Elaine wasn't okay when she called.

The sound of a photocopy machine droned in the background as she spoke, and she pictured Dylan, nodding and frowning as he listened to her. She finished the story and waited. He'd be thinking what was best, now.

'Holly, for God's sake. I'm in the middle of bloody mayhem in this place and I'm trying to catch up with my calls – important, work calls, Holly, and you phone me to say my mother overslept?' His voice was tight.

Holly flinched. 'I think Meg's afraid it's more than that. She said Elaine was dithery yesterday too. We need to make sure she's okay.'

'Meg's a hysterical teenager. And you're making sure, aren't you? It'll be nothing. Job done and thank you, Holly, genuinely, but I don't need a running commentary. I'll see you tonight.'

The connection broke. Holly stared at her phone, then stuffed it into her bag. What was going on with him? Even for a stressed-out business person, that had been harsh. Not to mention unfeeling. Work pressure was one thing; this was something else. How dare he speak to her like that?

———

MEGAN STEPPED out of the front door, then immediately stepped back in again. Gabe was leaving the house next door and no way did she want to walk all the way to school with him. He was always trying to sit as close to her as he could get in the classes they shared at school, and he was a bit over-enthusiastic for first thing in the morning when she was worried about Grandma. Megan heaved her rucksack over one shoulder and set off twenty yards behind him, then grinned at his back. Gabe could be annoying, but it was sort of nice too, to have someone gaping at her with his tongue hanging out – as long as none of her friends noticed, because she'd never hear the end of it if they did. The other kids were mean to Gabe; he got shoved around a lot, and the happy, eager-to-please expression his face was set in most of the time didn't help. He was a sitting duck for mummy's boy comments.

She pulled out her phone at the school gate and switched the sound off before stuffing it into her pocket where she'd notice when it vibrated. They weren't allowed phones on in school, but she had to know the minute Holly texted. Megan's stomach twisted. Please, Grandma, be okay. Because it wasn't just this morning, was it? Grandma'd been – different – a couple of times lately. She'd put her specs in the fridge last week. Seth had visited that day and Megan told him, but he'd only laughed and said that would be down to the sherry. Grandma did like a glass or two in the evening.

Tears pricked in Megan's eyes. Too much booze did you in. When Mum died, Grandma'd said it was the drink that did it. Mum had drunk a lot in the weeks before she died. Three or four bottles of vodka a week were too much – anyone savvy enough to go online and look up units of alcohol would know that in seconds. But Mum hadn't been like other people's mums. She'd been all about being who you wanted to be and fulfilling your destiny, whatever that meant. Mum hadn't wanted a husband but she'd wanted a baby, so Megan's dad had been allowed to swan off after he'd done the deed. He didn't know about her, and as nobody alive even knew who he was, she'd never find him. She'd never had a dad and now she didn't have a mum, and Grandma was old. She'd been forty-five when Dylan and Seth were born. Imagine having twins at forty-five.

Her phone vibrated during French, the second last class that morning, but Megan didn't dare look until the lesson ended. Miss Coulter ended every day with an impressive collection of confiscated phones, which she'd return after school along with some kind of punishment exercise. As soon as she was safely on the way to history, Megan opened her text: *Called Elaine, seems fine. Will come by 5ish today to make double sure. See you then. Xx*

Megan tapped to send a thumbs-up back to Holly and looked round for Susie and Hope, her best friends.

'Put that off, please, Megan.'

Mrs Dawson swept into the history classroom in front of Megan, and she stuffed her phone into her rucksack before sitting down. Mrs Dawson began the lesson, and Megan's eyes glazed as the fall of the Berlin wall washed over her head.

———

THREE O'CLOCK and school was done for the day, hallelujah. Just five more minutes and she'd see for herself that Grandma was okay. Megan rounded the corner into Oak Avenue and there was home, an ordinary semi that Grandma said was Georgian.

Footsteps thudded behind her, and who'd have guessed it, here was Gabe, all bright-eyed as usual, and she really wasn't in the mood.

'Hey, Meg. How about we go back to mine and do the physics homework together?'

Megan hesitated. It was a pretty okay idea, actually. Gabe was good at physics. But not today.

'Grandma's been a bit – not herself. Maybe another time?'

'Cool. Let me – or Mum – know if you guys need anything, huh?'

He gave her a metal-laden grin and loped up his garden path. Megan smiled back. He *was* nice… She turned up her own path, stopping to pick up an empty crisp packet that was caught in a bush at the side. Hadn't Grandma been out today? Megan fumbled the door open and went inside.

'Hello, lovey! Come and let me see you.' Grandma put her library book to the side.

Megan sat listening as Grandma talked about the Third World shop where she volunteered a few times a week. It all sounded so normal. Surely everything was okay?

Holly's car pulled up punctually at five, and Megan ran to the door. Holly was cool, and thank God she'd married Dylan, because the twins were both bleah. All those disgusting old jeans and ancient waistcoats Seth picked up in charity shops, and the way Dylan ruffled her hair when they met. She wasn't six any longer, and oh, why had Mum had to die? Holly was the only one who took her seriously. Holly and Grandma. And Grandma was… different, now.

Holly stopped to look at the rose bushes at the side. 'These could do with a prune. How's Elaine?'

Megan's heart sank all over again. Grandma had forgotten to prune her beloved roses. 'She was fine when I came home from school.'

'Good. We'll have a coffee and a chat, huh?'

Fred made a beeline for the living room, and Megan followed Holly through.

Grandma beamed from her chair. 'Hello, ah, dear. Lovely to see you. And my boy, he's a special boy, isn't he?'

She fussed over Fred, and Megan froze. That little hesitation – had Grandma forgotten Holly's name?

'I'll make coffee.' She vanished into the kitchen, leaving the door open so that she could hear Holly and Grandma. And come to think of it, Grandma was usually the one jumping up to make refreshments for guests. Why wasn't she today?

Holly talked about holidays while they were having coffee, and Grandma kept up her end of the conversation all right, even getting the chancellor of the exchequer's name right, but Holly's face was more thoughtful than Megan could remember seeing it.

Eventually, Holly put down her mug and smiled at Elaine. 'Can I borrow Megan for half an hour? I'd like to show her a new coffee shop in the village before it closes. They sell local craftwork too, and they have really funky earrings. Fred can stay with you, can't he?'

Grandma had barely touched her coffee. 'Of course, dear. I'll see you both later.'

Megan grabbed her jacket. Gabe was leaving the house with his skateboard as they got into the car, and he gave her a wide grin and almost waved one arm off. Megan rolled her eyes.

Holly gave her a nudge. 'One of your many admirers?'

'He's totes wet.'

Holly stuck the key into the ignition. 'He'll grow out of it. He looks like a nice kid.'

'He's okay. What did you think about Grandma?'

They were round the corner now, and Holly pulled over and faced Megan.

'It's hard to say. She didn't quite get my name, and her tone of voice wasn't what it usually is, did you notice? I don't know enough about it, Megs. She's nearly seventy-six – possibly you're allowed the odd foggy moment at that age. Let's see what Dylan and Seth think, and take it from there.'

Megan blinked hard to keep the tears in. Grandma was changing, wasn't she? 'Okay.'

Holly started the engine again and drove on to the village. 'People get older, but that's normal. We'll cope. Let's get you some earrings now, huh?'

Megan twisted her hands together. New earrings were no consolation when you were worried sick.

CHAPTER 3

WEDNESDAY, 12TH MAY

MEGAN STUFFED HER FRENCH BOOK INTO HER RUCKSACK AND headed for the door, ignoring the buzz of chatter around her. Time to go home, and was she glad or was she glad? Nothing was good about school this term; all they heard was exams this and exams that, all the bloody time. Who'd be sixteen? The sooner she got through school and was out earning her own living, the happier she'd be, but it would be years still before she was independent. Two more years at school, and then uni – would she still be at Grandma's all that time? It was crap when you had to worry about what would happen next in your life. She turned out of the school gate and set off downhill.

'Megan! Wait!' The voice came from behind.

Gabe. Megan shoved her hands into her denim jacket and marched on.

He trotted up and dropped into step beside her. 'Got much homework tonight?'

'Tons. I need to get my head down.' Megan sniffed. And it

wasn't even anything he could help her with. The physics she'd done alone yesterday evening had been a disaster.

'Pity. I thought we could go to the skateboard park – you know, by the river. I've got a new board, and it's ace.'

Megan screwed up her face. The skateboard park was new, and she'd hung out there last Saturday with Susie and Hope. Some of those boarders were cool, but – go there with Gabe? He shot her a sudden grin and wow, something was different.

'You've got your braces off!'

He nodded energetically, his face all pink, but he didn't look half bad without all those wires on his teeth.

Megan compromised. She really did have a ton of homework and it was history, so it would take her hours. 'How about another time?'

'Sure. How about kayaking, too? They're starting a kayak course at the sports centre soon.'

He might be okay, but kayaking was pushing it. Megan gave him half a smile as they approached home. 'I'll think about it.'

Gabe gave her another brace-free grin and turned into his garden. Megan walked on up the path next door, pulling her key from her inside pocket.

'Here she is! Come and have some cake, lovey!'

Grandma sounded chirpy, anyway. Megan flung her jacket on the stair post, then stuck her head into the living room. Grandma was sitting with a crumby plate, and a large chunk of Victoria sponge was waiting on the coffee table.

Megan plumped down on the sofa. 'Yum. Did you go to the bakery?'

'Seth brought it for afternoon tea. You've just missed him.'

Megan forked up some cake. Seth and afternoon tea weren't usually mentioned in the same sentence unless it was someone's birthday. Maybe Holly had said something to him about Grandma?

'What was he saying, then?'

'We were looking at your mum's bird book.' Grandma smiled her kind smile, and the cake-induced blink of sunshine in Megan's afternoon vanished. All those lines around Grandma's eyes... nobody could stop time, and Grandma was nearly sixty years older than she was. *Sixty years.* Megan almost choked on sponge cake and suppressed tears.

Grandma jumped up. 'I'll make you a coffee, shall I?'

She scurried into the kitchen, and Megan lifted the bird book on the coffee table. What happened after Mum died was enough to make her want to puke, even after all this time. Before the booze turned everything wonky, Mum had been a photographer. She'd started off with babies and weddings, but when Megan was five, she compiled a book of bird pics and had it published. *Birds in British Gardens* was a huge hit, so Mum went on doing nature books. Next was *On the Edge of the Ocean*, with wildlife pics in the Hebrides in Scotland, then another four from places all over the country and even one from France. There'd been a TV series too, and it had all brought in a shed-load of money so Mum made a will, leaving most of it in trust for Megan, but quite a lot to Grandma, too, for her old age. But when Mum died, Grandma'd gone and given her share to the bloody twins instead of saving it for when she was properly old, like Mum would have wanted. And the worst part of all now was watching Seth splashing Mum and Grandma's money on stupid concerts, and poncy Dylan getting posh clothes to swan around in, and they'd both bought a house as well, and it was all so crap, this uncertainty about Grandma, and – what was Grandma doing, actually? She'd had time to make six coffees now.

'You okay, Grandma?'

'Coming, lovey!'

A long pause, then the sound of the coffee machine droned

through from the kitchen. Megan cuddled Mum's bird book to her chest.

———

HOLLY COLLAPSED into her car at the end of her last farm visit. Spending the afternoon on the farms had kept Fred happy, though after half an hour with her arm up the back end of a poorly cow she was in dire need of a shower, and she wanted to have it before Dylan arrived. He'd spent yesterday evening – the little she'd seen of him, as he was late home – alternately snapping and silent. She'd suggested he visited his mother to form his own opinion about her state of mind, and he'd said he would, but he hadn't wanted to discuss it. Had he told Seth? Holly swallowed. This drifting apart was terrifying. She had to change that, and today was as good a time as any to make yet another attempt. Go home, Holly.

The Audi was hogging the carport when she turned into their driveway. So much for an early shower, then. Monday's journey home flashed into her head, and she peered into the Audi as she went past. The tray where she'd left the black-and-gold lipstick was empty, so Dyl had obviously dealt with it.

He was in the kitchen, emptying a bag of supermarket carrot salad into a bowl. Wonders would never cease; he was making dinner. He gave her a brief grin before wrinkling his nose.

'You stink.'

Holly gave him a careful peck on the cheek. Arriving home less than aromatic was a hazard of the profession for a vet.

He pushed her away. 'For God's sake, Hol – what was it this time, elephant poo?'

'Cow, and stop exaggerating. It's not that bad.'

He banged the carrot salad into the fridge and lifted a cucumber. 'It's worse. Go and shower. Seth's coming for grub to talk about Mum. He had coffee with her this afternoon.'

So he *had* told his brother about Megan's worried phone call. 'What does he think?'

'He thinks she's okay for her age.'

Holly sniffed, and left him slicing cucumber. Upstairs, a quick shower, a slosh of makeup and some perfume, and Holly the mucky farm vet was transformed into Holly the wife and hostess. She ran back down and began to lay the table. 'Did work go well today?' It must have done for him to be home so early.

He put a tub of spaghetti sauce into the microwave to defrost. 'Yeah, the new assistant's working out really well – her IT skills are amazing. You wouldn't believe the difference a few tweaks to the system have made already. Laura says we have to...'

He gushed on, not looking at her, and Holly blinked as Laura this and Laura that filled her ears. Brilliant. First he barely talked to her for weeks, now he was raving about another woman. Still, if this Laura had made his job easier after just three days in the company, more power to her elbow.

'Good she's so much help. Is she to be permanent?'

'No, she's with us for a couple of weeks to get things set up, then she'll be off again. I'm thinking we should have her here for dinner soon, as a thank you for all her work. I feel she has to help me more than the others as I'm so new to the managerial side. How about Friday?'

'Can we make it Saturday? I have surgery hours on Friday afternoon, and I'm not sure when I'll get home.'

A frown darkened Dylan's face. 'Laura's away at the week-end. We can make pizza or something – no need to have anything posh.'

Holly sighed inwardly. He'd invited the woman already, hadn't he? Rushing away to host a dinner party wasn't the best look when you were dealing with someone's much loved pet, but she'd do her best. 'Okay, Friday it is. But you're pizza chef, okay?'

'No problem. I'll get Seth to come and make up a foursome – Laura's single at the moment.'

Holly blinked. 'Seth?' That was unexpected. The brothers weren't what you'd call particularly close, and now they were having Seth to dinner twice in three days.

Dylan winked at her. 'I may have an ulterior motive. Laura's worried because she doesn't have anything else lined up when she finishes with us, and I know Seth's looking for someone to help with his everlasting concerts website. Win-win. Laura says...'

And off he went again. It wasn't clear if Laura was the main beneficiary here, or Seth, but – did it matter?

The doorbell ringing brought Dylan's rhapsody to an end, and Holly went to the door. Seth was his usual flamboyant self, wearing a purple velvet shirt and ancient bell-bottom jeans. He pecked Holly's cheek.

'How's things?'

'Oh, fine.' Holly hung up his jacket.

He raised an eyebrow. 'Sounds like there's a "but" in there?'

He was good at noticing people's moods. Holly dropped her voice. 'Just Dylan's work. He gets so stressed and grumpy, and it worries me.'

Seth gave her arm a little shake. 'Everyone gets stressed when they start a new job. Just be your usual understanding self for a bit, and give him time.'

Holly led the way into the kitchen. He could be right; maybe she should look at it more from Dylan's point of view. She took her place at the table as Dylan handed his brother a beer. It was always fascinating, watching the twins interact. Only their faces revealed the relationship between them – the same fair skin with a dusting of freckles over identical snub noses, same high cheek bones and brown eyes. But that was where the resemblance ended; Dylan's mop of dark blond hair was well cared for and shining; Seth did wash his, true, but he chopped chunks off as the notion took him and he rarely brushed it. The result was a not unattractive leonine look. Dylan liked designer stuff – tonight it was khaki chinos and a crisp black shirt – while Seth was what his mother described as 'a hippy in the wrong generation'. Managing concerts and so on was the perfect job for him.

She smiled at him across the table as Dylan handed out plates of spaghetti.

'What did you think about Elaine, Seth?'

He twirled his fork. 'To be honest, I didn't see much wrong. She was a bit hazy on Meg's GCSEs, but that's complicated stuff, and she was happy enough otherwise. I think Meg's seeing a disaster where there isn't one. Mum's always been fit and healthy.'

Dylan was nodding silently, and Holly grasped her courage with both hands. Neither of these two had any kind of medical training and she wasn't going to let them brush Megan's fears under the table.

She fixed her eyes on Seth. 'I wondered if she was a bit too bright? And sleeping in was unusual for her, too.'

He took a slug of beer. 'Don't you think that might be sherry-related? She'd have been sleeping off Monday night's indulgences.'

Holly frowned. Too much booze could be dangerous too. 'We shouldn't assume anything. Let's keep a close eye on her for a week or two, and then decide.'

Seth went back to his spaghetti. 'She'll be absolutely fine, you'll see.'

Holly squinted at Dylan. His good mood was gone; he was scowling as he ate, making no attempt to join the conversation. Seth started talking about the mini-festival he was arranging in Brighton the following weekend, and still Dylan hadn't said anything about Elaine. Frustration rose in Holly. It was his mother, for God's sake, and he'd been the one who'd invited Seth over to talk about it. You'd think it was at least worth a comment from Dylan, but apparently not.

Seth didn't stay long after the meal was over. 'Chill, bro,' he said in a phony American accent as he slapped Dylan's shoulder on the way out. 'It might never happen. You need more fun in your life. Doesn't he, Hol?'

Holly gave him a strained smile and stood waving as he reversed his dirty white van into the lane. Dylan was back in the kitchen, flinging plates into the dishwasher.

Holly lifted a cloth to wipe the table. 'You reckon he's right about your mum? He could be, of course—'

Dylan turned on her. 'He has no bloody idea, and neither do you. I have some overtime due, so I'll visit Mum on Friday afternoon and see for myself how she is. Now for God's sake stop going on about it.'

Holly flung the cloth down on the table and stamped out of the kitchen. Who the hell did he think he was, talking to her like that? She stood for a second in the hallway, taking deep breaths and trying to think what to do. Yelling back at him in that mood would get them nowhere, but, oh, it was tempting.

She was still weighing this up when a strangled gasp came from Dylan, immediately followed by the sound of running water. Holly turned and squinted into the kitchen.

He was standing by the sink. Appalled, Holly watched as he thumped both fists down on the work surface. And again, then his body bent until his head was almost touching the counter-top. She couldn't see his face, but his entire posture was one of anguish. Then he jerked upright, seized a glass and smashed it down on the floor.

Holly leapt back out of sight. Dear God – what was going on with him? This wasn't the man she'd married.

'Dylan?'

'It's nothing. Dropped a glass, that's all.'

Her heart thudding, Holly went on upstairs for a think. Whatever that had been, it hadn't been nothing. Obviously, she still didn't know the full story about his job issues. And what he'd said about Seth… 'He has no bloody idea.' About their own mother?

There was something about the brothers' relationship she just wasn't getting.

CHAPTER 4

DYLAN AND SETH: THE BABY DAYS

ELAINE STARED DOWN AT THE SLEEPING TODDLERS. HAVING TWINS at forty-five hadn't been her best move. Not that they'd been planned; she'd thought she was going through an early menopause when her periods stopped and exhaustion set in. That happened to more people than you'd think, according to her doctor as he sent her off to produce a urine sample 'to rule out' a pregnancy. According to her older sister, Dylan and Seth were 'a gift of God', but then Angela wasn't the one who had to get up ten times every night to deal with an unsettled baby. According to Bob, a bigger family would be the best thing ever. He'd been disappointed when no more kids arrived after Bryony, so when the twins were born and he got two sons in one go, well, he'd been over the moon – at first. Until the babies came home from hospital, Dylan at three weeks and Seth at ten weeks, and family life disintegrated into chaos that was still ongoing. Coping with a daughter about to hit puberty and now the boys meant that crippling tiredness had become a perma-nent feature in Elaine's life, and Bob was a rare sighting these days. He didn't get home from work until the twins were in bed, and as for her own career, she could forget that. Top secretaries didn't have bags under their eyes all the way down to their ankles. Why couldn't she be like those mums on the telly, juggling babies and housework and high-powered careers? Answer: she was twenty years too old for this game.

Holding her breath, Elaine stepped away from Dylan's cot, taking care to avoid the squeaky floorboard. The twins were well over two now, and their lunchtime naps were becoming ever shorter. Getting both of them off to sleep at once was a rare and major achievement; she should make the most of it. Holding her breath, she tiptoed from the room.

Downstairs, she sank into the armchair beside the wood-burning stove. They rarely used it now; even with a guard, the stove was dangerous. Seth was into everything these days, and Dylan would be too when he was steadier on his feet. Dylan had been a bum-shuffler; walking wasn't his thing. She'd taken him to the doctor eventually, but Dr Greyson only laughed.

'Don't forget they were born nine weeks early. And kids who bum-shuffle have their hands free quickly to play, and the rate he shuffles at, he gains time. Don't make things too easy for him. Have the interesting toys on the sofa, or somewhere he'll have to stand up to get at them. He'll soon get the idea.'

Elaine pulled a face at the memory. Dylan had soon got the idea, true, but having toys placed out of reach was the start of the terrible twos and the screaming temper tantrums for Dylan, and learning to walk – more or less – hadn't changed that. He still tended to crash from one item of furniture to the next, protesting loudly at each bump, and he had a voice that went right through your head.

A whimper came from above, and Elaine froze. There he was, bang on cue, but please, not yet. Let her have half an hour more with her feet up and no hot and sticky little hands pulling at her and demanding this and that.

Blessed silence descended again, and Elaine let her breath out slowly. If only they could put the boys in separate bedrooms. More often than not, poor Seth was rudely awakened by a shriek from his brother. It had been a real nightmare when they were babies, because the breathing problems that plagued Seth for months after his birth meant he needed more cuddles and attention, and more sleep, too. She'd never forget that heart-rending little catch in his breath as panic took hold of him – and of her. Oxygen cylinders had been a big part of life when Seth came home, but all that was over, thankfully, and at least the poor baby'd had something concrete to cry about. Dylan just grizzled in sympathy most of the time, and that was harder to bear, especially with Bob working all the hours God sent to afford them all and then relaxing at The Fox and Hounds before he came home. She had to deal with everything at home, and the only help available was Bryony, who was at school all day. Bry was good with Dylan when she was here, mind; she only had to say 'Smile, Dyly-Dyly', and he would. It had never worked for Elaine. She was just so damned tired all the time.

Okay. She'd had her hour's peace; it was time to lift them, or she'd never get them down tonight. Elaine pulled herself to her feet and trailed across the room. An hour and a half to get through before Bryony was home.

Upstairs, she peeked into the nursery, her heart melting in spite of the tiredness. Seth was awake, lying there waving his frog with the googly eyes in the air and babbling away. A huge beam spread over his face when he caught sight of her, then he scrambled to his feet and shook the cot bars.

'Want juice!'

Elaine gathered him up and kissed him, then set him down while she shook Dylan's shoulder gently. He whimpered, then opened his eyes and whimpered again. Elaine grabbed the dummy he'd lost in his sleep and jammed it into his mouth before depositing him beside his brother.

'Juice and biscuits, then we'll go and feed the ducks before it's time to meet Bryony after school. Come on!'

For a wonder, they got downstairs without a tantrum from Dylan, and Elaine set out juice mugs and custard creams. As usual, Seth insisted on sitting on her knee while he ate, and today, Dylan was happy enough to sit and eat. Biscuits didn't always work, but this was a good day.

Meeting Bryony from school was the daily ritual; they went even when it was raining, and fortunately, Bryony didn't mind being met. None of her friends had baby twin siblings, and all the girls thought the twins were 'gorgeous'.

Elaine waited by the gates as usual. The bell rang, and kids began to trickle out. Dylan saw Bryony first and screamed his delight. Elaine winced. Why couldn't the wretched child greet people normally? It was always either an ear-piercing shriek of joy or a howl of horror with him. She wiped her face with a shaking hand.

'You look tired. Are they still up at night?' Julia, a woman she knew from church, stopped beside her.

Elaine shrugged. 'Seth usually sleeps through, but Dylan shouts a lot in his sleep, so I wake up even when he doesn't.'

'Must be hard with two of them.'

Julia didn't add 'at your age', but the thought was there in the other woman's eyes, wasn't it? Elaine gave her a quick smile, then handed the twin buggy over to Bryony to push home and walked along listening to an account of her daughter's life since quarter to nine that morning. Thank God for Bry. Back home, Elaine settled the three children and a box of building bricks in the living room, then closed the kitchen door behind her and rootled in the cupboard under the sink for the sherry. Another hour or so and it would be time for a glass. She left the bottle and a glass ready beside the coffee machine on the worktop. Her daily treat, and just thinking about it helped.

A scream from the living room had her running from the

kitchen. That had been Seth. He held up a podgy hand when she went in, and my God – she could see the bite mark from the doorway.

'Dylan bit him, Mummy, but it was kind of Seth's fault too because he was taking all the bricks away from Dyl.' Bryony's expression was anguished.

Elaine scooped Seth up and kissed his hand. The skin wasn't broken, thankfully, but there would be a bruise. Bob wasn't going to be pleased. Elaine closed her eyes and rocked Seth, who was whimpering pitifully, his head tucked under her chin. Dylan, meanwhile, was chuckling away – he had the bloody bricks all to himself now. Infuriated, Elaine passed Seth to Bryony and swiped the bricks into their box, Dylan's chuckles turning to a shriek that rang round the whole house before he shuffled over to Bryony and held out a hand to his brother. Seth pushed it away. More shrieks, and Elaine closed her eyes. Dear God. She was so, so tired, and it would be years before the boys were anything like civilised. How was she going to get through it?

CHAPTER 5

FRIDAY, 14TH MAY

FRIDAY AFTERNOON SURGERY RAN LATE, AS SHE'D KNOWN IT would. There was something about an approaching weekend that sent people to the vet in droves, 'just to have it checked' before it was emergencies only for the weekend. Holly pulled into the driveway at twenty past six. Dylan was home already, presumably preparing for the pizza party, and hopefully he wasn't going to be crabby about the lack of a kitchen assistant. He'd apologised briefly for his outburst on Wednesday when she went back downstairs, then went on to talk again about holidays, which seemed to be his change-the-subject topic now. Holly decided to leave things there until the weekend when they'd have more time. But – it was getting harder and harder to reconcile the Dylan in front of her now with the man she'd fallen in love with, and she wasn't going to stand for being spoken to like that. And what the glass-smashing episode had been about, she had no idea. A constructive talk was a dire necessity.

She dropped her bag by the stairs and hurried into the

kitchen, where Dylan had two trays of pizza ready for the oven. One was tuna and olives, the other ham and peppers, and he'd got the good mozzarella from the deli, too, great. Dylan's pizzas were legendary, though it was a while since he'd made one.

He turned to lean back on the work surface. 'I visited Mum earlier and she was absolutely fine. We can stop worrying and relax now, huh?'

Meg had said Elaine was fine yesterday, too. Holly poured a glass of water and sipped. Maybe she'd overreacted about that. 'I guess you guys know her best. What time did you tell Laura and Seth?'

'Seven o'clock. Plenty of time for your shower.' He wrinkled his nose at her and stepped away. 'Don't tell me – piglet poo?'

Holly laughed. 'You're way out. Nothing but poorly cats and dogs all afternoon. Oh, and a hamster.' She ran upstairs. This was better – Dylan back to something like his old self, a nice dinner coming up, and she had tomorrow off, too.

Their guests arrived simultaneously at seven. Two car doors slammed, then the sound of voices on the drive floated in through the open window. Dylan rushed down the hall and flung the front door open.

'Come in, you two! Laura, you seem to have met Seth, and this is my wife, Holly.'

Holly had to fight to keep her jaw from falling open. Standing with Seth on the doorstep was one of the most glamorous females she'd ever seen, and certainly the most glamorous she'd ever invited to dinner. Laura was a tall, leggy blonde with a mass of hair arranged in one of those elaborately casual styles that took you half an hour and a ton of hair gel to create. Her bright red dress hugged a figure to die for, and shiny black stilettoes and perfect make up completed the model girl look. Holly smoothed her blue top over her wide linen trousers and swallowed. It was hard not to feel a tad inadequate. She grabbed Fred before he launched himself at their guests, then submitted to a double and fragrant air kiss from Laura and a pat on the shoulder from Seth. He was looking pretty swish too, in clean black trousers with a black satin waistcoat over a Poldark-style white shirt, though his hair was the usual messy lion's mane. Which was also pretty Poldark, when you thought about it. He presented her with a large bunch of gorgeous pink-and-yellow freesias, and Holly sniffed them. Wow. Seth's contribution to dinner was usually a few bottles of beer. Maybe his and Dylan's thirtieth last year had been a wake-up call that he should be more grown up. She kissed him, suppressing a smile. No, Seth was your original perpetual teenager.

Laura's voice was deep and husky, exactly what you'd expect from someone who looked like she'd just jetted in from somewhere exclusive.

'Good to meet you, Holly. And Seth too, of course.'

Dylan ushered them all into the living area, where Seth flopped down on the sofa while Laura took the armchair by the window. She pulled a small, flat parcel wrapped in blue tissue paper from her handbag and handed it to Holly, a faint smile pulling at her shiny red mouth. 'I thought you might like this. My brother paints. He does illustrations for children's books and magazine stories.'

Holly opened the parcel and found a little painting in a simple wooden frame – a sprig of vibrant green holly leaves, complete with glossy red berries on a snowy-white background.

'How lovely, thank you! He's very talented, isn't he?'

Laura smiled at the painting. 'He's one of those lucky people who can live from their hobby. He holes up for weeks on end in a cottage on the east coast and paints, then comes back to civilisation and sells them all.'

Dylan produced glasses and a bottle of prosecco. Holly listened as he chatted – he really was the perfect host. Efficient, too. In less than ten minutes he had Laura and Seth deep in discussion about Seth's business website and how it could be improved. He watched them for a moment, then caught Holly's eye and jerked his head to the kitchen. She followed him over.

'We can leave them to discuss it while we get the grub ready,' he murmured, his back turned to the other two. 'I'll stick the pizzas in the oven if you do the salad dressings, huh?'

Holly opened the fridge, where bowls of carrot, cucumber, and lettuce salad were waiting. Dylan had been busy.

The pizza was spectacular, and Laura kept them all in stiches while they ate, telling them about her crazy family in Wales. Seth matched the story with one about his and Dylan's Aunt Angela and the time she'd fallen into the river when she'd been on a summer visit one year.

'Good job it didn't happen this year.' Laura put down her glass and sat back. 'I drove beside that river for a while on the way here – it looked pretty full.'

Holly stood up. 'It is, though not half as full as it was a couple of weeks ago. It goes up and down a lot at this time of year.' She took the empty plates through to the kitchen, and heated chocolate sauce to drizzle over the vanilla ice cream. Dylan refilled everyone's glass then replaced the bottle in the wine fridge and stood beside her, his eyes flicking from the dessert to Laura and Seth at the table. The pair were in earnest conversation about the benefits of different ways to advertise, and a tiny frown had gathered between Dylan's eyes.

Holly squinted at him. What was wrong now? Tension was streaming out of him, though it was hard to see why. This was what he'd wanted – a thank-you dinner for Laura, and for her to organise help for Seth.

Laura's low laugh rang out, and Dylan breathed out loudly through his nose. He seized two plates and strode down the room.

'Pud coming up. Sounds like you're getting some good tips for your business, Seth!'

Seth beamed. 'I can certainly use them.'

Laura leaned over and patted his arm. 'We'll set up an advice session, if you like? No pressure to go with it unless you're confident it'll help, but most people find a more efficient set-up can swell the profits no end.'

Seth lifted his spoon. 'I would like.'

Dylan cleared his throat. 'Remember the ice cream we used to have as kids, Seth? At Brighton?'

The conversation was back to holidays, and to Holly's relief, Dylan's good mood returned. Though now that she was watching him, there was something a touch artificial about him tonight, as if he was acting out a part. The part of a happily married man? Oh, dear...

It was after eleven when Seth and Laura left. Dylan closed the front door after waving them off, and went straight to the stairs.

'I have some stuff I need to do for work while it's still reasonably fresh in my head.' He ran up without waiting for an answer.

At this time on Friday night? Stung, Holly took Fred out to the garden. Okay. Exploding at him tonight wasn't a good idea when she had the whole weekend to try something more constructive, like brainstorming how to get their marriage back on track. Some kind of date night every week? The anniversary of their first date was coming up on Tuesday; the ideal opportunity for a night out. Yes... She wouldn't make it a surprise because that might not go down well with Dylan, but a meal out together was a really good idea.

———

SHE STARTED the date-night plan the next morning. There was a limit to what you could organise for a Tuesday anniversary when you both had time-consuming jobs, but it didn't need to be anything elaborate. Holly booked a table at the Koh-i-noor in

Market Basing – yum, she could taste the pakora already. Another advantage of this place was that it was close enough to walk to, so they could both have a glass or two of wine.

Dylan gave her an odd look when she told him. 'Our first wedding anniversary's in a couple of weeks. That's a more sensible kind of thing to celebrate. Why not wait until then?'

'I thought it would be nice to do something together now, that's all. We haven't had much time for each other recently, and I miss that. We don't need to stay late.'

He tapped on his phone, chewing his top lip. 'Okay. Tuesday should be all right.'

Sorted, though he'd missed out the 'thanks, darling, what a great idea' bit. But it didn't matter. Baby steps.

The rest of the weekend went well, even if Dylan did shut himself into the study to work for a couple of hours on both days. Somehow, though, he managed to wiggle out of the constructive talk Holly wanted, but they'd visited Elaine, who seemed perfectly all right, and Holly had helped Megan with her maths. The poor kid was pathetically grateful, and Holly could sympathise. GCSEs were her worst school memories too.

She made sure she was home on time on Tuesday, and had a long shower with the posh shower gel her mother had given her at Easter. When she emerged from the bathroom it was half past six and still no Dylan; what a good job she'd booked for seven-thirty. She was standing at the mirror applying eyeshadow when her phone vibrated beside her. Holly's arm jerked, and dusky green smeared in entirely the wrong direction. Oh, no. It was Dylan – a message, and something was telling her she wasn't going to like it.

Sorry, Hol, panic++ here about new contract, not going to make tonight. Have cancelled restaurant. Holly sagged, frustration mingling with anger in her gut. What a bum he was. And somehow, the fact that he'd cancelled the restaurant before telling her was even more infuriating. She stared at her reflection, then grabbed a wipe and got rid of the green smear. Talk about all dressed up and nowhere to go... Well, she could visit Elaine and Meg and do some more maths. No point wasting all this make up on watching TV with Fred, was there? She collected her car key, whistled for Fred and left.

Elaine was home alone. 'Come in, Holly, dear. Megan's at Susie's – they're studying for the French exam.'

Holly made a mental note to buy Megan a good luck card. GCSEs were tough. Elaine made coffee, and Holly set out mugs while she explained about the non-celebration.

'Oh, what a pity. I hope you can go another time soon.'

'Me too. This new job of Dylan's is so constricting.'

Elaine stared into her mug. 'Yes... and he can be ruthless about things like that.'

'Ruthless' seemed an odd choice of words. Holly made an enquiring sound in her throat.

Elaine's eyes were still unfocussed. 'Dylan's always been a hard worker, right from when they started school. Seth was cleverer back then, but he didn't care enough to work hard. Dylan cared too much.'

That was an interesting thought. Elaine went on talking about the twins' childhood, and a somehow poignant picture of one little boy working his socks off while the other did little and had the better marks and all the kudos slid into Holly's head. Poor Dyl.

Elaine put down her mug. 'Of course, that changed when they were older. Seth left school as soon as he could, and Dylan was the one who ended up with the A Levels. Dylan always knew what he wanted, and he went for it.'

She went on to talk about Bryony, and Holly drove home an hour later wondering if the visit had cheered either of them up or not. But family stories like these were part of who Dylan was, so it was good to hear them.

It was almost eleven when he arrived home. He came

straight into the living room where Holly was watching the news.

'Oh, Holly, I'm sorry. But the situation at work is awful, it really is. It's all so much harder than I thought it was going to be, and if I don't make things work by the end of the month I'll be demoted again.' He sank down on the sofa and hid his face in his hands, rocking back and forwards over his knees.

Appalled, Holly switched the TV off. She'd misjudged him – she'd misjudged the entire situation. It was as Elaine had described it – Dyl working his socks off for little reward.

'Oh, Dylan.' She went to sit beside him on the sofa. 'I wish you'd told me this before. I thought Laura's help had improved things for you?'

He still wasn't looking at her. 'It is. It did. But that's only part of it. Tonight was a whole new area. I think I'm on top of it now, and Laura's going to help me again tomorrow, but the next couple of weeks are going to be crucial.'

'Is there anything I can do?' Holly rubbed his back. It wasn't the time to discuss whether the new job was worth it.

Dylan moved away from her and went to the drinks cupboard. 'Knowing you're here is enough.' He poured a glass of whisky and knocked it back. 'I'll go on up. I'm bushed.'

Holly stared after him, then poured a glass of wine and sipped. The next couple of weeks, he'd said. She could do that, couldn't she? Dylan was her husband and he worked too hard. She should be supporting him, not doubting him.

CHAPTER 6

WEDNESDAY, 19TH MAY

FIVE O'CLOCK, AND THANK GOD FOR THAT. HOLLY DROVE UP THE
main road in Market Basing and pulled up in the car park
behind the practice. A strenuous afternoon on the farms had left
her wiped out, and euthanising a cow hadn't improved her
mood. Time to grab her things from the practice and go home.

Fred stood up on the back seat, tail swishing through the
air. Holly turned and rubbed his head. 'I'll be two seconds,
okay?' She left him whining piteously, and loped to the back
door.

'A quick word, Holly.'

Jim Rosser, head vet and owner of the practice, was waiting
in the staff room when Holly went in to collect her things. He
motioned her into a chair, and she perched on the edge and
smiled at him. Hopefully she hadn't messed anything up; that
would just be the last straw today.

He was his usual placid self, though. 'I saw that poodle you
treated recently in the village today – he was looking pretty
perky. Well done. Holly, I have a proposition for you.'

Jim wasn't the kind of person you joked around with. Holly fixed on an interested expression, and he leaned forward.

'Adam Blake from the wildlife centre called. He was singing your praises, so well done again. The centre's main vet has had to leave for health reasons, and Adam asked if we could extend your hours up there. It would mean another three or four sessions a week plus the usual emergency work, and correspondingly fewer clinics and farm rounds here. Would you be agreeable to that?'

Holly's brain was buzzing. This was the best pick-me-up ever. At the wildlife centre she treated deer, foxes, badgers, water birds and anything else that lived outside, and it was always fascinating. The team there consisted of an enthusiastic band of volunteers as well as the paid team, which included Adam, the centre head, and a couple of animal nurses.

'I'd love that. Thanks, Jim.'

He grinned broadly. 'I had a hunch you'd be pleased! You can call Adam and set up a meeting to get things organised, then next week you'll have six half days there. We have the new vet starting here next month, so we'll need to juggle for the next couple of weeks, but then we'll be fine.'

Holly made her call, arranging a meeting with Adam at three on Friday, then collected her belongings and went back to Fred in the car. They passed the lane up to the wildlife centre on the way home and she slowed down to look, but the buildings were hidden behind tall trees. More than half her working week would be spent there now. Bring it on.

Turning into the driveway at home, she had to swerve to avoid clipping the back of Dylan's Audi, carelessly parked in the carport. Hopefully, Dylan home early meant Laura had been able to help him some more. She was leaving at the end of the week, wasn't she? Holly let Fred out, then locked her car. Was it stupid to hope that she and Dylan would be able to concentrate on themselves for a while soon?

She walked round to the back door after Fred. Dylan's voice on the phone floated through the open kitchen window, and Holly sat down on the step to wait until the call was finished. If Fred went in there now, he'd make a beeline for his master and Dylan might not appreciate the interruption. Best not to start the evening with aggro. She gazed idly over the garden. They should tidy up the strawberry bed.

'I couldn't agree more. It'll all be fine in the end, so don't worry, darling.'

Holly's head jerked up. Darling? Who the hell was he talking to? Fred, sitting patiently at her feet, seemed to sense that something was wrong. He gave a short bark.

Holly scrambled to her feet and stepped inside. Dylan was standing in the middle of the kitchen with a glass of beer in one hand and a pink face. His phone was on the table.

'Hello, you two! Good day?' He fussed over Fred, who lapped it up.

'Excellent. Sorry, were you on the phone?' Holly stood in the doorway clutching her bag. She'd never been in this situation; it was hard to know how to react. Thinking, 'who the hell were you talking to?' and saying it out loud were two different things.

His eyes narrowed. 'I had a quick word with Megan. About Mum's new blood pressure meds.'

Holly's brain whirled. Elaine did have new meds, and as it would be easy enough for her to check with Megan, it must be true about the call. Mustn't it? She glanced at Dylan, now sipping his beer, a sheen of sweat on his forehead. *Darling...* And that tone of voice. No, no-no. Something was off here and it wasn't her judgement. How stupid did he think she was?

Holly dumped her bag on the worktop. 'So, you call your niece "darling", do you?'

He thumped the glass down and beer sloshed onto the table. 'What are you accusing me of now? Nothing's ever enough for you, is it? I'm working the shirt off my back and all you do is doubt me. Get your act together, Holly – you're not the only person on the planet. I'm going out now to get a crate of that prosecco *you* like, for *you*, because the offer ends tomorrow and I'm doing my best for *us*. I suggest you do some thinking while I'm gone.' He snatched his car key from the table and was gone.

Holly stared after him. Was he right? She poured a glass of water and sat down on the bench by the back door while Fred ran around the garden. Okay, the bit about the blood pressure meds was true, but... She got up and walked down the garden, and Fred immediately ran up with his ball. Holly threw it for him a few times, then slid her phone from her pocket and stared at it. *Had* Dylan been talking to Megan? Oh, she wanted to believe him, but it was impossible to fathom out what was going on with him. All the overtime and stress and now this. And... and the lipstick in the car, and his weird outbursts of temper and – God forgive her, but she was going to check what he'd said. Suspicion was like poison when you started letting it in; it would spread through every cell in your body. She tapped, her heart thumping.

Megan took the call on the second ring, and Holly cleared her throat. 'I'm wondering if Dylan remembered to ask if Elaine's getting on all right with her new blood pressure pills?'

Megan giggled. 'He's just off the phone. Seth called earlier, too, Grandma said.'

'Oh, brilliant. Um, that's all, really.'

'Okay. I have to go, Grandma's making dinner and it's almost ready.'

Holly shoved her phone back into her pocket. She'd overreacted again, hadn't she? She shouldn't have doubted Dylan. Just – *darling*... But she shouldn't be so mistrustful. She was in the wrong.

It wasn't until she was back in the kitchen that a different thought struck. Dylan had left for the prosecco. Then she'd poured a glass of water, gone outside, chucked a few balls for

Fred, and called Megan. She'd given him plenty of time to pull over in the lane and call his niece, hadn't she? But now she was getting paranoid.

Dylan was back in less than half an hour with a crate of prosecco, and Holly did a major double-take when he marched in clutching an enormous bunch of pink roses too.

'Holly, love. I'm sorry. Work is a worry, but I overreacted. Once I'm settled in properly, it'll be all systems go again. It just needs another week or two, like we said last night.'

He squeezed her shoulder, gazing straight at her with sincerity streaming out of him, and tears came into Holly's eyes. What a cow she'd been, doubting him like that. The main problem wasn't his job; it was the fact that communication between them had sunk to sub-zero levels, and that was her fault too.

'A fresh start for springtime, huh? They're gorgeous, thank you.'

He leaned in for a kiss and grabbed her bum, but then stepped back. 'Stick them in water, and I'll phone for a takeaway. Then we'll have that talk we've been putting off forever. We'll get things back on track, never fear.' He pressed his lips to her forehead, then swung away to order the meal.

They ate in the kitchen, and oh, it was good to feel that Dylan was ready to work on their marriage again. Things like that really did take two. Holly watched him fork up green curry while he talked about his ambitions for the new job, and where he wanted to see them as a couple, and did she agree? A baby in two or three years, perhaps? Oh, yes, this was what they'd needed. It had been a long haul with his new job, but this could be them arriving in a better place at last, and hopefully her hours at the wildlife centre wouldn't be so complicated. Deer rescues and the like tended to happen in the evenings. She told him about the change, and Dylan listened, his face alive and interested. Wow, it was like having dinner with a different bloke. Jekyll and Hyde strike again...

He squeezed her hand. 'Sounds like a good opportunity to gain more experience, and it'll look good on your CV, too.' He rose to clear away the dishes, and Holly stood up to help, her reply dying on her lips when he grabbed her, twirled her round the kitchen then kissed her thoroughly. Well. They hadn't had much of that recently, had they? It looked as if all the worry about her marriage had been wasted time.

And of course he'd been talking to Megan...

———

THE SKATEPARK WAS BUSY, but wow, after days on end of the coldest, wettest weather since time began in this part of England, at long last the sun was actually hot. Well, hottish. Megan sat on a concrete slab near the pyramid and watched as Gabe whizzed round, soaring up the half-pipe then tanking along the flat stretch to skid to a stop beside her. He flipped the board up, caught it in one hand, then plumped down next to her. He wasn't half bad at this.

The weather wasn't the only thing that had changed. She and Gabe... they were seeing each other. They hadn't talked about whether it was exclusive or not or anything, but with exams and all the schoolwork, neither of them had time to see anyone else anyway. So in a way they were exclusive, but she hadn't told anyone that yet. The other kids would wind them up no end if it came out. Not what she wanted, and when you got to know Gabe, he was quite funny. Totally uncool, but funny, and Holly'd said he'd grow out of being uncool. The other kids shouldn't be so mean to him.

Megan pulled her jacket around her. An evening breeze was getting up, carrying with it the sound of the rain-swollen river behind them. It would go down as quickly as it went up; it always did. Until next time they had ten deluges in forty-eight hours. The good thing was, the kayak course had been cancelled, though Gabe was still keen to do one. The next was due to start in a week or two, so she'd have to think about that.

Gabe went off for another round of the park, but the arrival of a crowd of ten-year-olds meant they were soon in the middle of what felt like a primary school picnic. Megan looked on glumly as Gabe swooped down the half-pipe, then jumped off his board to avoid crashing into some random child. He trotted back to Megan with a face like fizz.

'This is hopeless.' He plopped down beside her and leaned across her to grab his rucksack. One of the badges he had pinned on it scratched across Megan's hand as he yanked it over.

'Ouch!'

'Sorry.'

And typical Gabe; it was the badge he was checking to see if it was okay, not her hand. Gabe was big on badges.

He unclipped his helmet. 'Let's go back to mine. Mum's making scones.'

Megan stood up. It was as good a suggestion as any. Susie and Hope weren't around, and it was no fun here with all these little kids hogging the place. She grabbed her bag and headed for the gate.

'Hey, Megs! And Gabo. Coming down to see the river?' It was Jay from school, meandering along the road with a group of kids from their year.

Megan turned to Gabe. 'Shall we?' It would be cool to see the river in flood.

He nodded and took her hand, and they tagged on at the end of nine or ten others. Further along, a narrow track led down through scrubland to the river bank, though it was more mud than path tonight, yeuch. Megan picked her way along the verge where there was more grass. Meh, she was going to have to wash her trainers.

The river was pretty impressive, tumbling and roaring across the rocks and flooding the narrow stony beach where they sometimes picnicked. No wonder the kayak course had been cancelled. A couple of the boys started kidding and shoving each other around, and Alma, one of the girls in Megan's form, shrieked as she was caught in the skirmish.

Megan gasped, but Gabe dived forward and grabbed Alma before she fell into the water.

He yelled at Steve, the boy who'd started the kidding. 'Watch what you're doing, brainless!'

Megan cringed. Jeez, Gabe could be brainless sometimes too. What an effing stupid thing to say to the biggest kid in their year. Steve was a bully, always mouthing off at the younger kids. Megan stood rooted to the spot in horror as he came right up and shoved his face in Gabe's.

'You do not. Call. Me. Brainless, Mummy's Boy. You hear?'

Megan pulled Gabe back, but he didn't know when to shut up.

'Loud and clear, so all you need to do is stop shoving girls around.'

'That right?' Steve grabbed Megan and pulled her towards the river and shit, no, he was holding her right at the edge of the bank; she was hanging over that horrible swift brown water and if he let her go…

Some of the girls screamed, then Gabe and Davey were there, pulling at Steve's arms. He kicked behind him, almost dropping Megan into the water, and now she was screaming. Then he whirled her back to the path, and shoved Gabe face down into the mud on the riverbank and kicked him.

Megan swore, and Steve swaggered off, dusting his hands on his jeans. 'Be careful, Mummy's Boy. Next time, you'll be in the water.' He swung round and leered at them. 'Or maybe your girlfriend will. Fancy a bath, Megs? Or are you more into crack, like your ma was?'

Megan pulled Gabe to his feet. 'He's a berk. Ignore him. You okay?' The other kids were standing well back, though two of Steve's mates were laughing. She glared at them. Mum hadn't been into cocaine – had she?

Gabe nodded, and the other kids began to wander off. Megan held his hand all the way back up to the road. Gabe wasn't as wet as she'd thought a few weeks ago. And see how his eyes were all shiny when he looked at her.

CHAPTER 7

DYLAN AND SETH: THE CHILDHOOD DAYS

IT WAS THE EFFING TWINS' EFFING FIFTH BIRTHDAY AND SHE HAD to stay at home on a Saturday afternoon to help with their effing birthday party instead of going up to London with her mates, because Mum couldn't effing cope with ten extra kids in the house. Bryony stood in the kitchen, dropping mini bars of chocolate into twelve party bags – because Dylan and Seth had to have a party bag too, didn't they, as well as all the presents. She swallowed yet another f-bomb as Dylan ran in and grabbed one of the lollipops waiting to be bagged up.

Bryony grabbed it right back. 'You can't have that, Dyl – at least, not unless you put it into your bag. Mum said no sweets before the party or you'll get a sugar rush.'

Dylan shrieked. 'You're mean! It's our birthday!'

'You'll thank me later.' Bryony dropped the lollies into the bags, then sealed them and attached one of the labels Mum had made, one for each child. Including Dylan and Seth. Because they always got everything.

In the living room, her mother was blowing up balloons

while Seth ran around like a lunatic waving one in each hand. And hell on earth, Mum was on the sherry already. Bryony peered down her nose at the glass on the coffee table. Mum hated it when she did that.

'Bit early, isn't it?'

'It's Saturday. And it's just a tiny one.'

This was true; Mum's 'tiny ones' barely made the inside of the glass wet. But short of watching her twenty-four/seven, there was no way to know how many 'tiny ones' she tipped down her throat every day. However many it was, the weekly shop always included sherry. Sherry was respectable, of course. Not like beer or vodka. Bryony rolled her eyes, and her mother sniffed.

'Wait until you're doing what I have to do. Your father pulled the long straw again.'

Bryony shrugged. Right again, Mum. Dad's new job on the rigs meant he was away for two weeks, then home for two weeks, minus the days he spent travelling to and from Aberdeen every month. And sometimes, he didn't hurry home. Dad's life was one long holiday, if you believed Mum.

Seth bashed Dylan's head with a blue balloon.

'I've got the biggest one!'

Dylan immediately snatched the balloon from Seth's hand and dived off with it, and now it was Seth who was shrieking. Bryony grabbed another blue one and handed it to Seth. Keep the peace, Bry, it's their birthday. And helping out this afternoon meant Mum would owe her big time.

The party guests arrived punctually and almost all together. Most of the mums barely waited long enough to get their offspring through the door, and Bryony grimaced as the noise level in the living room increased exponentially with each child. She would never have kids. Never. She swallowed her frustration as a crowd of small boys ran in circles round the room, pretending to be aeroplanes while Mum stood there like a lemon. Mum was good at seeing what was going on in her life. Problem was, she was rubbish at dealing with it. Look at her now, smiling vaguely while the kids bopped around like little maniacs, the twins the most manic by a mile. Seth was hyper because it was mostly his friends here – Dylan didn't do friends; he spent his time trying to edge into whatever group Seth was part of, so today he was hyper to make them notice him, which meant this party was out of control. Holy shit. Someone was going to have to take charge here, and that someone was her. As usual.

'First game! Listen up!'

Bryony yelled above the rabble, and the children gathered round, greedy for any treat she was going to provide. She grasped her patience and managed a smile. Think how different life would have been if it had been only Seth, or only Dylan. As things were, Seth was savvy enough already to know how to get all the positives. A proper little ray of sunshine he was on the outside; everyone loved him. Seth was his mother's favourite, and boy, did he know it. Annoying little bugger he was, too. The twins defended each other to outsiders, but you could see them looking sideways at each other too, each waiting for the chance to whisk the attention away from under the other's nose. Or the sweeties, or some toy. Dylan usually came off worst, whereupon he would scream or whine his little head off and make everything ten times worse for himself. Dyl was a poor little sod sometimes, but he was an annoying one too, the way he bulldozed around grabbing things and shoving people away. He hadn't clocked yet that being nice to people was the way to get what he wanted.

'Statues!' she announced. 'Run around until I clap my hands, then freeze. The one who stays still longest wins!' Best to get them all tired out as soon as she could; that way, the party had a chance of ending well. Maybe.

Bryony stood guarding the wood burner as the twins ran

around with their guests. One pigtailed little darling shoved Dylan when he pushed past her, and he fell.

Seth immediately whacked the girl with a cushion. 'Stop that!'

Bryony grabbed the cushion before a pillow fight broke out, then clapped loudly. Cue shrieks all round. Happy party, guys.

Three games later, merciful silence fell as everyone sat round the table eating too much sugar. Bryony gaped at her mother when she plopped more ice cream into the twelve Superman disposable paper bowls that Seth – of course – had chosen.

'Mum, we'll be up all night with them being sick.'

'It's their birthday. And at least it's keeping them occupied.' Mum dropped a kiss onto Seth's brow, and Bryony shook her head.

'You should have asked a couple of the mums to stay and help.'

Her mother gave her a look. 'You're kidding – you saw how quickly they all disappeared.'

Bryony sniffed. None of the mums wanted to be with the terrible twins, and they all wanted an afternoon off. And, lucky them, they had it. A wail came from one of the girls, and Bryony whirled round in time to see Dylan aim a jabby little finger at the girl's cheek, a pout pulling at his mouth. On the other side of his brother, Seth was at his most angelic, beaming away. No need to ask who had started this, and Mum had vanished into the loo. Gawd.

One little boy vomited onto the table, and Bryony's patience snapped. That was it. Mum could cope by herself for a change; she wasn't going to stay here a second longer. She'd run this party single-handedly for over an hour and she was done with it. It was time to go to Jan's for the rest of the weekend. Bryony shot off upstairs, grabbed the bag she'd packed earlier and fled, banging on the bathroom door on her way out.

The front door slammed shut behind her, and oh, how

amazing it was to escape into the great outdoors, away from shrieks and vomit and family. Family? That was a joke. Bryony scurried along the High Street to Jan's, a large bottle of coke in her bag. Jan's brother had given her a bottle of rum for covering for him last week when he'd been smoking weed or something; this was going to be good.

No, she would never have kids. They weren't worth the hassle.

CHAPTER 8

FRIDAY, 21ST MAY

Holly took a yoghurt from the fridge and pulled out a chair opposite Dylan, who was working his way through a bowl of cornflakes. It was the first time he'd sat down and had breakfast all week, so today must be a quiet day.

She opened her yoghurt and dug in. 'Have you heard if Seth has been in touch with Laura yet? This is her last day with you, isn't it?'

The corners of his mouth turned down. 'No. And yes. By the way, I'm going to an IT course in London this weekend. I leave tomorrow morning and I'll be away until Sunday night.'

He wasn't looking at her now, and hot frustration seared into Holly. So much for all the talk about getting their marriage back on track.

She persisted. 'I guess you'll be glad to be rid of the overtime every evening.'

Now he did look up. 'That's not a very dedicated way to look at it, is it? I don't see you refusing to do overtime when some mangy cat's brought in at five o'clock.'

Touché. 'I know. It's just you've had such a lot of it recently, getting to grips with Laura's changes and everything.' Holly glanced up at the picture Laura had given her. It fitted the space between the back door and the window perfectly. 'Maybe Seth'll have a thank you dinner for her sometime too.'

Dylan choked on his last mouthful, then took a large swallow of coffee. 'I would seriously doubt that.'

Holly breathed out slowly. As breakfast conversations went, this wasn't a great one.

Several hours at the practice gave her time to calm down, and she left again at twenty to three to drive to the wildlife centre and her appointment with Adam Blake. And just hopefully her new job wasn't going to lead to as much aggro as Dylan's had. Talk about a strain on your marriage... But she'd give him his couple of weeks to get the job stuff sorted before she brought the subject up again. They both wanted to make it as a couple, and that was the important thing.

The wildlife rescue centre was a motley collection of buildings near the top of Beecham Hill between Market Basing and Linton Keynes. Holly arrived at three and parked beside the centre's battered green van.

A door banged shut, and Adam, the guy in charge, strode across the forecourt. Holly hadn't had much to do with him on her afternoons here, but he was as much her boss as Jim at the practice was now. He was around her age and looked like a young version of Leo di Caprio, which had the added benefit of having every teenage girl for miles around queuing up to volunteer. Holly clipped on Fred's lead and went to meet him..

Adam pushed a mop of tousled hair away from his face. 'Hey. Great you're going to be our designated vet. Shall we do a quick tour and let you see what's in at the moment?'

'Sounds good.' She followed him into the main building, where a tiny office that doubled as staffroom was just inside the door, with the larger treatment room and an animal ward further down a dim corridor. The place smelled of animals and disinfectant. Nadia, the animal nurse, was in the ward dishing out food to a family of ducklings, and Sue, an older woman, was emptying the steriliser. Holly left Fred in the staffroom with Adam's dog and wandered round the cages, which held a selection of water birds, a squirrel and a tawny owl.

Adam waved at the ducklings. 'These little guys were orphaned yesterday, so they'll be with us for a few weeks. Come and see what's outside.'

Holly followed him to the back door, passing the treatment room where she usually worked. They had facilities for minor ops and X-ray here, and Adam was very proud of it, though the X-ray machine was anything but state of the art. He slung an arm across her shoulders as they walked across to the row of isolation huts behind the main building. Holly blinked. It was a while since she'd walked along like this with anyone other than her husband, but Adam was yakking away all the time about the hedgehog rescue they'd done on Wednesday.

The huts housed animals in need of rest and quiet. Holly looked in on a deer with a torn shoulder, a swan with an infected wound on one foot, and the hedgehog, who'd been stuck down a drain and needed fattening up. They walked on round the enclosures, which included two ponds, a home-made badger sett and a row of pens. Adam had moved away by this time, but he gave her shoulder the odd little pat as he made a point, and Holly relaxed. He was the touchy-feely type, that was all. She heaved a happy sigh – this was such a great place to work.

A gaggle of teenagers on bikes was approaching as they arrived back at the main building, and Adam gave them a wave. 'The after-school brigade.'

Holly watched as the teenagers dispersed around the buildings. 'My niece Megan would love this. I'll suggest she does a stint in the summer holidays.'

'We always need volunteers. Okay, let's go back in and sort out when you'll be here next week. Then I'm heading down to the river to release a duck, now the water level has fallen again. Want to tag along? We'll release you into the weekend when we're done.' He gave her his lop-sided grin.

Good, she'd be home well before Dylan arrived. With him away on his course, tonight would be their only opportunity to spend time with each other all weekend. Holly arranged her first shift for the following Monday and joined Adam in the centre's green van, the duck in a pet carrier in the back.

He drove the short distance to the river, which was still full, but much less violent now. They walked along the bank to the place the duck had been rescued, and Adam stood back with Fred while Holly crouched down and opened the pet carrier. What a special moment this was, the first time she'd released a wild creature back into its natural environment.

She waited, motionless, then a yellow beak emerged from the carrier, followed by a beady eye, and three seconds' flurry later, the mallard was swimming down the river, quacking loudly. Warm satisfaction spread through Holly as they drove back to the centre. This was perfect. Life was looking up.

She was getting into her own car when Dylan's text pinged in. *Late home, Laura's leaving do. Don't wait up.*

CHAPTER 9

WEDNESDAY, 26TH MAY

Everything stank this month. There was no school now, but all anyone had in their head was: exams, exams, exams. She'd spent all bloody morning doing physics and English, then she'd gone to the skateboard park with Hope and Susie after lunch to chill a bit before their afternoon study session at Grandma's. They'd do a couple of hours' work, have some grub then spend another hour or two swotting before they stopped for the night. It was easier to work when you had company. Megan's stomach churned every time she thought about the maths exam. Holly'd helped her with her revision too, but she was away this week. She'd got a last-minute cancellation place on a wildlife course in Cambridge and wouldn't be back until Saturday morning.

Gabe ran up to join them when they left the skateboard park. He took Megan's hand, but the others didn't go all 'oooh' when he did that now. They'd all been pretty quiet since the incident at the river. Alma's dad had complained to Steve's dad, and a few feathers had been ruffled. Good.

It was weird with Gabe; he wasn't like the other boys she'd

been out with. Okay, she hadn't gone out with hundreds of guys, but they'd all been keen to show off how cool they were and what kind of stuff they were into, and Gabe wasn't like that. He didn't care about things like what trainers were in or what logo he had on his T-shirts.

Hope, in front with Susie, turned round and walked backwards. 'Got some munchies at yours, Megs?'

Megan nodded. 'Grandma said she'd make ginger biscuits.'

'Can I come too?'

Gabe's eyes were fixed on her hopefully, but Megan hardened her heart. 'Nope. Girls only during the week.' She squeezed his hand to show she wasn't being nasty or anything. His face fell a mile, but he wandered up his own garden path with a very Gabe-like wave when they got home.

Megan called out as soon as she opened the front door. 'Hi, Grandma! We're here!'

Last time the three of them had come here, Grandma'd been snoozing in her chair when they arrived, and although she'd said it was because she was tired after her shift at the Third World shop that morning, she'd been pretty cross and embarrassed about it.

'Hello, sweetheart. Hello, girls!'

Grandma was folding washing in the living room and she sounded the same as always, but there was no ginger biscuit aroma floating out of the kitchen. Bummer.

A lump came into Megan's throat at the sight of Grandma's happy face. 'We're going up to my room to work for a bit. Are there any biscuits?'

'Take the chocolate digestives.'

Not a word about ginger biscuits. She'd forgotten. But it didn't matter, did it? Susie and Hope clattered on upstairs, and Megan went to put the kettle on.

'What's for tea?'

Grandma had followed her into the kitchen. 'Em... I

bought...' She opened the fridge, frowning, and Megan stared over her shoulder. There wasn't a lot in the fridge, and – she opened the food cupboard beside the freezer – no cereal. Either Grandma had forgotten a few things, or she'd forgotten to go to the shops this afternoon. She'd talked about it at lunchtime, too. Apprehension thudded into Megan's gut. That had never happened before. She wiped her face with one hand.

'Didn't you do the shopping? I can scoot up to the mini-market now, if you like?'

She mustn't let this be a big deal, because it wasn't. Who was she kidding? She was bricking it for Grandma all over again. No biscuits, forgotten shopping – it didn't sound like much when you said it quickly, but it wasn't like Grandma.

'Let's have this.' Grandma leaned into the cupboard and pulled out a jar of arrabbiata spaghetti sauce. 'I'll do the shopping tomorrow.'

Megan checked the cupboard and fridge, and yes, they had enough spag for four and an in-date packet of Parmesan. Sorted. She made four mugs of tea, left two digestives on a plate for Grandma in case Hope ate all the rest as usual, and took her tray upstairs, a nasty little worm of fear in her middle.

She needed to talk to someone about Grandma again. Holly was the obvious person, and roll on the weekend when she'd be home again, because this wasn't funny any longer. In fact, it had never been funny. And maybe it would be good to have a word with Seth, too, as he lived in Linton Keynes. She'd think about that.

———

IT WAS Friday before she made up her mind about speaking to Seth, and meantime, Grandma went right back to normal as if nothing had happened – it was hard to know if anything *had* happened. A forgotten batch of biscuits and the shopping a day late wasn't a disaster, was it? And she so, so needed Grandma to be okay.

There were three reasons Seth would be a good person to talk to about Grandma, though. One, Holly would have a lot to do at home when she came back from her course. Two, Seth had time off during the day so he could pop in on Grandma much more easily than Holly and Dylan could, and three, he had a new girlfriend, so it would be interesting to see how that was going. Megan grinned. When you thought about it, that was two reasons he'd be good to talk to about Grandma, and one because she was being a nosy cow. She'd met Seth and Laura in the mini-market on Monday, and to say Laura was different to Seth's last music-mad, guitar-playing, dreadlock-swinging and heavy metal concert-visiting girlfriend Roz was the understatement of the century. Laura was totally dead cool. Frosty. She looked like she'd spent about a million on her outfit, and her make-up was to die for. What on earth she saw in Seth was anyone's guess.

Megan handed in some stuff at the dry cleaner's for Grandma, then set off for Seth's place. Friday afternoon was a good time to find him in, getting ready for whatever gig was on that evening. She did a quick jog down the main road then turned into Ash Lane, and hooray, Seth's white van was parked outside his house, and so was a red Toyota. Seth's place wasn't as posh as Dylan's but it was still a nice house with a garden, bought as an investment – and paid for with Mum's money. Huh.

She was raising a hand to ring the doorbell when the door opened and there was Seth, a large cardboard box under one arm.

'Hey, Megs. Fancy a concert?'

He waggled his eyebrows at her, and Megan gave him what she hoped was a scathing look. His sense of humour was archaic.

'No, thanks. Can I come in? I want to ask you something

about Grandma. Is Laura there?' He might listen better if Laura was part of the convo.

'I'm here, but not for long. I'm off now, Seth darling.'

Laura appeared with her laptop bag slung over her shoulder, and Megan took a moment to admire the tight black trousers and bright fuchsia, over-sized shirt that sparkled when the light caught it, as did the matching headband tied carelessly around Laura's hair. Wow.

Laura smiled at her. 'Is your grandma all right, sweetie?'

'I don't know.'

Seth was making no move to stand back and let her in, so Megan told the story of the forgotten biscuits and non-shopping right there on the doorstep. Laura was listening, frowning slightly, but Seth was the one rolling his eyes now, and Megan finished with a sigh. He wasn't going to take this seriously, was he?

'Meggie, poppet.'

Poppet? Who the shit did he think she was? Megan folded her arms and glared, but he went right on moaning at her.

'Don't you think it's reasonable that you help out a bit more at home? Shopping and so on? Other kids seem to manage it.'

'I do help out! Even though I'm in the middle of exams! It's not about that – it's about Grandma forgetting stuff.'

'Everyone forgets stuff sometimes. Okay, Mum isn't getting any younger, but apart from that she seems to be doing well, considering she has a stroppy teenager living with her.'

Laura put a hand on Seth's arm. 'Not helpful, darling. Megan, how about if Seth and I popped in to see your grandma tomorrow?'

Megan gave up. She wasn't convincing them, and unless Grandma had one of her forgetting stuff episodes while Seth and Laura were actually with her, they wouldn't notice a thing. She said this, and Laura gave Seth's arm a little shake.

'We can go by tomorrow anyway, can't we, Seth darling? I'd like to meet your mother.'

Seth hefted the box he was still holding. 'Sure. I have to go, ladies. People to see, and all that. Mum'll be fine, Megs. You mustn't worry.'

He leaned over to give Laura a smoochy kiss – yuck – then shot Megan an odd little smile that wasn't a smile at all because it went nowhere near his eyes, and brushed past her to his van.

Megan stared after him. Weird. And she'd just had a bit of an aha moment. In behind that spooky smile, he was scared too, wasn't he? Scared that Grandma was changing, getting older and – not frail, exactly, but heading in that direction. He might be ignoring what was happening, but inside, Seth needed Grandma to stay the same as much as she did, even though he was grown up and could look after himself. But why? And – did Dylan? Megan pictured Dylan, with the same face as Seth but everything in behind it different. No, he didn't.

CHAPTER 10

DYLAN AND SETH: THE PRE-TEEN DAYS

SETH CRAMMED HIS MATHS BOOK INTO HIS SCHOOL RUCKSACK AND stretched. Secondary school was cool. He'd been worried about keeping up, but a year and a bit in, it was all so much easier than Mum and Dad and all the teachers said it would be. Easy peasy homework, though you'd never think it, the way Dylan moaned all the time. Dyl was pretty dumb, sometimes.

He looked around for his headphones, but they weren't in their usual place on the chest of drawers. He must have left them in the kitchen at lunchtime. Whistling, Seth clattered downstairs, and what did you know, an entire hour after arriving home from school, Dylan was still at the kitchen table doing maths, Mum bent over him like a vulture waiting to pick at a carcass. Mum was okay at maths, though that was something else you'd never know. Or not by looking at her, anyway.

'Oh, Seth, darling, see if you can help your brother with this, will you?'

Mum stepped back and gaped over her shoulder to where the sherry bottle was waiting beside the toaster. She didn't even hide it any more, not since the drinks police, aka Bryony, had left home. Mind you, Bry moaning at Mum for boozing was rich, when you considered she spent half her student loan on weed. That was all finished, though – the loan bit, anyway. Bry had finished her degree – art and design, no less, though she hadn't exactly shone all the way through it, and was sharing a flat with five other questionable people and working at some dodgy publication in Brighton. And smoking weed. And God knows what else. She never came home now, unless she wanted cash. So while Dad was on the rig, it was just him, Dylan and Mum.

Seth peered over Dylan's shoulder. Why he did his homework down here with Mum breathing down his neck all the time was a mystery, unless he was trying to impress her about how hard-working he was. And actually, that was most likely spot-on. Dylan spent a lot of time trying to get into Mum and Dad's good books. Seth smiled. Bad luck, Dyly. Mum and Seth were the dream team, weren't they? He tapped a finger on his brother's worksheet.

'You might want to rework this bit. Get the beginning right and you have so much more chance of landing on the right answer at the end.'

'What?' Mum bent over Dylan again, then she laughed and gave Seth a hug. 'I missed that. My clever boy!'

Seth wriggled free. 'Mu-um. I'm not a baby.'

She cuddled him again. 'You'll always be my baby.'

Dylan glowered. 'Is it too much to ask for a bit of quiet here?'

'Take it to your room, Dyly. Plenty of quiet there.' Seth jerked his head at the door. Poor old Dyl, having to depend on his brother's help.

Dylan swept up his books and stomped off upstairs, and Seth rootled in the fridge for a can of coke. One good thing was, he and Dylan had their own rooms now. Mum and Dad had insisted on hanging on to 'Bryony's room' while she was still at uni, but now even Mum had given up on Bry ever coming back here to live, so Seth had moved into the bigger bedroom.

Mum poured one of her famous tiny sherries and leaned back against the work surface, glass in hand. Seth raised his can and they clinked, and the usual goofy smile spread over her face.

'Your dad'll be going back to the rig tomorrow. And next week, Aunt Angela's coming for a few days, but don't worry, darling, she's staying with Maureen – you know, her old friend in Market Basing, so you and Dylan don't need to share while she's here.'

Good. 'Are you taking time off work?'

'No, but I'm rearranging my hours to give me a couple of full days off instead of every afternoon. I'll be depending on you to help your brother with his homework, mind. I don't see much of Angela, and I don't want to spend the time she's here worrying about Dylan's algebra and French.'

'Mais oui, Maman.'

She crinkled her eyes at him, laughing, then drained her sherry glass and poured another tiny one. Mum didn't as much drink the sherry as inhale it. Seth blew her a kiss and retreated with his coke and headphones.

———

IT WAS FRIDAY, Aunt Angela's last evening, and they were all going to the Italian restaurant in Market Basing. Seth stuck close to Mum in the scrum going in, and took the chair opposite Angela's friend Maureen, leaving Dylan to sit at the awkward end place with Mum and Aunt Angela on his right and left. It was a bit soppy, going out for a meal with basically three old ladies. Some of the kids in his class had grandmothers the same age as Mum was, and Aunt Angela and Maureen were even bigger dinosaurs. Still, the grub was good and it kept Mum happy, so it was worth doing.

When they were finished and outside again, Mum and Aunt Angela started bidding each other a fond farewell. Seth submitted to Aunt Angela's hug and even hugged back – she'd given him twenty quid, after all. It was going to be the start of his guitar fund. Aunt Angela and Maureen drove off in Maureen's car, and Mum linked arms with Seth as they went further along the road to the library, where Mum always parked because the spaces there were larger.

'It was a lovely evening, wasn't it, darlings? I wish Angela could come more often.'

Seth gave her his best smile. 'Won't be long until she's retired, huh? There'll be nothing to stop her, then.'

'True. You were very quiet tonight, Dylan. Are you all right?'

Dylan kicked a stone in the car park and it bounded up and hit the hub cap of Mum's car. 'Fine. Not that you and Aunt Angela talked much to me.'

'Don't be silly, you could have joined in any time.'

Dylan glowered. 'What do I know about all those things you were talking about?'

He immediately dived into the back seat, and Seth went round the car to go in the front. For some reason, Dyly seemed to prefer being alone in the back, and the stupid sod had just given him the perfect opportunity to score points with Mum. Dylan was his own worst enemy, sometimes.

Seth put on his best bright voice. 'It was interesting to hear what Maureen was saying about the hotel she sometimes goes to in Scarborough, wasn't it? Wouldn't it be great if we all went there sometime? We could make it so that Dad joined us on his way down from Aberdeen.'

'Oh, that's a lovely idea, darling. We might just do that.'

Mum started prattling on about Scarborough, and Seth gave himself a mental pat on the back. Everything was easier when Mum was happy.

The drive back to Linton Keynes was uneventful right up to

the last twenty metres. Mum turned the corner into their street and – oh God. Seth jerked straight in the passenger seat. A police car was parked outside their house, and two officers were walking down the garden path.

'Oh no. Not Bryony, please. All that stuff she smokes.' Mum pulled up behind the police car and shot out. 'Is something wrong?'

'Mrs Martin? Can we come in, please?'

The male officer looked like he'd swallowed a grapefruit, and Seth shivered. Something *was* wrong.

'Is it my daughter?'

Mum's hands were shaking so hard she couldn't get the key into the lock, and the woman officer took it from her and opened the door.

'It's not your daughter.'

Seth met Dylan's eyes, and saw his own fear mirrored in his brother's face. It was something bad, you could tell.

'Oh God, it's my husband, isn't it?'

The policewoman took Mum's arm and almost pulled her inside. 'Is this the living room? Shall we sit down? What are your names, boys?'

Mum plopped into her armchair while Seth mumbled both his and Dylan's names then sat down on the sofa with Dylan beside him, so close they were touching, because the policeman was there too and he was pretty big. Seth's stomach was churning and Mum looked like she'd seen a ghost.

'Mrs Martin, I don't know if you want the boys to stay?'

'Just tell us.' Mum was panting now.

The policewoman on the other armchair leaned forwards. 'There was an accident—'

'On the rig? Oh God, I knew it was dangerous to keep working there at his age.'

'No, not on the rig. It was a car accident, in Aberdeen, and your husband was involved. He suffered a bad head injury and was taken to hospital, but I'm afraid he died a short time later. I'm very sorry for your loss. Is there someone you can call now? You mentioned a daughter?'

Mum was crying, loud, high-pitched sobs that were shaking her whole body, and she was bent right down over her knees. Seth sat frozen to the spot. Dad wouldn't be home ever again. Everything was different now. Tears welled up in his eyes, and he grabbed a tissue from the box on the table beside the sofa. The woman officer stood up and took a couple over to Mum, and Seth squinted at Dylan. His face was like there was nothing in behind it; no tears, no nothing, just empty. He grabbed Dylan's hand, feeling the answering squeeze amid the shaking.

'I'll make you a cup of tea, shall I?' The policeman went into the kitchen and crashed about with the kettle.

Abruptly, Dylan got up too and went with him. Seth blew his nose. Mum was still crying and gulping, so it was up to him to answer the woman officer's question.

'My sister's in Brighton, and my aunt – Mum's sister – she's in Market Basing with a friend tonight but she's going home to Leeds tomorrow.'

The officer gave him a kind look. 'Good lad. Mrs Martin, do you want to call your sister? She's nearest.'

Mum gaped at him, then grabbed the phone beside her chair and tapped out Maureen's number. Her voice was like Dylan's face when she spoke, a nothing voice, except it was trembling like Seth had never heard it, and Angela's shrieks down the phone stretched all the way to the sofa.

The police officer leaned towards him. 'How old's your sister, Seth? What's her name?'

'Bryony. She's twenty-two.'

'That's good. You'll want to get hold of her too, I expect.'

Seth stared at his hands, clasped around the mess of snotty tissue. Getting hold of Bry on a Friday night might not be easy.

Mum put the phone down and sat rocking back and forward

in her chair. The policeman and Dylan came through with tea. Dylan still looked spaced out. He hadn't spoken a word since they came in.

Seth put his mug down on the coffee table, and went over and sat on the arm of Mum's chair. 'Mum? Do you want me to call Bryony?'

She grabbed him and pulled him right down over her; it was as if she was trying to get him onto her lap. 'Oh, Seth, darling. What are we going to do?'

The policewoman came to his aid. 'Mrs Martin, shall we call Bryony for you?'

Mum let go of Seth and passed him the phone. 'You call her, darling.'

The two officers exchanged glances, but they didn't say anything. Seth went round to the back of Mum's chair to call, because the cable wouldn't reach to the sofa. Bryony's phone rang eight, nine, ten times, and he was about to give up when a deep voice spoke in his ear.

'Hey, man. Where's the fire?'

Seth closed his eyes. This was Bry's flatmate Lenny, and judging by his voice, he was either drunk or stoned, which meant Bry would be too. He glanced at the officers, one on the sofa and one in a chair. This wasn't a good time to let Bry anywhere near a policeman.

CHAPTER 11

HOLLY DROVE HOME THROUGH HEAVY SATURDAY MORNING traffic. The wildlife course had been a real stroke of luck and well worth the time, even if it had taken her away from home all week. It would be nice to think that the few days' absence could have magically clarified things with Dylan – the texts he'd sent every day were pretty upbeat, actually. So maybe they were past the worst of the problems, and meanwhile, she'd be able to do her job at the centre with a lot more confidence.

She turned into their driveway just after ten to eleven to find the carport empty. He'd probably gone shopping. Holly lifted her case from the back seat and went inside.

Fred was ecstatic to see her home again, though the way he was nosing his bowl around the floor, you'd think he hadn't been fed all week. Holly gave him a chew and put the kettle on. Dylan had done well; the kitchen and living area were a whole lot cleaner and tidier than she'd found them last time she went away for a day or two. His way of making up to her for the last few weeks? She went on upstairs with her case, and wow, the bedroom was pristine too, almost like a hotel. Fresh bed things, not a stray sock in sight, and you could have done brain surgery in the en suite, it was so squeaky-clean. He must have been up at the crack of dawn doing all this.

She swung her bags onto the bed as car noises came from outside.

'Holly? Anyone home?'

He ran upstairs and wrapped her in a bear hug, and Holly held on tight. Please, please let all the see-sawing of emotions they'd been through recently be over.

She waved around the room. 'You've been busy!'

He laughed. 'I had the afternoon off yesterday. Though I hadn't planned on doing quite so much cleaning up here. I broke a bottle of aftershave, and the place smelled like a perfumery.'

Holly sniffed. 'Smells fine now. Shopping done?'

'The fridge is full.'

'Perfect.'

He hugged her again, then went back downstairs. The sound of dog food rattling into Fred's bowl floated up to the bedroom, and Holly froze. He hadn't fed her dog this morning. And in half a second, all the suspicions were tumbling back. Where had he just come back from? And... she stared around the room. He'd done a massive clean-up job, hadn't he? She sank down on the bed, her fists clenched hard. The misgivings she'd barely allowed to enter her head before were queueing up to get in now, and she was opening the door for them. Oh, no. *Darling...* Fresh bed linen. Spilled aftershave... or had it been *darling*'s shower gel and perfume making the place smell like a perfumery?

Dylan's phone rang in the kitchen, and he took it out to the garden. He'd been doing that a lot recently, hadn't he? Or was she being totally unreasonable? No... and this had gone on long enough.

She stamped downstairs and marched out to the back garden.

Dylan said, 'Okay,' into his phone, and came towards her. 'That was Seth. He and Laura are off to Brighton this evening – big concert tonight, apparently. Megan's been complaining about Mum being forgetful again, so they went to see her, but she was fine. I'm beginning to wonder if Meg's just attention-seeking with this? Setting it up as an excuse in case she fails her GCSEs?'

Holly gaped at him as uncertainty rose yet again. None of that sounded like someone who was having an affair. 'I shouldn't think for a moment she's attention-seeking; she's not six. Where were you today, Dylan? You were a bit late feeding Fred.'

His reply came easily. 'Sorry about that. I had to take my grey suit to the cleaner's as soon as they opened, because I need it on Tuesday, and I overslept, that's all.'

Brilliant. He'd managed to arrange the bedroom like a bloody show house before he left, but hadn't had time to feed a dog who'd have been trailing around after him whining its head off. Convincing? No. But it wasn't impossible, and that was the whole problem. Holly stared up the garden. She would think about it. Again. As for Seth and Laura, they were the most unlikely couple ever, but it seemed to be working, and it was good to know Laura hadn't noticed anything wrong with Elaine.

She spoke coolly. 'Do you want us to go and see Elaine too? We could go by later.'

'Good idea, but I'm sure you need some me-time now after your course. I'm playing squash with Joe at twelve. I'll look in on Mum beforehand.'

'Saturday morning might not be the best time to catch her at home.'

'If she's not in, that's another reason to be reassured, isn't it? Best if you talk to Meg alone sometime, too – give her some womanly advice or something.'

Fred bounded up with a ball in his mouth, and Dylan moved away to throw it for him. Holly stood watching as the game of 'fetch' began. Dylan's remarks about his mother were a shade off-hand, and that had been pretty patronising about Megan, too. But it might be better if she, Elaine and Megan had a chat without Dylan. His visit with his mother would be a short one if he was fitting it in before playing squash.

She matched his breezy tone of a moment ago. 'Tell you what, I'll come with you and see Elaine. Fred can come too. Megan might be glad of some help with her exam work, who knows?'

His eyes glazed over. 'For God's sake, Holly – you're making too much of this. Meg will be out with her mates on a Saturday, and supposing Mum's not at home either? Even if she is, she might have better things to do than entertain you while I'm playing squash. Joe and I said we might go for lunch after the game, too.'

Holly's breath caught. Every other thing he said today was making her suspicious. What was wrong with inviting your wife to join you and your friend for lunch the day after she returned from five days away from home? She stuffed her hands into her back pockets.

'If she's not home, I'll wander down the High Street and have a look at the shops. And I could have lunch with you too, couldn't I?' That sounded needy, but it would be interesting to see what she replied to it. And shame on him for putting her in this position.

Dylan's face was expressionless. 'Fine. We'll leave in half an hour.'

Holly trailed back inside. Okay, maybe he was playing squash with Joe, and not lunching with *Darling*. Come to think of it, *Darling* would have to be local if that was the case, which didn't fit with the lipstick in the car episode. He'd been in Croydon that day. Dylan ran upstairs, presumably to pack his squash kit, and a moment later the bathroom door banged shut on his voice on the phone. Holly called Fred inside and dried his feet ready for the ride in Dylan's precious Audi, misery swelling in her throat. They were back on the seesaw already.

The first part of the drive passed with Dylan lost in thought, and Holly was silent too. Should she suggest counselling? Marriage guidance? Did she even want that? Glory. She squinted across at him, and he caught her eye and grimaced.

'Sorry, babes. There's been a lot on at work, and I'm still a bit on edge about it all. I'll make it up to you, I promise.' He reached across and patted her leg.

The lump in Holly's throat was preventing speech while her pride prevented tears. They used to be so in love, and now she was suspicious all the time and he was – different. He smiled across the car, and there was something so *Stepford Wives* about his behaviour now, but she couldn't put her finger on it.

They turned into the High Street in Linton Keynes in time to see an ambulance speed through the lights further along and vanish in the direction of the river, sirens wailing. A police car and another emergency vehicle followed on, their sirens screaming too as they vanished from sight. Fred whined in the back, and Holly pressed a hand to her chest.

'Hope that isn't as bad as it sounds.' Dylan drove along Oak Avenue and parked outside Elaine's house.

Holly rang the bell, relieved when the shape of her mother-in-law appeared through the frosted glass of the door.

'Oh, hello, dears. I'm afraid I'm on my way to the Third World shop, and I can't be late, because one of the ladies has been taken ill suddenly, so poor Mary's there by herself and she can't work the till properly.'

Dylan was positively puffing his chest out, and Holly suppressed a grimace. She'd hear nothing but 'I told you so' later. Well, it was good that Elaine was well and happy, wasn't it? She was delighted to be wrong.

'No problem. Dylan's off to play squash, and I thought I'd

come and see if you were around, and if not, do some shopping. Is Megan at home?'

Elaine pulled on her jacket. 'She's out with Gabe. You should come with me to the shop, Holly – we have some lovely jewellery not long in. It's from Africa – big, shiny beads made with clay from Mount Kenya. The colours are wonderful.'

Holly followed Dylan back out to the car. He dropped her and Elaine at the shop, and Holly went in to inspect the jewellery. Elaine was one hundred per cent on the ball today, reassuring the other volunteer, a considerably older woman, that she would cope with all purchases, and not to worry. It was good in one way, but she could think of a couple of conditions that didn't exclude having fuzzy moments in between periods of normality. Mini-strokes came to mind, but then, Megan had never seen any sign of a movement or speech disorder. Seth and Dylan could be right; maybe you were allowed the odd fuzzy moment in your mid-seventies.

Holly bought a bead necklace, then wandered along the High Street. She still had nearly an hour before Dylan and Joe would be ready to go for lunch. She was walking past the café en route to the park and a good run for Fred when her name was called from behind.

'Holly! Were you at ours? What did you think about Grandma?'

Holly turned to see Megan in the café doorway and Gabe at a table near the window. She followed Megan inside, collected a mineral water from the counter and sat down beside Megan. Thankfully, Fred was excellent at cafés. Your typical hopeful dog under the table, in fact. Holly leaned over and scratched his head, then nodded at Megan.

'We took Elaine along to the Third World shop. She was absolutely fine, Megs.' She gave Megan's hand on the table top a quick squeeze. If by some chance Meg *was* exaggerating Elaine's symptoms, for whatever reason, it was best to sound clear about this. The girl could even be doing it subconsciously, out of fear that something would happen to her grandma. After Bryony's death, that wasn't impossible.

'Good.' Megan sipped her coke, and for the first time, Holly noticed how pale Gabe was.

'Are you okay, Gabe?'

It was Megan who answered. 'There was an accident at the skatepark. Sam – one of the kids in our year – went over the edge of the half-pipe and landed on his head.' Her lips trembled. 'He's really bad, Holly.'

'Oh no. Did you see it happen?'

'No, but we were there and we helped him afterwards. Gabe called 999.'

Holly touched Gabe's arm. 'We saw the ambulance drive past. They'll do their best for him.'

Megan was blinking hard. 'It was some kids being mean that made him lose concentration. They're awful, Holly. They ran off immediately after Sam fell. They didn't even wait to see if he was hurt.'

Holly flinched. Good God, kids could be brutal. 'I guess the police know all that?'

Gabe scowled. 'I bet nothing will happen to them. Or nothing that'll stop them being yobbish, anyway.'

The depressing thing was, he was right. Holly stayed with the teenagers for another ten minutes, then left them to it. Neither would be happy until they knew what had happened to their friend, and that could take a while. It wasn't what they needed at exam time.

A bus to Market Basing was approaching, and on an impulse, Holly jumped in. She would leave Dylan to lunch with his mate while she had a think about how best to tackle what was or wasn't going on with their marriage. The journey home took less than fifteen minutes, then she strolled up Farmer's Lane with Fred sniffing at every bush they passed. Home again, she pulled out her phone to text Dylan what she was doing. And send. Sorted. Now to unpack her course bag and get the washing machine on.

She was putting things away in their bedroom when she noticed Dylan's squash shoes halfway under the chair on his side of the bed. Oh. But you could hire shoes at the court, couldn't you? Yes, you must be able to, or he'd have come back for them. She put the shoes into the wardrobe just as his text pinged into her phone. *OK. See you around 4. xxx*

That was a long lunch… Holly stood taking deep breaths and trying to suppress the flutter of panic. He'd said things would be all right by the end of May, and they weren't. Or was it all her, being over-suspicious when there was nothing going on apart from work pressure? She'd been wrong about Elaine. Okay – she'd give him another two weeks, then if things hadn't improved, she would do something. God knows what, but she'd do it. She did *not* want her marriage to end like this.

What a coward she was.

PART II
IN SICKNESS AND IN HEALTH

CHAPTER 12

SATURDAY, 12TH JUNE

MEGAN SAT SOAKING IN THE SATURDAY AFTERNOON BUZZ AT THE skateboard park. She felt literally lighter today. A week after the accident, Sam was home again and recovering nicely, and Grandma had been fine all week. There was nothing left to worry about at home, though it would be nice if she could say the same thing about her GCSE results too.

She leaned back against the concrete plinth at the side of the park, watching Gabe as he swooped up and down on his board, giving her a big grin every time he passed. Loads of the other kids were checking him out, the way he'd slide across those bars, spin in the air, then land and roll back to collapse beside her. Wow, he was good.

Megan offered him a jelly dinosaur. Grandma'd been shopping again, though it was a long time since she'd come home with jelly sweeties for little Megan. Nostalgia thudded heavily into Megan's gut. That had been in the days when Mum was alive and Grandma'd come to visit them in their flat by the river and life had been happy and safe.

Gabe laid his helmet on the plinth, and his damped-down hair blew about in the breeze as it dried. Megan sighed happily. He was one of the cool guys now, and the other girls were looking at him with their tongues hanging out, but no danger either she or Gabe would start anything with someone else because they were officially exclusive now. Gabe wanted to buy her a soppy locket to put both their pics in, but they hadn't done that yet.

He took a couple of jelly dinos and chewed. 'We could go down to Brighton tomorrow and paddle.'

Megan wrinkled her nose. Maybe not so cool. 'It's going to rain tomorrow.' She stuffed the empty jelly dinos packet into her rucksack. 'Let's see what next week's like, huh? I was thinking of getting some stuff in and having a party, actually.' That would impress the kids from school, and Grandma wouldn't mind, would she?

'Stuff? Booze? That's daft. With a bit of cash, we could do something real in the holidays. You coming on the kayak course?'

Megan rolled her eyes. He was back to being wet. 'Can't. I'm getting a job. My aunt works in the wildlife centre, and they're looking for people.'

'Getting a job' sounded so much better than volunteering to muck out sheds. Megan got up. 'I should go. It's after four, and I told Grandma I'd make dinner. You coming?'

'Nah. I'll do another few rounds here, first. I'll text you.' He grabbed his rucksack from the plinth and slid off on his board, giving her a cheery wave as he went. Two of the girls nearby whistled at him, and Megan glared.

Back home, she hung her denim jacket on the stair post before heading into the living room.

'How about… Grandma? Are you okay?'

Grandma was leaning all squint in her chair, staring at the

window, her face pale and blank and a thin stream of dribble glistening on her chin. *Jesus.* Megan stumbled across the room.

'Grandma?' She shook a bony shoulder.

'Haaa…'

Thank God, she was breathing. Megan fumbled for her phone, fingers shaking, and hell, she was out of battery. She turned to the landline phone, but the receiver wasn't there, and it wasn't on the coffee table either and she was wasting time here, she had to—

Grandma jerked upright. 'Oh! Megan, love.'

Blue eyes were gazing at her, and Grandma was wiping her chin with one hand. Her mouth was still squint. Megan sank down on her knees beside the chair, clutching her phone. Should she call 999? Or the doctor?

'Are you all right? I thought you were ill! Where's the phone?'

Grandma yawned, but she didn't cover her mouth like she always did. 'Nothing a cuppa won't sort, lovey.'

She didn't sound right. Megan headed for the kitchen and plugged her phone into the charger. Seth and Laura had gone to Paris for the weekend, so no point calling Seth. Dylan? No, Holly would be better. Megan tapped, and thank God, Holly took the call on the second ring.

'Grandma's had a funny turn. Can you come?'

'Oh no – what kind of turn? Do we need a doctor?'

'I don't know.' Megan described what she'd seen.

'I'll call 999 for you, okay? Be with you in ten.'

Megan made tea, and there was the bloody landline phone in the fridge again. She took a cup through to Grandma just as Dylan pulled up outside with Holly in the passenger seat. Megan ran to open the door, her legs all trembly with relief that someone who knew what she was doing had arrived. An ambulance pulled up outside, and two minutes later the living room was full, with one green-clad paramedic taking care of Grandma while Holly stood with an arm around Megan and another paramedic asked her question after question and Dylan hovered behind Grandma's chair with one hand pressed to his face as if he had toothache. Grandma was looking from one person to the next, saying 'I'm all right, really' every ten seconds, and her mouth did look better now, but Megan shivered all the same. No one was saying this was nothing.

The paramedic went back to his colleague and Grandma, and Holly gave Megan a little squeeze. 'It could have been a mini-stroke, Megs. Do you know what that is? They'll do tests at the hospital to find out.'

'I guess. Will she have to stay in?'

'Depends what they find.'

The two paramedics were helping Grandma into a wheel-chair, and all of a sudden, she looked like a real old lady, all bowed on the chair, one hand clutching at the blanket they'd wrapped round her. Megan stood on the pavement, wiping away tears as the ambulance with Grandma and Dylan inside vanished round the corner. They didn't have the siren on; that was a good sign, wasn't it?

Holly took her arm. 'Come on. We'll get some things ready for Elaine in case she does have to stay in. Dylan will call as soon as there's news.'

Upstairs, Megan pulled out two clean nighties for Grandma, then went through to the bathroom with Grandma's toiletries bag. This was like the worst was happening to her and she couldn't even moan about it because what was happening to Grandma was worse again – what would she do if Grandma died? She put the toiletries bag into Grandma's weekend bag, and Holly zipped it up.

'We'll hear something soon, Megs. Mini-strokes are treatable, but it's a worry. I wonder if Dylan's called Seth yet.'

Megan wilted. Even thinking about calling Seth when he was away for the weekend was proof this was bad. Holly's phone buzzed, and she put it on speaker.

Dylan's voice was calm. 'They're keeping her in – her blood pressure's way up. She's going for a scan, then they'll know more. She'll need some stuff from home.'

'We'll bring that. Have you called Seth?'

'We'll wait for the scan results first.'

Holly ended the call and they set off in Dylan's car, dark thoughts circling in Megan's head all the time. Was this the end of her life in Linton Keynes with Grandma? Please, please no.

A text from Gabe pinged into her phone. *You okay? Mum saw an ambulance.*

Megan tapped. *G's bad, in hospital. Going there now.*

The reply came a moment later. *Let me know if I can help.* A kiss and a heart emoji ended the message, and tears rushed into Megan's eyes. Gabe was so lovely.

———

THEY HAD to wait ages before Grandma came back from the scan room. Megan stood to the side with Holly and Dylan while a nurse helped Grandma into a bed in a four-bed room in a ward. Grandma was awake and her mouth looked normal, but she wasn't saying much, and she closed her eyes as soon as the nurses were gone. Dylan went to look for a doctor to speak to, and Megan and Holly sat by the bed. Megan clasped her hands together hard. This was scary, as scary as when Mum had died. She'd had to wait with Seth then while Grandma and Dylan were at the hospital with Mum, then they'd come back and everything in her whole life had been different. Now it was happening again, maybe in slow motion this time because no one was saying Grandma's life was in danger, but people of Grandma's age weren't very strong, were they?

Dylan beckoned them from the door, and they stood in the corridor talking in low voices. You couldn't tell at all what Dylan was thinking.

'It was a mini-stroke, but they've given her clot-busting drugs and that should do the trick, along with getting her blood pressure down again. The doctor thinks she might have been forgetting to take her pills – did you notice anything, Megan?'

Fucking hell, was this her fault? Megan burst into tears. 'No! I'm sorry! But I'll watch carefully from now on. I'll make sure she takes them!'

Holly put both arms around her and Megan leaned in, crying onto Holly's blue sweatshirt and smelling her perfume, and oh God, would they let her take care of Grandma?

'Megan, darling, it's not your fault. No one could have known this was going to happen. We'll have to wait and see how Elaine gets on, and then – then we'll fix something.'

That meant nothing, did it? Megan wiped her eyes on the tissue Dylan was holding out.

'Holly's right, Meg. The doctor said she'll be out for the count for the next few hours. Let's get your things from home and go back to our place, and I'll call later to see how she is.'

Still with Holly's arm around her, Megan followed him back to the car. Nothing was going to be the same again.

Had he called Seth yet?

CHAPTER 13

DYLAN AND SETH: THE LAWLESS DAYS

Dylan kicked Seth's CD box under his bed. With bloody Bryony living back at home, he and Seth had to share a room again. It was the pits, and that's what Seth's side of the room looked like too, a pit, with clothes strewn all over the place and the bed permanently unmade. And just typical that Mum let him get away with it.

His sister's voice arguing with their mother in the kitchen floated up the stairs, and Dylan shoved the bedroom door shut. Bryony was a mess. Her flat had been raided, and two of her flatmates were arrested and charged with possession and dealing of drugs. They'd all been taken in for questioning, and Mum had to go to Brighton in the middle of the night to pick Bry up and bring her home, and she'd bloody been here ever since. 'It's cheap. I'm saving for better things,' was all she said about it. Ha. That would take a while, considering she worked at the supermarket in Market Basing where she was basically a skivvy, paid by the hour.

Dylan rolled his eyes. It was incomprehensible why anyone

would want to stay here. He couldn't wait, he absolutely could not wait to get away. He'd be off to uni or college or some kind of training course just as soon as was physically possible, and you could bet your life he wouldn't be caught dead living at home again once he'd left. He wasn't going to throw himself into a dead-end job, but leaving home earlier and spending a little longer doing courses and climbing the career ladder slowly would be more than acceptable.

Seth banged into the room, headphones on as usual, and dropped down on his bed without looking at Dylan. Dylan didn't even try to hide his grin. Look at the scowl on Sethy darling's face. It wasn't so easy to chum up with Mummy dearest now, was it? All his life, Seth had spent every available moment sucking up to Mum in the hope she'd give him what he wanted, which nowadays was hard cash. And attention, of course. But that didn't work quite as well with Bryony around, did it?

Dylan turned his back, still grinning. He'd worked out ages ago how to balance things in his favour in this dysfunctional family he was – unfortunately – part of. All he had to do was not care. Not caring gave you the power. For as long as he could remember, Seth had been the favourite. That was just the way it was, but one day, he'd find someone who'd think he was as much the bloody bee's knees as Mum thought Seth was. Dylan sniffed. What Seth thought, he had no idea. Anyway, with Bryony living at home, Bry and Seth were permanently at war with each other for Mum's attention, not to mention her cash. Special boy Seth was usually successful about the cash bit, but as Mum said, Bryony was a grown up with a job and she didn't get pocket money any more. Ha bloody ha.

Bryony's feet thundered up the stairs, then her bedroom door slammed shut. You'd think someone of twenty-five would have a bit more self-respect, wouldn't you? Dylan left Seth twitching in time to whatever he was listening to, and jogged along to the bog. He was poking at his forehead in front of the bathroom mirror when a thud came from further along the landing.

'Seth! You in there?'

Bryony, and she was at their bedroom door. What the shit did she want with Seth? She spent as much time ignoring his existence as he did hers. Dylan inched over to the bog door and listened.

'Seth!'

A low mutter from Seth, then Bryony again. 'Come to my room. I need to run something by you.'

Well. That was interesting. Dylan waited until Bryony's bedroom door closed, then marched out of the bog, stamped along to his room and put a CD on. Then he crept back along the landing and stood with his ear right up against Bryony's door.

'...and Mum's on my back about Lenny. She's always sneaking around in my room, so I need you to look after it for a day. It won't be longer than that, and I'll make it worth your while.'

'What is it?'

Bryony's reply was inaudible, but it made Seth choke, so 'it' must be something big. Not weed, then?

Silence, then Seth again. 'How much?'

Another inaudible reply, but Seth agreed pretty smartly. 'Okay. When will you get it?'

'Tonight. Len's giving it to Tina and she's leaving it out the back for me. I'll bring it to your room late this evening, then it'll be gone by tomorrow night, and I'll be off too. I have enough cash to start off with, and I need to get away from Len. He's taking too many risks now. You won't need to do it again after this, but I have to go to work tomorrow because it's payday, and I can't exactly leave a package in my jacket on the coatstand, can I?'

'Okay. I'll take it to school and leave it in my locker. Mum might find it in my room.'

'Yes. It won't be a big parcel, don't worry.'

'Where are you going?'

'Best if you don't know, kiddo.'

A floorboard creaked, and Dylan shot back to his room. *Very* interesting, and potentially something he could use.

He made a point of moaning about how tired he was that night, and went up to bed shortly after ten. Bryony was faffing around in her room as usual, and Seth, of course, was down in the living room yakking to Mum, who was lapping it all up. Also as usual.

Dylan lay awake, eyes open, until Seth came up at half past ten. He had to close them then, and lay biting the inside of his cheek to stop himself falling asleep. He'd heard nothing from the garden, so Tina had either sneaked very quietly along the lane at the back, or she'd left the parcel there before ten. He was still fighting sleep when footsteps sounded on the stairs and a soft tap came at the door.

It happened in seconds. Seth opened the door, closed it again, and the footsteps moved on along the landing. Then a thud and a familiar rustle and click, and Seth was back in bed. Dylan relaxed. Whatever the parcel was, it was in Seth's school rucksack. Now all he needed to do was have a look when Seth wasn't around tomorrow.

Luck was on his side, because Seth woke him the following morning falling over his own trainers on the bedroom floor. Dylan grunted, then pretended he hadn't woken up. The moment Seth went out to the bog, he leapt up, opened Seth's rucksack and rummaged. And there it was, a small package wrapped in cloudy plastic with about six elastic bands around it. Dylan lifted it and rubbed at an odd little mark on one side, like a Chinese or Japanese symbol; that must mean something. But what? The bog flushed and the bathroom door opened; gawd,

Stinky wasn't having a shower. Dylan shoved the package back and leapt into bed. It might be worthwhile getting some photographic evidence of that parcel... He wasn't going to tell, or use what he'd seen, or not yet, anyway, but knowledge was power. And power was everything, ha.

He didn't get a chance to take a pic before they left for school, but once they were there, Dylan made a point of not going to the lockers with Seth. Then as soon as his brother appeared back in the corridor in the middle of a crowd of boys, Dylan was on the case. Thank God he knew where Seth kept the spare key to his locker.

The package was on the top shelf, skulking at the back behind a deodorant and an empty bottle. Dylan moved these and aimed his camera, making sure to get the pics and stuff Seth had taped on the inside of the locker in the frame too. There. Pic taken, and a backup just in case. He might never use them, but he had them. The power was his.

Home again, he made a point of hanging around in the kitchen, where Mum was making lasagne for tea. Seth was in their room listening to his never-ending music, then Bryony rushed in at half six.

'I'm off to Pat's for the weekend, Mum. See you on Sunday night!'

'Oh! All right, but you will be good, Bryony darling, won't you?'

Dylan nearly choked at this. How old did Mum think Bry was? And did she think for one moment that Bry was going to be 'good'? Apparently she did, because she was perfectly happy with her sherry and her lasagne at dinner time, and she'd agreed to Seth having two of his mates round to listen to some new CD Seth had bought. That meant Dylan was banned from his own bedroom, but it didn't matter. It was actually quite peaceful watching one of Mum's soppy films with her and planning what he could do – one day – to get his revenge. Revenge for being permanently the odd one out in this bloody family. After all those years of favouritism, he had the upper hand.

It was Sunday evening when Mum's happy – ha ha – family illusion came to an abrupt end. The three of them were in the kitchen when a police car drew up outside, and two officers arrived at the door.

'We're looking for Bryony, Mrs Martin. Is she at home?'

Mum trotted out about Bryony being expected home soon after spending the weekend with Pat in Eastbourne, then asked, 'She isn't in any trouble, is she?'

'No. But we're keen to trace one of her friends, Lenny Carter. Any ideas? Boys?'

Head shakes all round, and by the look on Seth's face, you'd think he really didn't know what Bry was up to.

'She'll be back soon,' trilled Mum, as the officers left.

She wasn't.

Months passed before Bryony next turned up on the doorstep. Dylan answered the doorbell, and his shout had Mum and Seth running to see who it was.

'Hey Mum, hey twinnies,' said Bryony, as they all stood gaping at the bundle in her arms. 'Meet Megan.'

CHAPTER 14

'THANKS, ADAM – CALL THE PRACTICE IF YOU'RE WORRIED ABOUT anything.' Holly tapped to end her call to the wildlife centre. She'd been due to check on a deer that day, before it was released. But Adam could deal with that, leaving her free to concentrate on the family. And oh, hell – poor all of them.

Dylan strode into the kitchen and attached his phone to the charger. 'I called the hospital. Mum slept well, and they'll be doing more tests over the next day or two.' He flipped the kettle on.

'Dylan – you have to call Seth.' Holly put a hand on Megan's shoulder as she passed. The girl was bent over the kitchen table, and she slumped even further at Holly's words. The poor kid must feel as if she didn't have a home to go to any more, and what was going to happen there was anyone's guess.

Dylan glared at her, then looked away, and Holly pressed a hand to her mouth. Things had been bad enough before. She'd been a coward, not pinning him down for a frank talk before now, in the hope that things would improve by themselves.

Nothing had changed. Dylan was still stressing about his job, still swinging between pseudo-normal and downright dismissive towards her. Laura and Seth, meanwhile, were as loved up as any couple she'd ever seen, and to say she hadn't been envious of that weekend in Paris would be a lie, but now the family was facing a real problem and Seth was unaware of it. Dylan had refused point-blank to call his brother yesterday, saying there would be no point interrupting Seth and Laura's well-earned holiday if Elaine was allowed home the next day. They shouldn't leave him in ignorance any longer.

Holly cleared her throat. Patience, woman, and be kind. His mum – and Seth's – was in hospital. 'If it was the other way round, wouldn't you want to know? I would. No matter how much we think Seth needs a break, we should tell him.'

Several expressions chased across Dylan's face at that, and none of them were complimentary.

'Have it your own way.' He pushed his chair back and took his phone out to the garden.

Holly stood at the window as he paced up and down the patio with his phone, his voice inaudible behind the double-glazing. Oh, glory. She'd been so in love with this guy, but that had retreated into once upon a time. Would they ever get the feeling back? She stared at the mystery of Dylan's face, serious as he spoke to his brother, then breaking into a brief smile.

He ended the call as she watched, and joined them in the kitchen. 'They're going to see about flights back.' He scowled at the table. 'I guess I should let Aunt Angela know, too.'

Megan heaved a huge sigh, and Holly thought back to her own teenage days when her grandmother had taken ill and then died. Helping Megan through this wouldn't be easy, but please God Elaine would soon be home.

Dylan went upstairs to the study, and Holly made toast and persuaded Megan to eat a slice. They were still at the table when Dylan clattered downstairs again.

'The ward sister called. They've said we should take Mum some clothes in, and a pair of supportive shoes for walking, too. Why don't you two go over and collect some bits for her, huh? You'll know better than me what she'll need.'

———

IT WAS STRANGE, being in Elaine and Megan's home like this. Holly left Megan examining shoes in the hallway and went up to Elaine's bedroom, where a stale, unused smell was hanging in the air already. She traced a finger through a layer of dust on the dressing table. She hadn't noticed this yesterday, and oh, dear – Elaine wasn't coping with this big house, and Megan was too busy with school to think about things like dusting her grandmother's bedroom occasionally. Holly lifted the photo frame on the chest of drawers. Elaine and Bob with Bryony and the twins; a happy, smiling family, and this was possibly the last family photo before Bob's death. How young the twins looked.

Tears in her eyes, Holly opened the wardrobe. Trousers would be best. She was folding blouses when her phone rang.

'Dylan?'

'I'm on my way to the hospital. They called again – she's taken a turn for the worse. I'll let you know what's going on ASAP. Stay where you are with Meg.'

The call ended abruptly, and Holly pressed her lips together. That was pretty macho, but who wouldn't be stressed out in those circumstances? And Megan was going to go bananas at this news.

She was right about that.

'I want to go now! Please, Holly! If – if you don't take me, I'm getting a taxi. You can't stop me.'

No, she couldn't. 'It's okay. We'll go. Bring the bag.' Holly locked the front door behind them and reversed out of Elaine's driveway, Megan hyperventilating beside her. Dylan had made the wrong call, though she could understand why he'd made it. Sixteen-year-olds were too young to be dealing with this.

The hospital was twenty minutes away by car, and Holly drove swiftly along deserted country lanes. They pulled up in the main car park, and Megan was out of the car and scurrying to the entrance before Holly had the car key in her handbag. She ran after the girl.

Dylan was sitting in the corridor outside Elaine's room, his face white and set. His eyebrows jerked up when he saw them, but he took the hand Holly offered.

Holly put her other arm around Megan, her mouth going dry. This was looking scary. 'What's going on?'

'I don't know. The doctor's with her now. I think she's unconscious – they said they'd come and tell me when she's been examined.'

It was another ten minutes before a grey-haired doctor came and invited them into his office at the end of the corridor. Holly's heart thudded. This wasn't going to be good news, was it? She took Megan's hand.

The doctor came straight to the point. His eyes swept round all three of them, then rested on Dylan. 'Your mother appears to have had another stroke, a larger one this time. I'm sorry. We'll know more after another scan.'

Megan's hand in Holly's was shaking. 'Is Grandma – she'll be okay, right?'

Holly held her breath, but the doctor gave Megan a kindly look. 'After the scan, we'll be able to plan what treatment to give her. I can't say more at the moment, I'm afraid. We're taking good care of her, don't worry.'

He stood up, again looking at Dylan. 'I'll come and find you when we have the results, and we'll have a chat.'

Holly led the way out, with Megan still hanging onto her arm. They stood in an unhappy little group in the corridor, Megan wiping her eyes. Dylan cleared his throat.

'There's no sense in us all hanging around here. Holly, why don't you and Megan wait at Mum's, and I'll call as soon as there's any word? It's not as if she's conscious and wanting us here.'

Holly agreed. Another scan would take a while, and Elaine's home was close enough to get back quickly, if she woke up. Back in the car, Megan sat slumped in her seat, eyes half-closed, and Holly gave her arm a quick squeeze.

'Try not to worry too much. They might be able to treat it quite successfully. She could have physiotherapy as well as medication. Let's wait for more info, okay?'

Megan turned big eyes to Holly, then her face crumpled, and Holly's heart ached for the girl. Depending on what the doctors found, there could be difficult days ahead for Megs, and finding a good solution for everyone wasn't going to be easy. A bigger stroke meant Elaine wouldn't be home any time soon.

They drove on in silence, then stopped off at a café to buy sandwiches for later. Megan scurried up to her room the moment they arrived at Elaine's, and Holly took the sandwiches through to the kitchen. Her phone rang while she was waiting for the kettle to boil.

'Seth? Where are you?'

His voice was shaking. 'At the airport. I've just called Dylan – he should have let me know immediately Mum was worse! He said they were still doing tests. Have you seen her, Holly? How bad is it?'

'Oh Seth, I didn't see her, no. Meg and I are at Elaine's now. Dylan will give you the latest news from the hospital.'

'We'll be back this afternoon. Oh Christ, Holly, this is awful.'

'I know. Let me know if you need a lift or anything.'

The connection broke, and Holly lifted the kettle. Hadn't he believed what Dylan had told him? Or did he think she would give him better news? Her poor family.

Megan crashed in, and the kitchen door slammed against the fridge. 'Was that Dylan?'

'It was Seth. He'll be here late afternoon. Let's have those sandwiches, Megs. We don't want to be passing out from lack of food later on.'

Megan slumped. 'S'pose. Grandma will need us.'

Holly bit her lip. Please, please let that be true. Let Megan have her grandma – preferably at home like before – for a little longer. Please.

————

IT WAS the most unreal afternoon Holly had ever spent. Dylan stayed at the hospital, but either he didn't know how Elaine was, or he wasn't sharing it with her and Megan. All he told them was that the new scan showed another stroke and they were busy 'stabilising' Elaine. Normally, she'd have gone straight to his side whether he wanted her company or not, but there was Megan to consider now too. The poor kid was barely coping here at home; a long wait in a hospital relatives' room would be infinitely worse for a nervous teenager. At two, Seth texted that he and Laura had arrived at Heathrow and were going straight to the hospital. A sick churning began in Holly's stomach. Had Dylan told Seth more than he was telling her? Would Megan want to see her grandma if Elaine was going to… Stop it, Holly. If Elaine was going to die, wouldn't Dylan have told her? She glanced at the pale teenager jabbing at her phone on the sofa. Maybe not.

It was almost six and they were having yet another cup of tea when Holly's mobile rang again. Dylan. Megan jerked upright, then stared at Holly with anguished eyes.

'Put it on speaker – please!'

Holly hesitated, then complied. She would have to tell Meg whatever Dylan was going to say, anyway, wouldn't she?

Dylan had never sounded drearier. 'She's gone. Mum's gone. She stopped breathing and they – they couldn't help her.'

Megan burst into tears, and Holly grabbed hold of the girl. 'We'll come straightaway, Dylan, love.'

Seth was there too; she could hear him in the background, his moans echoing strangely down the phone. Dylan ended the call without saying more, and Holly held on for dear life while Megan's skinny body shook with sobs.

CHAPTER 15

SUNDAY, 13TH JUNE

MEGAN MASSAGED HER FOREHEAD WITH THE FINGERTIPS OF BOTH hands. She and Holly were in the car, rushing to the hospital to get to Dylan and see Grandma, except Grandma wasn't there any more, just a dead body. Would they let her see a body? She didn't even know if she wanted to. The reality of Grandma being dead was so awful everything inside her was numb, and the whole world looked different, as if she was in a parallel universe populated by aliens instead of people. She hadn't felt like this when Mum died. But she'd only been twelve then, young enough to be confident that someone – Grandma – would look after her. Now she was grown up and Grandma wasn't here, but she wasn't eighteen yet so she'd still need someone to 'look after' her, and that someone would have to be Dylan or Seth. Oh, *God*.

Holly turned into the street where the hospital was, and Megan pressed her hands between her knees. Please God, let her stay with Dylan and Holly. Dylan was a berk and Seth was almost as bad, but Holly was okay. You felt safe with Holly.

God only knew why she'd married Dylan, but imagine if she hadn't.

At the hospital, the other three were waiting in the relatives' room at the end of the corridor in Elaine's ward. Seth's face was tear-stained, and he was holding onto Laura's hand as if his life depended on it. Dylan stood up when Megan went in, and she tolerated a hug but moved away as soon as she could and grabbed Holly's arm again.

'I want to see Grandma.' Her heart had decided without her.

'We'll ask about that, sweetheart.'

Holly ushered Megan over to a chair, and they all sat in a horrible little row with Megan between Holly and Dylan.

Dylan cleared his throat. 'They said they're – getting her ready.' He bent forward over his knees, underarms propped on his thighs, his head sunk. Megan leaned back as Holly reached across her for his hand, but he ignored it, swallowing loudly.

Megan glanced along at Seth and Laura, who were still entwined, and a shiver ran right through her. Seth's face... She'd never seen him look like that. The memory of that glimpse of neediness for his mother flashed back into the front of her mind. But Seth looked more than gutted; he'd gone all red in the face and blotchy, and the hand that wasn't clutching Laura was in a tight fist like he was angry, too. Because he wasn't here when Grandma died?

An older nurse came in while she was still thinking about this. 'If you want to see your mother, I'll take you in now.'

Dylan stood up and so did Megan, but Seth shook his head, which was bent so far over his knees he was almost falling forward. Laura grabbed him and held him on her shoulder.

'I'll stay with Seth.' She spoke against Seth's head, gaping up at Dylan, her lips trembling.

Megan walked along beside Holly, her trainers squeaking on the shiny green floor of the corridor. The nurse took them past Grandma's old room and stopped outside a door right at the end of the ward. She was the ward sister, according to her name badge, and she put a hand on Megan's arm.

'You can stay as long as you want to, pet, and you can touch your grandma. Don't worry, she won't feel – or look – very different.'

Megan's legs were shaking so hard she could hardly stay upright. She followed Dylan into the room, which was tiny with only one bed, and on it lay Grandma. Megan choked, and Holly helped her onto a chair beside the bed, then sat down beside her. Dylan stood at the foot end, his hands clasped together, saying nothing.

Megan forced herself to look. She had to do this right, because she wouldn't see Grandma like this again. Soon, she'd be in a coffin, definitely dead, and then she'd be gone forever. Do it, Megs. She reached forward and touched Grandma's forehead, surprised when it was still warm. It was Grandma's face, but oh, the grandma inside was gone, wasn't she?

Two minutes was enough. Megan stood up. 'I think I'll go back now.'

She stepped away from the bed, away from Grandma, and – oh! Dylan was crying, big, silent tears that he made no effort to wipe away. Why couldn't she cry too? She'd loved Grandma more than she'd ever loved anyone, almost. Maybe even more than she'd loved Mum.

In the relatives' room, Seth was leaning back in his chair, eyes closed and his head resting on the wall, still clasping one of Laura's hands. Megan slunk to her chair, then a nurse came in and said she'd bring tea in a moment.

Laura gave Megan a tiny almost-smile as she sat down. 'All right, sweetie?'

No, she wasn't, but that wasn't what Laura meant, was it? Megan wiped her face with a scrunched-up tissue, then froze as she noticed Seth's left hand, the one that wasn't clutching Laura's.

He was wearing a wedding ring.

———

HOLLY DROVE the Audi back home, leaving the Corsa for Laura and Seth, who had come from the station in a taxi. There was nothing more they could do tonight except be with each other and try to help Megan. Tomorrow, they'd have to start the paperwork, organise an undertaker and fetch Elaine's death certificate from the hospital. All the usual death procedure, except it wasn't usual when you were doing it for the first time. Dylan and Seth had worked through it all four years ago when Bryony died, of course, but they'd had Elaine to help them then. Holly tapped her fingers on the wheel. She'd have to tell them at work that she wouldn't be in for a day or two, and they'd need to sort out something for Megan. Oh, glory. And how much worse this must be for the guys and Meg.

At home, Megan went straight up to the spare room, saying nothing. Dylan poured a large whisky and took a big swallow.

'I'll go on up,' he said, not looking at her. 'I'll call Aunt Angela. She should know tonight.'

Holly winced. Telling an almost eighty-year-old that her sister had died – that must be one of the worst jobs ever, especially when you were talking about your own mother. Holly stretched a hand towards him, but he moved away and took another swig of whisky.

'I need some space, for God's sake. I'll sleep in the study tonight.'

Heck. Megan was in the spare room, of course, and the study wasn't much more than a boxroom with a single bed. Holly gave herself a shake. He'd lost his mother; anything he wanted was okay by her. In spite of the problems they were having, she should show she was there for him. Holly stepped forward and held him close, rubbing his back, but Dylan stood like a stick until she let go.

She gave his arm a little pat. 'Come and get me any time if you want company. Shall I bring you a cup of tea?'

Dylan refilled his glass. 'Hell, no.' He grimaced at her and went on upstairs.

At least he hadn't taken the whisky bottle, but this wasn't good; he wasn't letting her anywhere near him. Look at the way Seth had clung on to Laura – that was how couples should be, under stress. Supporting each other. Tears burned in Holly's eyes, and she had no idea if they were pity, or self-pity. It was hard not to feel rejected, impossible not to think back to the *darling* phone call. Was he wishing *Darling* was with him now – and who the hell was she?

Holly trailed into the kitchen and opened the back door for Fred.

'Out you go, Freddo. And perhaps you can sleep in with Megan tonight.'

Megan trudged in and sat down. 'I'd like that.'

Holly grabbed a couple of mugs for tea. The poor kid's face seemed to have sunk inwards, somehow.

'I'm here any time you need to talk, or just be with someone, Megs. It's all very raw at the moment, I know.'

Megan cupped her hands around the mug of tea Holly set in front of her. 'Did you notice Seth and Laura are wearing wedding rings?'

Shock rippled through Holly, and her arm jerked, slopping tea onto the table. '*What*? Are you sure?'

'Yes. I saw Seth's first, then Laura's later when he let go her hand. I guess that's why they went to Paris.'

Holly's thoughts were racing. 'I don't think they could have married there.' Her brow creased. 'Married' didn't sound like Seth, and the couple had only known each other five minutes. And why the secrecy? 'I guess they'll tell us about it tomorrow.'

Megan swirled the tea around in her mug. 'Will I be living here, now? Or...?'

Holly grasped Megan's cold hand across the table. 'As far as I'm concerned, you have a home here, lovey, and I'm sure Seth will say the same. We'll need to talk when we're all together, though. Dylan's calling Aunt Angela. She and the guys are your relatives.'

Holly went up with Megan and settled Fred in his basket in the corner of the spare room. They'd need to turn this into 'Megan's room' as quickly as possible, even if the girl stayed with Seth some of the time too. The days of her and Dylan being alone here might be gone soon, and a teenager in the house wouldn't make things any easier for a couple who were having what you might call major communication issues, on top of Elaine's death. Whatever happened now, life would be different for them all.

CHAPTER 16

DYLAN AND SETH: THE DISCO DAYS

SETH TURNED OUT OF THE SCHOOL GATE IN THE MIDDLE OF A crowd of kids, pulling his jacket collar up against the stronger-than-usual east wind. He sniffed the air – they didn't often get snow around here, but maybe this year would be different. A white Christmas would be cool.

He punched out a few fist-bumps to his mates and headed for the High Street. Dylan was at his maths tutor group today, so no point hanging around waiting for him to come out. Dyl's days of struggling at school were over, and as Mum said, it was all down to hard work and perseverance. Seth snorted. Persevering with hard work wasn't how he wanted to live his life, was it – where was the fun there? Love what you do was his motto, and he sure as hell didn't love maths and history et al.

He stopped outside the charity shop, Linton Keynes' newest addition to the High Street. They'd had some really wacky stuff in the window the other day, and he needed some gear for the school Christmas disco next week. Those jeans in the corner looked as if they were genuine 1970s. Wow. In you go, Seth.

Back home, he was showing Mum his purchases – one pair of bell-bottom Levis, a white shirt with a ruffle down the front, and a denim waistcoat someone had sewn cloth badges all over – when Dylan arrived. As expected, he immediately put on a sniffy expression.

'You're never wearing that crap to the disco?'

Seth folded his gear back into the bag. 'Sure am. Sadie's wearing something retro too. The others'll be all over us, you'll see.'

Their mother rushed in to keep the peace. 'What are you wearing, Dylan, darling? And who are you taking?'

Seth pretended to fuss around with his new clothes. Dyly wouldn't answer if he thought his darling brother was interested in the convo.

Dylan scowled. 'My black trousers and a shirt. And I don't know yet.'

Seth squinted up. He'd seen the way Dylan's tongue hung out every time he looked at Natasha, and as far as he knew, she wasn't going to the disco with anyone yet. Not that it was obligatory to go in pairs, but some kids were. It was more than his life was worth to say anything about it, though – Dyly was touchy about stuff like that. He didn't have what you'd call a great chat up line. The poor sod needed to chill more.

Mum left after tea to babysit for Bryony, who now thankfully had a flat of her own and a proper job at a photographer's. The downside was the job sometimes involved evening work; the upside was Bry was turning out to be pretty good at it. She'd done loads of courses and stuff at the Open University, so even though she spent her life bribing them all to babysit, it was sort of worth it because she paid for it. Seth quite liked babysitting. Megan was a cute little thing, toddling all over the place now.

He watched telly for a bit, then went up to his room. Dylan's door was open, and Seth glanced in. Dylan was at his desk, and he immediately whisked a sheet of paper into the drawer, glaring at Seth.

Ah-ha. What was that? Seth leaned on the door frame. 'Much to do?'

'Geography. Done yours, have you?'

'Just about to.'

Seth left him to it. He looked over the unit about the prairies of North America for his last mock exam, then faffed about in his room for a bit. After a while Dylan went downstairs again. Seth waited until the TV blared out, then scuttled along to Dylan's room and eased the desk drawer open. As he'd thought, Dyly hadn't bothered to hide the paper he'd slid in there. Two seconds were enough. All there was on the sheet were the words 'Natasha' and 'Tash' about fifty times in different kinds of lettering, linked by the odd little heart. Jeez, Dyl was so wet. He needed a helping hand here.

———

DYLAN PULLED on his black trousers and added the black shirt Mum had ironed for him. It was the school disco tonight – did Natasha like black? Mum said he'd look as if he was going to a funeral, but black was always in. A funeral would probably be more fun, anyway. Discos were meh, and someone was bound to have smuggled in some booze, and after seeing what it did to Mum and Bry – silly giggling didn't come into it – he wasn't into booze either. Or anything else.

Seth was downstairs with Mum, and she lifted her car key as soon as Dylan appeared.

'Come on, you two. I'll be at Bryony's until about ten, don't forget, but I'll be home before you're back.'

Out at the car, Seth jerked his head towards the front seat, and Dylan got in without a word. He scowled out the window as they drove off. The disco was to be in the community hall on the other side of the village, and why they couldn't just have had it in the school hall he did not know. They were picking Sadie up on the way, then her dad was bringing them all home again.

Sadie was waiting at her gate for them. She got in beside Seth, bringing a cloud of musky perfume with her.

'Ooh, you do smell nice, love.' Mum set off again.

Sadie clicked on her seatbelt. 'Thanks. You bringing anyone, Dylan?'

'He bottled it, didn't you, Dyl?' said Seth cheerfully.

Dylan could have strangled him. 'Most of the guys aren't, you know.' He stared straight ahead.

'I think you'll find the cool ones are.' Seth whispered something else to Sadie, and she giggled.

Dylan sniffed. 'If that clobber you're wearing is cool, I'm glad I'm not.' Wow. For once he'd got a good reply in.

Mum pulled up by the community hall, and they all got out. 'Have a lovely time, darlings!' And she was off again.

Seth slapped Dylan's back on the way in. 'You're cool in a different way, Dyly, don't worry.'

Dylan shrugged. That had been kindly meant, and this was where he should say something brotherly too, but the moment was gone. He stared after his brother as Seth and Sadie took their jackets over to the cloakroom. He was always the odd one out, and he didn't want to be.

He wandered over to hand his jacket to the cloakroom attendant, and that was when the evening exploded. Dylan turned back towards the main hall, where Rihanna was blaring out at full volume. He'd said he would see Paul and Jay inside. Someone pulled at his arm, and he turned to see Sadie gesticulating towards the door with her other hand.

'Look – here's Natasha. You should wait for her, get a dance in with her.'

'Oo – er. Going to ask Tash for a dance, Dyly?' Greg from their tutor group was there now too, and Dylan shrugged.

'Seth said he wanted to ask her to go with him, but he bottled it.' Sadie sounded nothing but cheerful, and Dylan glared at her. Seth was nowhere to be seen.

'Ooh, Dyly, you need to get your finger out if you want a girl to go with you.' Greg was laughing hysterically now, beer fumes from him mixing in with Sadie's musk. Dylan hesitated, and Rick swaggered over. He was Greg's mate, and he had a mouth like a sewer.

'It's not his finger he wants to get out. Is it, Dyly? Or should it be Dicky?'

Howls of laughter came from all around, and Greg slapped Dylan's back. 'Go on, Dyly-dick – ask her!' He propelled Dylan towards Natasha, who was putting her cloakroom ticket into her bag. 'Hey, Tash! Little Dick wants to ask you something!'

Dylan lashed out and managed to free himself. 'Fuck off, all of you!' He spun round and pushed through the growing crowd, ignoring the calls of 'hey, Dick, come back!'

Dylan charged into the gents and almost fell over Seth at the end basin. He was poking at a spot under his chin.

'Does this show much?'

Dylan shoved his shoulder. 'You told Sadie I bottled asking Natasha here!'

Seth shrugged. 'It's not like it's a secret, Dyl. Everyone knows. You can ask her to dance, though, can't you?' He wiped his hands on a paper towel and left, cries of 'where's little Dick?' floating into the gents as the door opened.

Dylan leaned on the sink, his stomach heaving. Why were they so cruel? Just because he didn't jabber and joke all the time, just because he worked hard. He'd never hear the end of this now. He'd be 'little Dick' forever. Natasha would be laughing her head off with the rest, or worse still she'd be embarrassed and angry. She'd never look at him now.

More calls from the hallway. 'Dick-y, Dick-y. Come on, Dick-y…'

Dylan retched. This was all Seth's fault, and it was – unforgivable. Yes. He stared at his reflection in the mirror, breathing deeply.

One day, he'd get his revenge.

CHAPTER 17

MEGAN WAS STILL ASLEEP WHEN HOLLY TIPTOED PAST THE SPARE room door. Or if she wasn't asleep, she was being mighty quiet, and Fred wasn't moving around either. Holly paused outside the study door, but all was silent there too. Best leave Dylan to sleep; it wasn't even seven yet and he'd probably lain awake for ages last night. She had, too.

She was organising ingredients to make scrambled egg and bacon when the shower in the en suite bathroom started. That must be Dylan. Holly switched on the coffee machine to heat up.

He appeared ten minutes later, unshaven but otherwise looking okay. Holly gave him a hug, which he reciprocated for about half a second before moving away. He was shutting her out, and while it was par for the course they'd been on for the past couple of months, it still made her feel guilty today. She was being a crap wife. He pulled out a chair and dropped into it, his face dreary.

Holly handed over a coffee. 'Did you get much sleep?'

A shrug. 'Some. Let's eat. There's so much to do today.'

'I'll help all I can.' Holly gave his shoulders a rub, and now even this – a perfectly normal thing to do when your partner was upset – felt wrong. It wasn't what she wanted; she wanted them to be back to the way they were before his bloody promotion, but it was all so complicated and horrible, and it must be so much worse for him. And heck, she'd need to mention Seth and Laura's wedding rings in the next few minutes, because that wasn't the kind of thing you could ignore. Had Dylan noticed? But he'd have said if he had – wouldn't he? Or maybe he'd known about it beforehand. But he'd have told her. Wouldn't he? Oh, God, this was dire.

He was silent as she scrambled eggs and grilled bacon, answering her question about toast with a nod. Holly waited until he put his knife and fork down.

'Dylan, I don't know if you noticed yesterday... I didn't, but Megan said later that Seth and Laura were wearing wedding rings.'

Her words hung in the air. Dylan froze, staring straight ahead with no expression on his face. Holly waited, her heart pounding. It felt like forever before he heaved a sigh and pushed his plate away, not looking at her.

'Yes.'

'You knew? Are they properly married, or...?'

He leapt up, leaning over until his face was inches from hers, his eyes blazing and his fists balled. Holly shrank back.

'For fuck's sake, Holly. Just leave the gossip alone, can't you?' He yanked the back door open, stepped out and slammed it shut behind him.

Shaking, Holly rose to clear away the plates. He'd been within an inch of hitting her there. It was the new worst hour of their marriage, and she had no idea what to do about it.

IT WAS EXACTLY the same as when Mum died. For half a second when she woke up, everything in Megan's world was normal, then – wham. Here she was in Holly's spare room, and Grandma was dead. She would never kiss Grandma again. And she didn't want to kiss Dylan or Seth. She had no relatives left to kiss except Aunt Angela, and she didn't count because they only saw each other once or twice a year. Was there anyone left alive who even loved her?

Megan rolled over and lifted her phone. She'd missed a message from Gabe last night: *Is everything okay?*

Her fingers flew over the screen as she tapped out the bare essentials and pressed send. Fred was standing watching her, whining, and Megan got up to open the door for him. He ran downstairs, and now she was all on her own in a bedroom in someone else's house. Her phone rang when she was pulling the duvet back over her head. Gabe.

'I don't know what to say, Megs. I'm sorry. Can I do anything?'

'Thanks. No.' Megan cleared her throat. 'I don't know what's happening now. Today.'

'Shit. Text me later when you do know. I'll come and see you.'

Did she want that? Megan put off the decision. 'I'll try. Thanks. See you soon, anyway.' She ended the call and breathed out. She'd been dreading talking to people, but that hadn't been too bad. Gabe was kind. But Susie and Hope would be full of questions – wanting to help, sure, but no one could. Megan flopped back on the bed. Did you go through this every time someone died?

She trailed downstairs half an hour later to find Dylan sorting papers on the kitchen table and Holly emptying the dishwasher. Dylan gave her a nod and said 'Meggie', like he used to when she was tiny, and Holly came to give her a hug.

'Come and have breakfast, Meg. We're working out what needs doing about the funeral, so you can think if you have any wishes about it. We'll try to have it on Thursday or Friday.'

'Okay.' Megan accepted Holly's offer of scrambled eggs because it was easier than refusing, and grabbed her mug to cuddle in the meantime. 'What are we doing today?'

It was Dylan who answered. 'Paperwork at Seth's first. Laura says he doesn't want to leave the house, so we'll go there once I've got this lot sorted. And Aunt Angela's coming this afternoon. She's going to stay at Mum's until after the funeral.'

Megan sat straighter. Wow. She could go home for a few days and stay there with Aunt Angela. Except Aunt Angela was almost a stranger, and yet again she didn't know what she wanted to do.

They left when she'd finished pushing scrambled egg around on her plate. Dylan drove, although he was in a total funk, barely speaking to anyone. Megan undid her seat belt as soon as the car pulled up outside Seth and Laura's. She hadn't dared mention Seth and Laura's wedding rings, but Holly would have told Dylan, wouldn't she?

It was Laura who let them in. 'Seth's in the study. He's still in a state – why don't you and Holly join him, Dylan, and Megan and I'll bring coffee in a few minutes? We won't be able to help much with your mum's business stuff.'

No one was saying anything about weddings. The others traipsed into the study on the other side of the hall, and Megan grabbed Fred and followed Laura up the hallway. You could tell Laura had moved in properly. The kitchen here was pretty old, but the sink was clean now and the worktops were full of swanky kitchen stuff like a bread maker and a pestle and mortar. Laura was obviously a much better cook than Seth was.

And Grandma would never cook again. Megan flopped down on a wooden chair. That was how it went. For a few moments, something would distract her from the awfulness of what was happening, then it would hit her all over again and the sick, heavy feeling in her middle would pin her down so hard she could barely move.

Laura pressed buttons on the coffee machine. 'Cappuccino?'

Whatever. Megan nodded, then stirred in the choc powder when her mug arrived. Laura was doing her nails, and Megan watched as she dipped a cotton bud in nail polish remover and wiped round each nail in turn. Yesterday's bright red was gone; today's colour was muted pink. Because Grandma was dead? Megan barely suppressed a sniff. She would never be happy again.

Laura leaned over the table. 'Oh, Megan, sweetie. It's hard. But it's better for Elaine that she doesn't have to suffer for months and years after her stroke. And you won't always feel like this, you know.'

Megan shrugged. As if Laura, who'd known her for half a second, could see into her head. A housing brochure of some kind was on the kitchen table, and Megan twisted her head to see it. Someone had circled an advertisement for a house in Sevenoaks and put a large tick beside it. Megan's heart thumped – were Seth and Laura planning to move away? Sevenoaks would be closer to Laura's work in London, but most of Seth's concerts and things were between here and the south coast. Maybe Laura had found him a posh new job in London to go with her own posh job.

Abruptly, Laura shoved the biscuit tin across to Megan, lifted the brochure and jammed it into the shoulder bag hanging on the back of her chair. Megan glowered. Obviously, she wasn't supposed to see that.

'Have a biccy. I'll pop in and see if they're ready for coffee yet.' Laura gave Megan a little smile – at least it wasn't a big bright one – and left her alone with Fred.

The business bit couldn't have been difficult, because Laura was back in half a minute saying, 'On you go through, Megan. Take the biscuits, and I'll bring the tray.'

As if they were having a bloody coffee morning. Megan grabbed the biscuit tin and stomped through to the study. The other three were sitting round the desk, but Dylan got up as soon as she went in.

'Let's take this into the other room.' He brushed past Megan into the living room and flopped down on the sofa.

The others followed dumbly, Holly with a hand on Seth's arm. He looked shocking, huge panda eyes in a white face. Megan blinked at him. Had he slept at all last night? It didn't look like it. When Laura had brought in the coffee, Dylan cleared his throat and looked at Megan.

'We're waiting with the funeral arrangements until Aunt Angela's here too. I'll fetch her from Heathrow this afternoon.'

'I'll stay at Grandma's with her while she's here.' Megan braced herself to argue, but no one objected.

Holly leaned forward. 'I'm going to Heathrow with Dylan, Meg – do you want to come too?'

'No. No-no.' That would be the worst ever. Imagine standing waiting at arrivals and Aunt Angela appearing and hugs and tears and – oh, God. 'I'll, um, stay at home and get a bed ready for Aunt Angela.'

Holly looked from her to Dylan as if she couldn't decide what to do, then she nodded at Megan. 'That would be a real help, if you're sure you don't mind being alone for an hour?'

Laura was leaning towards her too. 'Megan darling, I'll – Seth and I'll only be a phone call away if you need us.'

Megan pressed her back into the sofa and stared at Seth, who was sunk in misery or whatever in the armchair by the window. Obviously, he and Dylan needed more looking after than she did. Good.

CHAPTER 18

HOLLY TOOK A DEEP, APPRECIATIVE BREATH OF GARDEN AIR. IT WAS almost the longest day and summer had arrived, in between the monsoons they were having this year. And with all that was going on, it was a huge relief to be alone here for an hour or two to recharge her fading batteries. Being with Dylan, trying to reach into his grief and help him was as exhausting as it was futile. This afternoon, though, he'd gone to Seth's, and as Megan was at Elaine's with Aunt Angela, Holly and Fred had the place to themselves. The garden was bursting into life; it needed taming, and a bit of weeding would be balm to her soul. Holly fetched a basket for the weeds and crouched down by the strawberry plants. Runners everywhere... She started snipping them off.

Was she expecting too much of Dylan? It could be a Venus and Mars kind of thing; men would grieve differently, perhaps. Holly's shoulders slumped. What was happening to them had started long before Elaine's death and wasn't just odd, it was terrifying. Dylan. The man she loved. The man she wanted to have children with, grow old with, and he was becoming a stranger. Last Christmas, everything had been fine. Then he started that bloody job and it all went pear-shaped. She scowled as yet another runner appeared from under a strawberry plant, then snipped it off and tossed it into the weed bucket. They didn't need more plants for next year, though by the look of things, this year's crop wasn't going to be the bumper that last year's had turned into. Strawberry plants didn't enjoy on-off torrential rain all spring.

Her phone buzzed in her pocket, and she stood up to answer it. Oh – it was Adam, which must mean they had an animal in dire trouble, because he knew she was in the middle of a family crisis.

She was right. 'Holly, can you possibly come in? We have a swan here. He's swallowed a fish hook and there's a mile and a half of line attached to it. We took an X-ray – the hook's clearly visible and I can feel it from the outside, but we can't get it out and his breathing's getting laboured. If you can't, I'll try else-where, but…'

He was panicking. 'With you in ten.' Holly hurried inside for her bag and car key. Swans, with their long, elegant necks, could have real problems if they swallowed something they shouldn't. You didn't need much swelling to close off a swan's neck. She shut Fred into the kitchen and left him in an insulted heap on the floor.

The swan was a young male, one of last year's cygnets by the look of him. His head was resting on Adam's shoulder and he was frighteningly still for a wild creature. Holly's heartbeat increased. They didn't have much time here, and if Adam hadn't been able to work the hook up the neck and out through the creature's mouth, she certainly wouldn't be able to. The alterna-tive was making an incision in the swan's neck.

Adam's face was set. He touched the side of the swan's neck about halfway down. 'The hook's here.'

Holly ran her fingers over the place, then went to look at the X-ray. 'Let's try as small an incision as possible to get it out through the neck wall.'

'Agreed.' He had a tray all ready with the necessary instruments, and Nadia reached for the anaesthetic cone.

Holly bent over the swan as she worked. Two minutes had the neck open, then she reached for the surgical tweezers and grasped the hook, manipulating it round and out of the swan's oesophagus. She pulled gently, and a long stretch of fishing line came with it.

'Excellent. We'll check there's no more line in the mouth when you've closed the wound.' Adam's relief was almost palpable.

Twenty minutes later, the swan was lying in a shed. A day or two's peace and quiet was what it needed now. Holly circled aching shoulders, then walked back to the main building with Adam.

He slung an arm around her. 'That was brilliant. Well done and thank you so much for coming out.'

His hand rubbed her shoulder, and Holly blinked up at him. Adam was the huggy type, and it was oddly unsettling after the coldness Dylan was sending out towards her these days.

'No problem,' she said lightly. 'I'll get off home, now. Dylan's at his brother's, so poor Fred's home alone.'

'We owe you an afternoon off sometime.' He lifted his arm in a wave.

Home again, Holly released Fred from the confines of the kitchen and jogged to the compost heap at the back of the garden with the abandoned bucket of weeds. If only her relationship with Dylan was as effortless as her relationship with Adam. It had been, once upon a time.

———

MEGAN STOOD at the top of the stairs. Silence was everywhere. Aunt Angela had gone to Seth's for a last funeral talk before tomorrow, so she was here on her own, and that wouldn't often happen after this. They'd want to sell Grandma's home, wouldn't they? Oh, Grandma.

The stairs creaked as she went down. Normally she didn't notice; now each step was a nostalgic shriek in the silence. The house was hurting, too, but at least home still smelled the same. Megan stood in the front hallway with her eyes shut, breathing, in, out, and if she could just stand here doing this for the rest of her life, nothing would have changed so horribly. But she couldn't, and everything had changed. She crept into the living room, sat down on Grandma's chair and had a good cry.

She was drying her eyes when her mobile buzzed. Seth – why didn't they leave her alone? She didn't need a babysitter, and this would have been Laura's or Aunt Angela's idea anyway.

'You okay by yourself, Megs?'

'Fine. I'm – having a tidy.'

'Okay, if you're sure. See you soon.'

He ended the call before Megan realised it would be the adult thing to ask him if he was okay too. She trooped through to the kitchen and began a desultory tidy. Grandma had always said Aunt Angela was still as pernickety as when she'd been head teacher at school, and she'd been right.

The doorbell rang while she was dusting the living room. Gabe was standing there, his face creased.

'You okay? Mum said she saw your aunt go out.'

Megan choked, and he stepped right in and closed the door, then held her while she cried all over again.

'I'm scared, Gabe. I don't know what'll happen to me, without Grandma. She's gone, just like that.'

'I guess you'll stay with one of your family.'

She dabbed at her eyes with a tissue. They'd talked about this over lunch on Monday. 'I've to be at Seth's during the week until

I start my job at the wildlife centre. He and Laura are at home more, and they all think I shouldn't be sitting alone at Holly and Dylan's all day. Seth's gutted about Grandma but he's a creep, and Laura's a – a stranger. I'll move to Dylan and Holly for the rest of the school hols when my job starts.' She stopped. If Seth and Laura were moving to Sevenoaks, she would have to live with Dylan and Holly permanently, always supposing her GCSE grades were enough to get into sixth form. Did they actually want her there full time? Grandma's house would be sold and there wouldn't be anything left of her old life in Linton Keynes, and it was all so complicated and horrible.

More tears spilled over, and Gabe pulled her in for another hug. Megan inhaled sharply, then pushed him back. He was being nice, but this was more than a 'make Megan feel better' kind of hug. Gabe was enjoying it for a very different reason, and that was – perverse.

Not having a home was the worst ever.

CHAPTER 19

DYLAN AND SETH: THE SOLO DAYS

'Is that you, Seth? Are you working tonight, love?'

Mum's voice floated through from the kitchen the moment Seth stepped in the front door, and he winced. That meant she needed him to do something, and as he had no plans for the evening, it would be hard to say no.

'Nope. Why?' He left his jacket on the stair post and went through. She'd been a bit distracted today, though she hadn't said anything, which was unusual. When Mum had a problem, she generally told you ALL about it.

'Bryony called while you were out. She's at her important meeting about this bird project she's working on, and it's running over. Megan's gone to play at a little friend's house, but we need to collect her at half five and I'm waiting on a call from Angela. She hasn't been well. Can you go for Megan? It's 17, Elm Street, so you'd be there and back in a few minutes.'

He hadn't heard about Bry's important meeting, but as favours went, this wasn't a biggie. Seth glanced at the clock on the microwave and grabbed his jacket again. 'See you in ten, then.'

He plodded along an icy pavement and into Elm Street. Bryony was doing all right for herself these days. Who'd have thought it? Her photography had really taken off and she was building up a very respectable freelance photography business of her own, her and her camera. It was amazing how many people wanted baby pics and wedding pics and God knows what else pics, but Bry did them all, with the help of a little studio in the flat she and Megan lived in on the edge of Linton Keynes. A bird project sounded as if she was branching out. Good for her. At least she was doing real stuff, not like that ponce of a brother they had.

Megan came hurtling down the stairs as soon as Tanya's mum opened the door. She zipped up her jacket, her little face full of happiness, and Seth's heart melted. Aw, she was pleased to see him.

'Is Mummy still at work?'

'Yup. Will I do? Say bye bye.'

She waved to Tanya and her mum, then grabbed his hand and launched into her usual chatter about school and lunch and what Mummy said about this and that. Seth listened with half his attention. Yes, Bryony was sorted. A cute daughter, a growing business and babysitters on tap. Dylan was sorted too, in that he was at uni in Bristol, of all places. He'd said it was the best place for business courses, but the real reason would be to get far enough away so that he couldn't possibly come home every weekend to help his mother. Seth swallowed a laugh. Guess what, brother dear. We don't miss you one bit. He and Mum were still the dream team.

Seth bit his lip. Making out he didn't care was a lie. Dylan had never forgiven him for what happened at the Christmas disco that time. Oh, he'd apologised – not that it was his fault, really – but even now, Dylan still spent half the time looking at him with scary eyes. Poor sod had been slagged off for the rest of the time he'd been at school, too; the other kids didn't like Dyl much. He hadn't gone out with a girl until he'd left.

His mother was on the phone in the living room when Seth and Megan arrived back home, so they tiptoed past and went into the kitchen.

'I have homework. Will you help me?' Megan opened her schoolbag and produced a worksheet from her folder.

Seth sat down, watching as she filled in the letters to make animal names, then coloured them in. His mother came in when Meg was almost finished, and the school and lunch and what Mummy said chatter began all over again. Seth sat back. She was a bright little kiddy – it was fun, being part of her life.

They were finishing Meg's favourite chicken pie and peas when Bryony arrived. She pulled a blue bottle from her bag and stuck it in the freezer.

'We'll give it ten minutes.' She plumped down beside Megan and beamed round the table. 'You. Will. Never. Guess. What.'

'We never will, so you'd better tell us, darling.' Mum fetched Bryony's plate from the oven. 'I kept it warm in case you were hungry.'

'Mummy? Is it something nice?'

Bryony kissed Megan's head. 'I'll say. I have a book contract. They – the publisher – liked my work and my idea for a bird book. I've got six months to get the photos finished and organised into seasons, then it'll be published in the autumn ready for people buying posh books next Christmas. They want another one, too.'

Seth whistled. Wow. His sister, the author. Were people who created photo collections authors? He sat listening to his mother rhapsodising about the bird pics while Bryony chomped her way through her grub, spluttering pastry at them as she answered.

Seth pushed his empty plate to the side. 'Don't writers earn peanuts?'

'I'm not a writer. There'll be a sentence or a label on each bird, but it's the pics they want. And I'm getting an advance. A big one.' She got up and organised fizz glasses before rescuing her bottle from the freezer and opening it with a pop that made Megan shriek.

Seth opened his mouth to say 'how much?' then closed it again. Not your business, Seth. He accepted a glass of bubbles from Bryony and clinked with her while Mum poured apple juice for Megan.

His womenfolk went on talking about birds, and Seth sipped morosely. He was glad for Bryony, really he was, but this wasn't half making his job as roadie cum mixer cum manager for the band a few of the guys had got together look inadequate. The pay was pretty inadequate too, but having said that, they had double the number of bookings this winter compared to last, so things were looking up. Problem was, Bry and Dylan had their independence, and he couldn't afford not to live at home. He was living the life of Riley, according to his mother, and in many ways she was right. Meals cooked, practically no rent, and if he had to do some odd jobs for Mum now and again, he could do that. What he couldn't do was fling parties like most of his mates did, and having Mum and often Meg around was more than a touch style-cramping when he wanted to bring girls home. He needed to get his own place. Forcing a smile for his mother, Seth tuned back into the birds conversation.

Maybe Dylan'd had the right idea.

———

IT WAS ALMOST twelve before Seth was up on Thursday. The band had a once-a-week Wednesday night spot in a Brighton pub, and it had been after two when he arrived back in Linton

Keynes. He rolled out of bed, grabbed his clothes and opened the bedroom door. Mum was talking downstairs, so she was either on the phone or— No, hell! That was Dyl answering her. What was he doing back home in the middle of the week? Seth pulled on his clothes and ran downstairs.

Dylan was sitting in the kitchen with Mum, a mug of coffee in front of him and an annoying pleased-with-himself expression on his face.

Seth clicked on the kettle. 'Morning, Dyl...an.' Calling his brother 'Dyly' now was enough to get the scary-eyed glare again.

Dylan looked pointedly at his watch. 'Afternoon. Busy night at the pub?'

'It was, yes. Wednesdays always turn in a good profit. Lectures finished for today, then?'

'You two!' said his mother. 'I hope that's what you call friendly bickering?'

Seth swished his tea bag around in the mug. 'Absolutely.' Not. Friendly bickering was a thing of the past. Dyl's bickering was deadly serious nowadays.

Dylan leaned back in his chair. 'I'm here for my ski things, if you must know. A couple of us have rented a chalet in Aviemore for the weekend. We're driving up tomorrow.'

'Aviemore, how lovely. Seth, darling, I'm about to make spaghetti for lunch. Do you want some too?'

'Sounds like a plan. Thanks, Mum.'

She patted his shoulder on her way past. Dylan rose abruptly and went upstairs to bang around in the attic, and Seth slurped his tea. Skiing in Scotland, huh? Now that was living the life of Riley. Ominous thuds vibrated down from the attic, and his mother looked at the ceiling.

Seth sighed theatrically. 'Want me to go and see what the hell he's doing?'

'Give him a hand, darling. Skis aren't easy to shift down that ladder.'

And Dylan was more the type to yank stuff around and do things by force instead of applying a little dexterity. How he managed to stay upright on skis was a mystery. Seth dumped his mug in the sink and meandered upstairs. Dylan's ski boots and helmet were lying at the bottom of the ladder up to the attic, and Seth dodged to the side as a ski pole dropped from the trap door in the ceiling.

'Hey, you should look before you chuck things around. Pass them down to me.'

The second pole whizzed past, and Seth swore. 'Dylan! What are you doing?'

More thuds. 'My skis have fallen behind those bloody TV aerials. They're all tangled up.'

Seth grasped the ladder. Mum's retro aerial collection from the dark ages might even be worth something one day. He climbed the ladder and stuck his head into the loft. The roof was too low to stand up here, and Dylan was kneeling at the far end, holding one ski and trying to disentangle the other from a mass of wire.

Seth crawled over. 'Here. You lift the aerials and separate them, and I'll pull the skis out.'

'Be careful with them. They're expensive, you know.'

Seth took hold of a ski. Typical Dylan, always buying stuff to show off with. Normal people who skied three times a year max would hire their equipment, but not Dyl. He splashed the cash like a bloody millionaire. He had a part-time job as well as his student loan – which he'd have to repay, of course. It wasn't the way Seth wanted to go.

A brief tussle with the aerials, and the skis were freed. Seth reversed back down the ladder, took the skis from Dylan at the top, then pushed the ladder up when his brother arrived back on the landing.

Dylan was making a meal out of arranging the skis, binding them together and fussing around hanging the poles over one end. What an irritating bugger he was; not a thank you to be heard.

Seth folded his arms. 'You're welcome,' he said, injecting as much sarcasm as he could into his voice. 'You owe me, huh?'

Dylan jerked, then looked Seth straight in the eye and hissed. 'Owe you? Oh, I don't think so, do you? I reckon you owe me. Big time, as they say.'

Seth gaped. 'How d'you make that out?'

Dylan gave his smarmy little smile, and Seth raised his eyebrows. What was coming now?

'Because, brother dear, in spite of your efforts at making me look like a halfwit at that disco, I've kept my mouth shut about that dodgy little package you had in your locker at school a while back. Remember? The one with weirdo symbols on one side? Tut, tut. Imagine if Mum got to hear about it. You'd be out on your ear without a penny to your name, wouldn't you?'

Jesus Christ. How the shit did he know about that?

'I don't know what you're talking about.' Except he did, didn't he? Bry's bloody package of whatever it was.

'Oh, I think you do. Want to see some photographic proof? You'd better be nice to me, brother dear.'

Dylan smirked again, then manoeuvred his way downstairs with his ski gear.

Seth stood still. *No.* Holy shit – had Dyl taken pics of the bloody parcel? Or was it a bluff? This was going to need a bit of thought, because Dylan was right about one thing. After all the aggro with Bry, and with her lovely new life being a grandma, Mum had zero tolerance about anything drug-related these days. Not that it stopped her swigging sherry, and Bry was pretty good with the booze too, but that was different, apparently. It would be finito dream team if Mum found out about that package, and while she might not chuck him out on the street, she'd be disappointed and horrified and all the bad stuff, and that was *not* what he wanted.

'Lunch, Seth darling!'

Mum's usual bright and breezy call came a few minutes later. He wasn't going to do anything to lose that, was he? And he mustn't let Dylan do anything, either.

'Coming!' Seth fixed on a smile and ran downstairs.

CHAPTER 20

THURSDAY, 17TH JUNE

Sunlight chinked through the gap between the leaf-green
bedroom curtains and flickered on Holly's face. Still half-asleep,
she stretched a hand out, but the other side of the bed was
empty. As it had been all week. And oh, no, today was Elaine's
funeral.

The entire week had passed in an unreal, empty, echoing
way, but maybe time always seemed like that after a death.
Visiting the undertaker, making the arrangements, talking in
hushed voices that didn't belong to them. Still three separate
families, with the difference that it was Angela staying at
Elaine's house with Megan. That would change soon; Angela
was going home on Saturday. Holly flung back the duvet and
grabbed her bathrobe.

Downstairs, Dylan was hunched over the kitchen table, a
mug of coffee and a pile of funeral paperwork in front of him.
Holly touched his shoulder as she passed. He had closed right off
from her; it was terrifying. Inside, he must be craving love and

warmth, but the fact that he'd been cold towards her even before Elaine's death wouldn't help him accept the warmth she was still trying to show him. Holly shivered. It was anyone's guess if their marriage would survive this, long term. She had no idea what he was thinking.

'The arrangements are perfect, Dylan. You did a great job.' Funeral arrangements had fallen to him, as apart from helping with some details about Elaine's life, Angela had left things to the brothers, and Seth had been much too emotional to deal with anyone outside the family. Who'd have guessed that happy-go-lucky, easy-going Seth would fall apart so thoroughly? Your mother's death was a huge thing, she got that, but she hadn't realised how close Seth had been to Elaine.

Dylan stuffed his paperwork into a plastic folder. He still hadn't spoken to her, and Holly forced back choking resentment. He was grieving, she had to make allowances, this wasn't the time – etc. etc.

'You'll feel different after the funeral, Dylan.' Now she was spouting platitudes.

He glared. 'How can you possibly know that?' He drained his coffee mug and pushed his chair back.

His feet thudded up the stairs, and a moment later the shower in the family bathroom started. Well. She'd asked for that. And yet... Holly stared outside where Fred was sniffing around the hydrangea bush. Was it really her job as Dylan's wife to take the flak for everything when he was grieving? Well, yes, perhaps it was, and perhaps she should be happy to. That she wasn't was possibly an indicator of the state of their marriage.

They arrived at Elaine's much too early, but Seth and Laura were there before them and Angela looked as if she'd been sitting in her funeral clothes for hours. Holly's heart ached at the sight of Megan's bleak face. Dylan squeezed onto the sofa with Laura and Seth, leaving the other chair for Holly. She patted the arm, glad when Megan came over and perched. The hearse wouldn't be here for another half hour, and all they could do was wait, with Dylan stiff as a poker and Seth sunk in misery while Angela fidgeted with her handbag. It was left up to Holly and Laura to fill the silence with the odd remark.

A sharp intake of breath from Megan alerted Holly to the hearse pulling up outside, a black funeral car behind it. Seth grabbed Laura's hand in both his own, and Dylan went to help Aunt Angela from her chair. Holly concentrated on Megan. This was her job, today.

The neighbours had gathered on the street, ready to follow the hearse, and Holly was glad to see Gabe there too. He stepped forward and gave Megan a white rose, how lovely. Holly blinked back tears while Megan whispered her thanks.

The service was mercifully short, and Holly kept a firm hold of Megan's hand for the duration. Funerals were tough, end of. At the end they sang 'All things bright and beautiful' as the curtain across the front of the chapel jerked shut, and the coffin was gone. Seth was shaking visibly now, and Dylan's face was white. Holly shuddered. One day, she too would go to her mother's funeral, and who could tell if she'd cope any better than these two? There was no real closure when it was your mum. As the teenager beside her knew all too well. Holly inched her chair closer to Megan's. A few more words from the vicar, and people started filing out.

Megan stepped towards the front, the rose Gabe had given her still in her hand. 'I want to put this on the coffin.'

Holly went behind the curtain with her, and yes, this was good, a moment of peace for Meg, here with her grandma where no one else could see her. Megan ran her hands up the coffin and laid the rose at the top end, her lips trembling.

Holly stroked a stray wisp of hair from the girl's forehead. 'You never lose the love, Meg.'

'I know.' Megan turned away.

Holly ushered her out through the chapel entrance, where people were gathering to say goodbye. That was when she noticed Seth. He was clinging to Laura, his face twitching, and his eyes – his eyes were wild.

———

MEGAN SLUMPED down in the funeral car as it drove them back through the village to the hotel that was providing a soup and sandwich lunch for the funeral party. Round tables were laid for eight in a sunny room overlooking the garden, and Megan took her place between Holly and Aunt Angela. She had to force the food down, but eating the ham soup and a cheese and cucumber sandwich helped. She could do this.

After the meal, Holly joined some of Elaine's neighbours at the next table while Gabe came over to Megan. Dylan had gone to another table too, and Seth, Laura and Aunt Angela were joined by a couple of elderly ladies who were chatting with do-you-remember expressions. Megan glared at her coffee cup. This was crap. Why did funerals always end up being just normal meals out? At least Gabe was here, being properly quiet and respectful to Grandma.

Megan stared up the table. What the hell was Seth doing? It was like watching a car crash in slow motion. Seth started to shift around in his chair, then he wiped one hand over his face and blew his nose on a large cotton handkerchief that was prob- ably Laura's contribution to his outfit. Laura was muttering in his ear now, but whatever it was, Seth had heard enough. He pushed his chair back and swayed across the room, crashing into an empty table as he went. A chair clattered to the floor and the room fell silent, apart from the thud of Seth's feet staggering across the wooden floor. Laura and then Dylan ran after him, and they all stood in the corner talking in low voices before Seth flung his arms up and strode from the room.

Heart thumping, Megan jerked round to exchange glances with Holly at the next table. Holly shook her head. Okay, Laura and Dylan were enough people to help Seth. The two had their heads together now, murmuring, then Laura went out after Seth.

Dylan came over and bent his head to Megan's. 'Seth's upset. He's gone for a breath of fresh air. He'll be okay, don't worry.'

He walked on to his place at the next table, and Megan turned to Gabe. This was all just way too much. 'I want to go outside too.'

And it was nice, the way he stood up straightaway and took her hand.

The rose garden was deserted, which was just as well because it was tiny, and if anyone else had been out here they'd have had to whisper not to be overheard. Megan drifted round a circular bed with yellow and orange roses, her hand held tightly in Gabe's. This was better.

Eventually, she sat down on a green bench by the garden wall. You couldn't walk in circles all the time. Gabe sat down too, then inched along the bench and put his arm around her. Megan stiffened, but he didn't move away.

'Meg – I hate seeing you so alone and lost like this. I want to look after you. Let's go public properly. I want people to know we're a couple, don't you? I should have been sitting beside you today.'

He was right up close now, and – no! His head swooped forward to kiss her, his hands pulling her closer, and why the shit did he think she wanted this at Grandma's funeral, for God's sake? Megan shoved him back as hard as she could, then leapt to her feet and ran.

'Meg! Wait! I'm sorry!'

She wheeled round. 'It's my grandmother's funeral, Gabe. Not your best move, was it? Stuff going public. We're done.'

Brilliant. She'd dumped him at Grandma's funeral. Life could not get any more sick and depraved than this. Megan stamped back to the hotel, Gabe trailing after her bleating, 'Wait, Meg, please!'

Back inside, people were beginning to go home, and Holly and Dylan were in the foyer saying goodbye. Megan went to stand beside Holly.

'Bye for now, Megan, love.' Sonya, Gabe's mum, gave her shoulder a pat. 'You're welcome at ours anytime, you know that. Is Gabe...?' She looked around.

'He's outside.' Megan swallowed, and Sonya moved on to say goodbye to Dylan.

Holly gave her a little hug. 'You did well today, Megs. Are you okay?'

Oh, she was fine, apart from a few minor details like no Grandma and no home and now no boyfriend because he'd turned into a sex-mad wanker. 'S'pose. But – I only have two more nights left at home, don't I? Ever.'

Holly pulled a face. 'I know it's not the same, Meggy, but you'll have a home with us – and with Seth and Laura – for as long as you need one.'

Megan sniffed. 'Not if Seth and Laura move away I won't.'

'They're moving away? First I've heard of it.'

'Laura was looking at a house closer to London. Bet you anything you like she gets her way, too.'

Holly handed Megan the car key. 'Let's leave that for another time, huh? Can you take Aunt Angela to the car while Dylan and I say thank you to the hotel people – and don't worry, Megs.'

Megan rolled her eyes. Her life was one long worry. She took Aunt Angela's arm, and they walked to the Corsa, which Holly and Dylan had left here ready for them. Aunt Angela huffed and puffed as she got into the passenger seat.

'Are you… are you okay, Aunt Angela?'

The old lady reached out to take Megan's hand.

'You're a good girl, Megan. Holly's another. You can trust her.' She turned away and stared out of the window.

Megan looked too. Dylan was striding across the car park, Holly trotting along a few yards behind him, as if she was trying to catch up.

———

It was nine o'clock that evening when they left Elaine's house. Holly reversed out of the driveway and gave a wave to the forlorn little face in the living room window. Megan was going to need a lot of support over the next few weeks and months. Hopefully volunteering at the wildlife centre would help the poor kid find her feet in her new world, and Fred would help too, bless him. Dogs knew where they were needed.

Dylan was tapping on his phone. 'Seth's gone to bed. Laura says he had a good cry, then they had a talk about Mum and he went off to bed with a sleeping pill.'

He was communicating with her. Thank God. Holly reached over and touched his arm. 'He'll need time, but we can be there for him as much as he wants us to be. Are you okay, Dylan?' She'd have said, 'Dylan, love?' a few short weeks ago.

He looked sideways at her. 'It's tough, but – we have to carry on, don't we? It'll get easier.'

Correction. He was communicating in clichés. Holly reduced speed to let a van swing past. 'Megs told me something just before we left the hotel. There wasn't time to get the whole story and I thought it would be best to leave it for another day, but – she said Seth and Laura are looking at a house closer to London. She had the impression Laura wants to move.'

Dylan slapped his hand on his knee. 'Oh, for God's sake, don't be so bloody ridiculous! Why would they want to move?

Megan's a hysterical teenager and you should know better than to believe everything she says.' He jerked away from her as far as the confines of the car allowed him, and gave his full attention to his phone.

Holly breathed in deeply. Okay. It had been a hard day and Dylan was grieving. She had to make allowances for him. Again.

CHAPTER 21

DYLAN AND SETH: THE UNCLE DAYS

DYLAN TAPPED OUT OF HIS INTERNET BANKING AND MENTALLY ticked the 'reorganise savings' box in his head. He leaned back in his chair, swinging it gently from right to left. It was very satisfying, how the cash was coming together. Another couple of years, and he'd be able to afford the deposit on a place of his own, one he could do up and improve the value, live in for a year or two, then sell on. His flat here in Croydon was nice enough, but renting wasn't the best way to go.

An email pinged into his account, and he opened it. Ah – from Megan: *Hi Dylan, thanks for my birthday money. I'm going to buy a colour-changing lamp for my bedroom. See you soon, love from Megan x*

Nice. Money was the easy option when it came to presents, of course, but what did he know about twelve-year-old girls? At least she'd get something she wanted. Mum had bought her some riding lessons, and knowing Seth, his contribution would be some weird T-shirt or a ticket to a concert Meg didn't want to go to. As for Bryony…

Dylan rubbed a hand over his face. Bry was a mess. You'd think after having six books of bird and wildlife photos published, making a television documentary on how to take bird pics and bringing in an absolute shedload of money, his sister might consider herself established enough to make a home for her daughter and relax into life as a respectable photographer, but that hadn't happened. When the last book came out, Bry had declared a book a year was too much and she couldn't be arsed to do another, and fallen into a bottle full time instead of every third week. Like mother, like daughter, though Mum never took it to the lengths that Bryony did – which was fortunate, as Mum was the one who had to look after Megan most of the time. Family was complicated, and his more so than most.

Dylan scowled as he closed the laptop. His family wouldn't be half as complicated without Seth. What a bugger he was, still scrounging off Mum. Oh, he didn't live there now; Seth's pad was a dingy flat in Linton Keynes that he shared with two others who worked in his new 'business'. Arranging concerts wasn't a proper business. Or not one that would pay your food and rent bills – pay for a normal life, in fact. And yet Mum was still falling for it, like she always had, giving Seth handouts now as well as looking after Megan and propping up Bryony, while he'd had to work hard for everything, all his bloody life. It was sheer favouritism, and it still made Dylan's blood boil. If she knew what he knew... The usual rage flashed through his soul when he thought about Seth and the drugs package – and those awful kids at that disco and how they'd ruined his life back then. But the best way to deal with his family was to ignore their existence as much as possible, so that was what he did. He had a good job, a nice flat, and one day he'd find a lovely girl who'd love him the way no one had ever loved him, thanks to Seth. That was all anyone wanted, wasn't it? Unconditional love. So put the whole bloody Martin clan out of your mind, Dylan, and get on with your life.

The call came three evenings later.

'Dylan, I'm having problems getting hold of Bryony. I don't suppose you know where she is?'

Why on earth would he? 'I've no idea, Mum. It's not as if Bry and I live in each other's pockets. I should think Seth's more likely to know. Or Megan? I guess she's with you?'

'Yes. She came after school, but Bryony was supposed to pick her up two hours ago, and she always calls if she's going to be late. And Seth knows as much as I do.'

'Try some of her friends?'

'I have, but no one's seen her today. I'm getting worried. Meg said she was a bit down this morning.'

'Maybe she went up to London for some retail therapy? Or maybe she had one over the fifteen at home to drown her sorrows, and is sleeping it off.'

Silence while his mother chewed this over. Then: 'Hm. I'll go round there now.'

Dylan ended the call. Good thing Mum was an old hand at this. It wouldn't be the first time Bry had knocked herself out with the contents of a vodka bottle.

He was faffing around ironing a shirt when his phone rang again. His mother's voice was a high-pitched squeak.

'I had to call 999. They're here now. I don't even know if she's breathing. Can you come to the hospital? Seth's staying at home with Megan.'

It wasn't the time to ask for details. 'Be with you as soon as I can.'

She was sitting in the relatives' room at A&E, shaking and tearing a tissue into tiny pieces, and one look at her face told Dylan all he needed to know. He dropped into a chair beside her.

'Oh God. She's dead, isn't she?'

His mother gave a tight nod. 'She choked on her own vomit. She was barely alive when we got here, and they couldn't help her. They're cleaning her up, and then we can see her. What am I going to tell Megan?' She pressed a clenched fist to her mouth.

Dylan gave her back an awkward rub. They weren't a family for hugs and kisses. Or he and Mum weren't, anyway, and tonight it felt as if they were a million miles apart. Why had she even asked him to come here? They were two separate people in two separate worlds with no bridge. He leaned his underarms on his thighs and stared at the floor.

'Tell her the truth, I guess. But leave out the details.'

'Yes. I'm glad she's used to staying with me.'

Dylan said nothing. Megan would be staying with Mum full-time now. It wasn't as if there was anyone else.

He patted his pocket. 'Would you like me to call Aunt Angela for you? And what about Seth?'

'Let's wait until we get home. I need to tell Megan face to face.'

There was nothing he could think of to say. Mum wasn't talking either, sitting there with a frozen, blank face, fingers still working at the shreds of the tissue. A nurse appeared a few minutes later and took them quite a long way down a corridor into a side room. Dylan stood beside his mother, staring at the body of a woman he barely knew.

———

THE NEXT SHOCK – albeit a pleasant one this time – came several months afterwards. Dylan was jogging home through city streets, the business podcast he'd listened to in the park switched off, because you needed your wits about you when you jogged through crowds. He passed an undertaker's window, and a picture of Bryony lying in her coffin swam into mind. It was the last time he'd seen his sister, and now her death had retreated into something right on the edge of his life. Oh, he thought about her occasionally; in a weird way he missed her.

No, that wasn't true. It was the idea of Bryony alive in his life that he missed. They'd been good friends when he was a little kid, but that connection hadn't survived Bryony's teenage years, and somehow it was as if she'd been a non-presence in his life ever since. Or maybe he was the one who'd changed.

Dylan shivered, bobbing up and down as he waited for the green man. He had three people in his immediate family now, but did he love them? Did they love him? Not the real kind of love that held you up and helped you be a better person, anyway. Maybe you only got that from a partner.

Back in his flat, he tapped into the dating app he had installed. It was lots of fun, but so far, he hadn't found anyone he wanted to spend his life with. On the other hand, thirty was plenty of time to settle down, and he had a bit to go before he hit that milestone. Your twenties were for having fun, weren't they? So – oh – he had a missed call from his mother. He tapped to connect.

'Ah, Dylan. I'm glad you called back. Just to tell you that Bryony's estate is settled.'

'That's good.' It was good, too, for Mum and Megan, who'd inherited Bry's considerable fortune. Photography was lucrative when you did it like Bry had. What a waste of a life. The lion's share of the estate went to Meg, of course, but Mum had come into a nice sum too, lucky lady, though no doubt she'd end up giving most of it to Seth, loser that he was. Dylan grimaced.

She hadn't finished. 'I'm going to split what Bryony left me equally between you and Seth. I'm fine here with my savings and my pensions, and Megan is well set up too. I don't need more money in the bank to worry about, and you boys will be able to use it much better than I can.'

Dylan sat down suddenly. She was giving him forty thousand quid, *bloody* hell. 'Wow. Thanks, Mum, but I – we can't let you do that. You might need it later.'

'If I do, you'll hear about it, don't worry. But I'm sure I won't, and this is what I want, Dylan. Your share will be in your account tomorrow. Be careful with it, for me and for Bry. But you'll know how to invest it much better than I would.'

They chatted a few more minutes, then Dylan rang off. The future he was saving for was a whole lot closer than it had been half an hour ago. Okay. He had the money, but he still needed the love. Back to the dating app, Dyl. You need someone to celebrate with.

CHAPTER 22

HOLLY LOADED THE BREAKFAST DISHES INTO THE DISHWASHER, then sat back down at the table. It was two days after the funeral, and last night Dylan had slept in their bed for the first time since Elaine's death. He hadn't touched her, but it was a start. It didn't seem right to give up on her marriage yet. He was head first into yet another pile of papers now, and he'd done little else all week. What was there left to do? Asking would be inviting a snub, though.

She cleared her throat. 'Do we know who's going to the airport with Angela this afternoon?'

Dylan snorted. 'I don't imagine my brother will be queuing up to take her, and I'm sure Megan won't want to go, either. I'll go, and you can help Meg sort her things out.

Holly went to separate her phone from the charger. 'Okay. Do you want to check in with Seth and Laura, or shall I do that too?'

Dylan's face as he considered this reminded Holly suddenly of a lost child, and her heart ached. Heck, this was a family who didn't know how to support each other, and heaven only knew what would happen to them now. Elaine had been the main point of connection between the brothers. Dylan and Seth would have to reforge their relationship, for Megan's sake as well as their own.

Rather to her surprise he pulled out his phone and tapped. 'I'll speak to Seth. You can call Megan.'

Holly took Fred out to the garden to throw a few balls for him while she made her call. The poor creature hadn't had much in the way of long walks recently, but that was another thing that could get back to normal. And now to see what Meg wanted to do.

Megan was clear about this. Waving Aunt Angela off at Heathrow was a definite 'no', and Holly agreed. It was important for the girl to feel she was in charge of at least some things in her life. 'You can get the rest of your stuff packed, then we can drop your things for Seth's off when I pick you up later.'

She could hear the shrug in Megan's voice. 'I expect I'll be back at Grandma's often when seeing Hope and the others. I can get anything I need whenever.'

Holly made a mental note to sit Dylan and Seth down to talk about selling the house ASAP. Grieving alone in an empty house might not be the best idea for Megan's state of mind. Though watching her old home being dismantled wasn't going to be great for her either – the poor kid couldn't win no matter what happened.

She left Fred sniffing around in the garden and went back inside. Dylan was fathoms deep in his paperwork again, so she ran upstairs to the spare room. They should call it Megan's room now, and there was a load of sundry items she'd need to shift out of here before Meg took possession.

The small fitted wardrobe contained little but their suitcases and a couple of boxes of things from Dylan's childhood. Holly put the boxes on the landing to go up in the attic, then went back to tackle the chest of drawers, which held things like sheets and towels they didn't use, and Dylan's ski gear. This could all go in the suitcases for the moment. She swung the largest case onto the bed to fill.

The top three drawers were quickly emptied, then Holly opened the deep bottom drawer and hesitated over Dylan's winter sportswear. But he wasn't going to need any of this for ages, so it could go in the attic in the meantime too. She stuffed ski underwear and goggles into a case, then paused as a small-sized plastic bag from a chemist's fell out from the middle of a pile of ski socks. What was this? She peered inside, then dropped it onto the floor beside the chest of drawers, her heart pounding.

Condoms. A good handful, five or six in all. And – she tipped them out onto the bed and grabbed the receipt that fell out with them. It was from a shop in London, and was dated the fifteenth of April this year. *This year.* The world swam.

She was still frozen, staring at the condoms with her heart beating wildly, when Dylan's phone ringing in the kitchen had her scrambling to her feet. She stuffed the condoms into the bag again and crammed it and all the ski gear back into the chest of drawers before banging the drawer shut. What was she supposed to make of this? Dylan wasn't the kind of person to sleep around. On the other hand, his behaviour over the past few months had shown her loud and clear that she didn't know him as well as she thought she had. No, no-no – she was jumping to all the wrong conclusions here, she must be. And yet... that *darling* phone call. And – oh glory, the lipstick she'd found in the car. Not that either had to mean he was sleeping with someone...

She would have to confront him about this, so much was clear, but she needed to think first. Barging into a 'WTF were you doing with these' kind of accusation wouldn't get her far. Tears shot into Holly's eyes, and for the life of her she didn't

know if they were tears of rage or frustration or sheer gutted-
ness, but it made no difference. She couldn't tell anyone about
this, not yet, though all she wanted to do was howl on the
nearest shoulder. Her oldest friend Valerie in London was the
obvious choice to provide one, but knowing Val she'd be on the
next train down here to check Holly was okay, which would be
complicated too. And there was Megan to think about. The back
door banged shut downstairs, and a moment later Fred burst
into the room. Holly crouched down and put an arm around his
warm back, and he cuddled up close. Her dog was providing the
shoulder, bless him. Dear God in heaven. *What was Dylan doing
with those condoms?*

That had to be the most stupid question in the world.

———

AUNT ANGELA WAS BUSY PACKING. Megan went upstairs with a
bag of pills Aunt Angela had left on the kitchen table. She took
even more pills than Grandma had, and it was all so horrible,
thinking about people getting older and then dying and there
was nothing you could do about it. Megan tapped on the spare
room door and went in.

'Oh, thank you, love. You can put them beside my handbag
over there.'

Megan sat down on the bed beside Aunt Angela's weekend
case. She'd spent the day with Hope and the others at the
skatepark yesterday, so she hadn't seen much of her oldest rela-
tive. She'd been dreading meeting the other kids, but everyone
had been kind, and Hope and Susie'd made sure no one asked
too many questions. She hadn't told them she'd dumped Gabe,
but thankfully he'd had an orthodontist appointment in London,
so she hadn't had to face him yet. Today, she was moving out of
this house for good, so she wouldn't see much of him at all now
– and she would hardly see anything of Aunt Angela after this.

'What did you mean on Thursday, that I can trust Holly?' She'd wanted to ask ever since, but she'd never found the moment.

Aunt Angela put her black cardie into her case and smoothed it down. 'You need a – a mother figure in your life, Megan. Another woman.'

She smiled, but her eyes only met Megan's briefly. Megan shrugged inwardly. She trusted Holly more than Seth or Dylan, sure, but it wasn't because Holly was a woman.

Aunt Angela closed the case and pulled the zipper round. 'You know where I am if you need me, dear. Now, shall I help you pack?'

Megan shot off the bed. 'No, thank you – I just need to sort through a couple of things and then I'm done.' No way did she want Aunt Angela or anyone else shifting her stuff around.

'All right. I'll have a lie down for a little while, then we can have a cup of tea.'

Megan swallowed. Aunt Angela was going away. 'Okay. I might take my school things over to Seth's. I'll be back in an hour.'

She fled to her room and grabbed the box with her sports stuff and a few other bits she'd need after the holidays, and shoved everything into Grandma's suitcase that was her suitcase now. Taking these things to Seth's before Holly came for her meant they could go straight back to Market Basing and she could forget about school completely for a bit.

Megan grabbed her denim jacket and left the house, and oh, God, this was the last time she'd leave this house to pop out somewhere and then come home again, wasn't it?

The street was deserted, and Megan scurried past Gabe's place with her head down. The more she thought about that almost-kiss after the funeral, the angrier she became. What had he thought he was doing? He hadn't been thinking with his brain, anyway. Berk.

Laura answered the door when she rang the bell. 'Come and have a coffee – Seth's still asleep, and I don't want to wake him. He's still in a bit of a state, poor love.'

Megan opened her mouth to say she would just leave the case, then closed it. A coffee with Laura would be better than a cup of the builder's tea Aunt Angela was so fond of. She followed Laura into the kitchen and sat at the table while Laura fussed around with coffee capsules. No sign of house brochures or anything this time.

Fortunately, she didn't have to say much because Laura chatted on about when she'd been at school in London all the time they were drinking weird coffee with cinnamon, then a bang came from upstairs and Laura cocked her head to the side.

'There we go. I'll pop up and see him, then you can take your things to your room.'

She ran upstairs, and Megan swivelled round to see the oven clock. It was nearly eleven; she should go soon.

Five minutes later there was still no sign of Laura or Seth, and Megan abandoned her coffee mug in the dishwasher. It might be best just to take the case upstairs and call goodbye. She carried it up, creeping past Seth's mumble in the master bedroom, then stopping in her tracks as Laura answered.

'Don't worry, love, I know you have more than enough on with your family at the moment. I'll do everything about the house.'

Megan scowled. What a heartless person Laura was, talking about buying houses when Grandma wasn't even a week dead. Another mumble from Seth, then weird noises. Yuck, they were kissing. Megan abandoned the case, retreated halfway down the stairs and called out.

'I'll leave my case now – Aunt Angela's expecting me back.' She thundered back up the rest of the stairs and shoved the case into the room that was to be hers.

Laura's head appeared round the master bedroom door. 'Sure. We'll be round later to say goodbye.'

Megan managed a smile, then fled. Get out of here, Megs.

————

HOLLY DROPPED into a garden chair while Fred careered around the garden. It was a good thing they had such a large plot here; at least the poor mutt had space to race around in, even if he was missing his beloved woodland walks.

It was hard – no, impossible to work out the best thing to do. Obviously, she would have to ask Dylan about the condoms and see what kind of excuse he was going to produce, but was two days after his mother's funeral the best time? Was there ever a best time for this? A hidden bag of new condoms could only mean one thing.

The church clock chimed half past one, and Holly came to a decision. She'd have a go at a proper talk with Dylan right now, but she wouldn't start with the condoms. She'd say she wanted them to work on their relationship, see how he reacted and take it from there – and she'd better be quick. They'd be leaving for Linton Keynes in an hour, in two cars because Dylan was taking Angela to Heathrow while she and Megan came back here. God only knew when there'd be time and privacy for a real chat after this, with both of them at work all day and Megan here too.

Dylan was on the sofa, tapping away at his phone. Holly perched beside him.

'Paperwork done?'

He grunted. 'As much as I can do, alone and at the weekend. We'll need to sit down with Seth and Laura and talk about selling the house, but that'll have to wait until Seth takes his head out of a bottle. Laura says he's barely been sober since the funeral.'

Holly winced, then clenched her fists. Go for it, woman.

'Dylan, this is a hard time, and I'd like to be able to help you more. I feel we've become – distant, recently, and I've hated it. Can we try to put things right?'

He stared past her, his eyes unfocussed. 'For God's sake, Holly – I've had job stuff up my eyes for bloody weeks, and now Mum. Cut me some slack, huh?'

She clasped her hands. It was important to stay calm. 'I feel Laura's helping Seth through this much more than I'm helping you. What can I do?'

He snorted. 'I told you. Cut me some slack. As for Laura and Seth – he's a mess. It wasn't a great time to get married, was it?'

Oh, for heaven's sake. 'They couldn't have guessed Elaine would die when she did.' The couple must be devastated, and they still hadn't got together as a family to toast them and hear all about it. Laura must feel her wedding was jinxed, poor soul, and every anniversary they'd be remembering Elaine's death too.

Dylan shoved his phone into his pocket. 'Whatever. I'm going to get ready.'

He stood up without looking at her, and something in Holly snapped. She had to do something pronto or she wouldn't be able to look herself in the face again.

'Oh, I started clearing the spare room for Megan. The bottom drawer up there is full of your ski gear – I'll put it all in the attic, shall I?'

Now he was looking. Glaring, in fact, his lips as thin as she'd seen them.

'You can leave it alone. I'll see to it.' He literally fled the room, and Holly listened as his footsteps above moved around the spare room before going into the bedroom. If that wasn't an admission of guilt, she didn't know what was. But she'd seen the last of the condoms, anyway.

CHAPTER 23

MORE BLOODY RAIN. MEGAN HUDDLED UNDER AN INADEQUATE umbrella with Hope and Susie as they walked along Grandma's street. They'd been hanging out at the skatepark, but that was no good in the rain so she was going to Grandma's to pack up the last of her stuff to go to either Seth's or Dylan's. Holly was coming to help her later, and this was the first time since Grandma'd died that she'd walked back – home – with her friends, almost as if nothing had happened. But it had, and it would probably be the last time she'd do this, too.

'Megan! Wait! Please!'

Megan rolled her eyes. He wasn't going to give up, so she might as well get the convo out of the way and be done with it. She disentangled her arm from Susie's and stepped back.

'Don't get too far ahead, huh?'

The girls walked on, and Megan waited until Gabe trotted up, all panting and eager. At least his brolly was a large one.

He held it over her. 'Thanks for waiting. Megs, I'm sorry. I truly am. About your grandma and – everything.'

155

Megan shrugged. 'Okay, but you can't change what happened, can you?'

'It was a mistake, a moment. I've said I'm sorry.'

He fell into step beside her, and Megan made sure they stayed within calling distance of the girls in front. Grandma'd always said, you learn by your mistakes. And, you're allowed to make mistakes. Okay, Gabe's had been a big one, but he'd been part of her life since he moved to Linton Keynes a year and a half ago, and lately he'd been a friend. A good one. Maybe they should go back to that.

She stuck her chin in the air. 'Okay. We can be friends. But that's all, until you learn when someone needs a hug and when they want more than a hug. And—' She swerved away as he moved to put an arm around her. 'And right now, I don't even want a hug, Gabe. I want a mate. One I can depend on not to use a God-awful situation for his own needs. Got it?'

'Loud and clear.'

They walked on, and Megan breathed out. It was lousy when you weren't on speaking terms with someone, so it was good they'd sorted that.

He touched her arm quickly. 'I'll see you at the skatepark next time, huh?'

They were nearly home. Hope and Susie were waiting by Grandma's gate, and Megan stopped at Gabe's. 'Maybe. You can text me when you're going.'

He zoomed up his path, almost bloody skipping. Jeez, he could be weird. Megan grinned reluctantly and went on to say goodbye to Hope and Susie. Sorting her things out was something she had to do alone.

The moment she opened the front door at Grandma's, it was as if reality reared up in front of her and slapped her on the face. The house smelled all fusty and unlived in, not a trace of Grandma's flowery perfume or dinner simmering on the cooker or even the yucky air freshener Grandma always had in the downstairs loo. Megan hurried past the living room door so she didn't have to look at Grandma's chair, and made a cup of tea to take upstairs. They'd brought some removal boxes over on Monday evening when she and Holly had packed up a shedload of books, and Megan took a couple upstairs with her. She moved around her bedroom packing her winter gear and the other clothes that were still here. That was quickly done; it was the rest of the stuff that was more difficult, stuff that was scattered around the whole house. Books, Grandma's ornaments – how many of these did she want to keep? She was trying to decide about a pile of kids' CDs when the doorbell rang. Twenty to five – too early for Holly, so a hundred to one, this was Gabe.

It was. He was standing with a hopeful expression on his face and a tea tray in his hands. Two mugs of coffee and two of his mum's scones with jam were sitting there.

'Thought you might like this.'

Hell, he was nearly in tears now. Megan stepped back to let him in.

'Looks fab. I made tea, but this is miles better.'

He brightened up about five hundred per cent, and they sat on the stairs and had a little picnic as if they were six, and it was good. She'd missed the Gabe who was her friend.

'What's it like, living at Seth's?' He finished his scone and chased crumbs around the plate with one finger.

'Worst ever. It's like I'm there, but I'm not part of their lives. And Laura keeps yanking Seth into other rooms to snog him, and he's all ooh-er. It's better at Dylan's, except he and Holly hardly speak to each other.' That was the new big worry. She'd be staying with Holly and Dylan full-time from next week, when her job at the wildlife centre started – but what would happen if they split up? That would be the worst nightmare come true, because if Holly left she'd have to stay with Dylan, wouldn't she? Seth had barely said three words to her since the funeral. Even she could see he needed bereavement counselling or something.

He was a mess, and Laura kept giving him ultra-thoughtful looks and smoochy kisses. Bleah.

Gabe finished his coffee. 'Ah well. Two more years and you'll be off to uni.'

Happy thought for the day. Megan stood up and brushed the crumbs from her sweatshirt, and wow, Gabe's mum must have had a word because he lifted his tea tray and went to the door.

'I'll leave you to it, huh? Or d'you need a hand?'

Megan opened the door for him. 'No, but thanks. I'm the only one who can decide what to chuck out and what to take to which house.' Nobody knew what it was like, having your things spread over the district like this.

Then he went and spoiled it all. 'We'll get back together again soon, though, won't we? Officially, I mean. I want to be with you, Megs.'

He wanted sex, that was what.

'Leave it, Gabe. You're pushing it now.'

She shoved him out and closed the door behind him, then went up to Grandma's room with its ordinary, old-fashioned wooden furniture. Blinking hard, Megan opened the wardrobe and ran her hand along the row of blouses and jackets hanging there. The smell of Grandma was still here. Just. It would soon be lost forever.

———

PONCY DYLAN WAS his usual stuffy self at dinner time.

'I need to talk to you about Mum's estate, Megs. I spoke to the lawyer today, and as you know, Mum left everything to be split evenly between you, me and Seth. There's more than I'd thought there was. Your share will go into your trust fund for you along with Bryony's money, but it'll be a while before we get it all finalised, of course.'

Megan sniffed. 'And the house?'

As if she cared about money. But at least Dylan was talking to them tonight, and at least she was here, not at awful Seth's. Holly had brought her back along with the boxes destined to stay here, and invited her to stay for dinner. Sitting at Holly's table was infinitely preferable to sitting at Laura's.

'We'll get it cleared, and put it on the market. Don't worry, you can keep anything you want from it.'

'I don't know if I want it to go on the market.'

Dylan gave her one of these exaggeratedly patient looks that weren't really patient at all.

'Megan, what would any of us do with that house? You'll be off to uni before you know it, starting your own life independently. You don't want a house in Linton Keynes to worry about.'

Megan forced back tears. He was right, she didn't need a house, which meant she wasn't going to have a say in this, was she? Holly's phone buzzed, and she took the call, said 'okay' a couple of times then disconnected and stood up.

'I have to go to the wildlife centre. Badger with a nasty head wound. Want to come, Megs? I'll take you back to Seth's afterwards.'

Megan jumped up. Anything not to have to sit and talk to Dylan. Not that he'd be doing much talking; he was heading upstairs to his study already.

Holly must have been worried, because she drove to the wildlife centre much faster than usual in spite of the driving rain. The badger was in a bad way, according to Adam, with a wound it must have had for a while. Megan shivered. Hopefully the badger would be okay; she didn't know if she'd cope with watching it being put to sleep.

Adam was waiting in the treatment room with Nadia and the badger. His face was bleak, so he obviously wasn't expecting much from them. But he was allowed to put animals to sleep too, so he must have a tiny doubt about it being the only thing to do.

Holly bent over the badger while Megan hung round at the back of the table and crossed her fingers. The wound was right across the poor badger's head, and it was smelly. Yuck. It had probably been hit by a car days ago, according to Adam. Holly stood straight again, and Adam leaned forward expectantly.

'I'm wondering about trying some super-strong antibiotics?'

Holly chewed at her top lip while Megan held her breath.

'I don't know, Adam. You've said yourself that wild creatures have a built-in instinct about when to fight for betterness, and this one isn't fighting, is it? I suppose we could try, though, and keep it sedated. If it isn't significantly better by the weekend, we euthanise. It's not fair otherwise.'

'I know. But we can try. Thanks, Holly – if anyone can do it, you can.'

Adam gave Holly his lopsided grin, and Megan's radar bleeped. Oops. What was going on there? He didn't look at her – or Nadia or any of the others here – like that.

Holly pulled up the antibiotic and injected the badger, and Adam clapped her shoulder.

'You're a star. We'll put him in a shed overnight.'

Megan watched as he gathered up the badger to go to a shed, cuddling it to him as if it was a baby. She held the door open for him, then gave Holly a pointed look.

Holly grabbed her bag. 'Come on. Seth and Laura are expecting you.'

'D'you think it'll make it?'

'The badger? Fifty-fifty at best. But Adam likes to give an animal a chance.'

'He likes you, too.'

The sentence hung in the air, then Holly swallowed loudly.

'I don't know, Megs. Best to keep things simple, huh?'

Nothing was simple in their family, was it? Megan shrugged, and neither of them spoke during the short drive to Seth's.

Holly put a hand on Megan's arm before she left the car. 'I'll see you on Friday after work, then. You can come to the centre with me at the weekend too, if you like.'

Megan smiled briefly, and ran for the front door. It was raining again.

CHAPTER 24

DYLAN AND SETH: THE DATING DAYS

SETH PULLED ON THE HANDBRAKE, GRABBED THE BAG OF PRESENTS from the passenger seat of his van and headed for his mother's front door. It was Mum's birthday, and they were having a little tea party for her. Megan was even making a cake, so hopefully she'd deign to speak a few words to him while they were eating it. They wouldn't all be here – Dylan wasn't coming down until the weekend. Tuesday tea parties didn't fit into his work schedule, apparently, but that was just fine. Seth shuddered. Being in the same room as Dyl and Mum was nerve-wracking; he never knew when Dylan would take exception to something or other and squeal to their mother about that drugs package and what had happened at that bloody disco. And Dylan took a positive delight in flinging his brother looks that said 'I've got something on you, don't forget' every time they were both with Mum. It was dire. But he could forget it today, at least.

'Happy birthday!' Seth pecked his mother's cheek and handed over the bag.

'Oh, you shouldn't have!' She pulled out the bottle of sherry.

'It's the good kind – thank you so much, darling. And my favourite chocolates. You're spoiling me.'

She patted the sofa beside her and Seth sat down. Dylan wouldn't be happy if he knew about the sherry, but it was Mum's birthday. A little of what you fancied did you good, didn't it?

The front door banged open as Megan came in, dumped her school rucksack at the bottom of the stairs and came through.

'Made it – I thought Mr Clay was never going to finish his stupid chemistry lesson. Shall I make tea now?'

'Hello to you too,' said Seth, and she put out her tongue at him.

'That would be lovely, darling. I'll help with—'

Seth stood up again. 'No, you sit down, Mum. Meg and I will do the needful, and you should be taking it easy at your incredibly advanced age, y'know.'

Megan gave him a dirty look, then flounced into the kitchen. Seth followed, grinning, but it wasn't funny, was it? Meg was your typical stroppy teenager now, and he and Dylan were the main targets. She hadn't found out Mum had given him and Dyl so much money until about six months after the event, and to say she'd been furious was like calling an Ebola outbreak in the village a minor inconvenience. He'd borne the brunt of her anger, as Dylan wasn't around most of the time, and the only way he'd found to get past it was to ignore the frequent barbs and filthy looks. According to Megan, Bryony would have wanted Mum to keep the cash for her old age, and to be honest, that probably wasn't far off the mark. But Mum had made her own choice. Seth watched indulgently as Megan made tea and lit the ten candles on the cake before carrying it carefully to the coffee table. Meg loved her grandma; that was clear as the sky was. Yes, she was sniffy with him, but she was a good kid. She'd put the open warfare to the side for an hour.

Seth did his bit by singing Happy Birthday along with

Megan, then Mum blew out the candles and they all sat forking up carrot cake.

'Lovely, darling. Much better than shop-bought, isn't it, Seth?'

'I'll say. Have you decided where you want to go for the birthday dinner on Friday?'

'I thought we could try the new Indian place near the post office? I haven't had a curry for a long time. And Seth, darling, would you and Dylan like to bring someone – a girlfriend?'

Ha. This was Mum's way of finding out if she'd be mother of the groom sometime this century. Neither he nor Dylan were doing their bit there, unfortunately. Dyly had a different elegant lady on his arm every time you saw him nowadays, and – Seth chased a few stray crumbs round his plate. Roz was his woman at the moment, but Mum had never met her and she'd be seriously taken aback by Roz's appearance. Dreadlocks, tattoos all over and piercings on the bits in between weren't quite Mum's style, though Roz was lovely and Meg had liked her, the time they'd met by accident in the village.

He compromised. 'Not sure Roz is free on Friday, but I'll ask her. Are you bringing someone, Meg? Got a boyfriend yet?'

She sniffed. 'Hope's coming. Not that it's any of your business.'

Mum was milking her birthday. 'Seth, maybe you could call Dylan and ask him if he'd like to bring someone? That way, he'd feel free to do whatever he wanted.'

Seth winked at Megan. 'Will do, Mum.' It was always fun, meeting Dyly's ladies. Maybe he would bring Roz.

He called Dylan on his way home. It was great having a place of his own – thanks, Mum. Home was an elderly house on the other side of the village. It had 'potential', according to the estate agent, and one day he'd do it all up and make a profit with it. Seth put the phone on hands-free and drove along the main road. The van was another thing he owed to Mum's generosity.

'Hey, Dyl. Phoned Mum to say happy birthday yet? We're going for a curry here on Friday night, and she said to bring a date.'

There was a short silence. 'Ah. Okay. I do have a date, but I'm sure she'll be happy to come to Linton Keynes.'

He'd forgotten, hadn't he? Seth prodded. 'Have we met this one? What was the last one's name again? Jamie, wasn't it?' He grinned, picturing Dylan's glare.

'Martina, actually, and no, you haven't met this one. Text me the time and place and we'll meet you all at the restaurant. And please refrain from talking about Martina or any of the others on Friday, or I'll drop a few bombshells over the pakora. Might have a word with your boss, too.'

Seth crashed gears as he skidded round the corner. Jeez. Dylan wasn't going to forget about that package of drugs, was he? Mum knowing about it would be bad enough, but... Seth swallowed. His latest job was events assistant with a company that organised concert tours and the like. A lot of them were for youth organisations, and they tended to have a zero drugs tolerance policy. A packet of coke in his past wouldn't go down well, and this job was one he wanted to keep. What a bugger Dylan was.

———

FRIDAY EVENING STARTED WELL. Seth picked up Roz first – she looked stunning in a high-necked purple dress that covered most of the tattoos, and a black-and-orange scarf holding the dreadlocks in check.

She got into the van and twisted round to see the back, where he'd put the seats up to transport the dinner guests. 'How old's your mum, then?'

'Seventy-three and counting. Dyl and I were what you might call a late surprise.'

'Good for her. She made a good job of you, didn't she?'

That was why he liked Roz; she was always kind. It was a pity she was going up to Newcastle this summer to do another degree. Her roots were there so she'd feel at home, but he was hoping she'd be back one day.

Mum and the girls were ready when they arrived, and Roz shifted into the back with Megan and Hope. Dylan's car was already parked outside the restaurant – good. Seth took his mother's arm on the way in.

'Can't wait to see the latest offering from Dyly's dating app,' he whispered, and she giggled. Gawd. She'd been at the sherry already, hadn't she?

Dylan was alone at the round table by the fireplace. He stood up to kiss his mother and Megan and shake hands with Roz and Hope. Formal as always, but he'd missed out the brotherly hug, hadn't he?

'Didn't you bring anyone, Dylan darling?'

'She had an emergency at work, but she texted she's on her way now.'

The arrival of one waiter with menus and another to take drinks orders filled the next few minutes, and Seth squinted at his brother. Dylan looked different tonight. More – peaceful, somehow. He hadn't even looked scornful about Roz's dread-locks, and he was usually pretty scathing about people who dared live their lives as they wanted to and not how Dylan thought they should.

'What do you think, Seth, darling?' Mum was peering at the menu.

They were in the middle of a discussion about naan bread versus chapattis when Dylan stood up.

'Here she is!' He strode across the restaurant to greet the woman coming in.

Seth blinked up. Was this the reason for the good vibes Dyl was sending out tonight? Dylan's date was around the same age as they were, with shiny mid-brown hair just past her shoulders and wearing black trousers and a silvery top. Dylan kissed her cheek and escorted her back to the table.

'Mum, this is Holly.'

Another round of hellos and handshakes began, then they settled into choosing the meal. Seth watched as Holly chatted about food to Mum and the girls then complimented Roz on her outfit. The waiter took the order for a taster menu for seven, and the conversation went on. Holly was a vet, which went down well with Megan and Hope, and yes, Dyl was different with this one. Gone was the man who'd emanated peevish jealousy all his life; this new Dylan was flying high, full of the joys of spring, in fact. Even his voice was different, and look at the way he and Holly kept glancing at each other with a little smile.

Mum was patting Dylan's hand now, and Seth sipped his wine. Something was telling him Holly was going to be around for a bit. Had Dylan found in her the elusive thing he'd spent his life looking for? Hm. Maybe, maybe not. Holly would last for a while, yes, but knowing Dylan, sooner or later a new best thing would come along. And new love was always the sweetest, wasn't it?

CHAPTER 25

MEGAN STOOD WATCHING A GROUP OF ORPHANED DUCKLINGS swim around the pond while Adam moved a few steps away to answer his phone. Holly had checked the badger – which was doing better than anyone had expected, though it wasn't out of danger yet – then left to go for lunch with some old school friends. She'd asked Megan along too, but no, she wasn't ready for lunch with a load of strangers yet. Much better to be here, doing something uncomplicated like transporting a young duck family from the tiny pond into this big one. Adam said they'd be ready for release soon, but the river was high again after all the rain they'd had in the past few days. Today was the first completely dry day since Wednesday, but it was going to rain again tonight, Adam said. Megan looked down at her feet. She even had her own pair of wildlife wellies now – working here was going to be good, and best of all, she was full-time at Holly's for the summer now. She was moving the last of her things from Seth's place this weekend.

Adam came back and clapped Megan's shoulder. 'It's after two. You can get off home, Megan – you've done well.'

She hadn't done anything, hardly, never mind doing it well; he was just being nice. Megan went to leave her wellies in the container by the door. She had a wooden clothes peg with 'Meg' written on it in red marker pen to clip the boots together and make sure nobody else swiped them. She would learn a lot here. Mum would have approved, and come to think of it, maybe she could do more stuff that Mum would have approved of. Take photos of the animals, for instance. Her phone camera would do to start off with, and if she liked it, she could get a proper camera and do a photography course sometime. Wow. A plan for the future. And it was a good one.

Her phone vibrated silently in her jeans pocket, and Megan's brief moment of optimism vanished. That would be Gabe. Again again again. He'd tried to call about ten times since they'd made up, and he'd sent literally dozens of messages, too. It was getting intrusive, and she hadn't worked out if she wanted to go back to being his girlfriend yet or not. Didn't people deserve a bit of space and consideration after someone had died and they'd lost their home?

Megan rejected the call and went inside for her bag. She'd have to decide about Gabe soon; he wasn't going to let this go. The way he'd been so nice after Grandma died was lovely, and so was the rose he'd given her, but then to kiss her at the funeral – that was too much. Not a good idea, Gabe, and he hadn't even left it being an idea. And if she did agree to getting back together with him properly, he'd want to do more than kiss her, and she wasn't ready for that yet. Loads of the others had done it, but... Did all guys have one-track minds?

Megan trudged round to where her bike was parked, grinning faintly as she remembered the struggle they'd had that morning to fit it into the back of Holly's car. But biking home alone was still better than going to lunch with Holly and her friends.

Back at Holly's, the driveway was empty – good. Peace and quiet and no Dylan was perfect. Megan was pulling on clean jeans after her shower when her phone buzzed again. Hell. But she'd have to talk to Gabe at some point, and this was as good a time as any, and – bummer. She was almost out of battery. She searched around for a moment, but she knew where her charger was: plugged in behind her bedside table at Seth's. Holly's was in the kitchen, though. Megan ran downstairs, but bummer again, Holly's charger was for an iPhone and Dylan's was nowhere to be seen.

Megan sighed. The other two wouldn't be back for ages. The best thing was to go for her own charger now, then she'd have it. It was an okay afternoon for a bike ride, although Adam was right – those clouds gathering in the west were going to swamp the lovely summer weather before the day was out. It was being one of those wet British summers, but it kind of matched the way she was feeling.

She was halfway to Linton Keynes, enjoying the wind in her hair in spite of the permanent ache in her gut about Grandma, when her phone rang. What was it they said about last straws? Megan pulled up at the roadside and swiped to take the call.

'Gabe, leave me alone. I don't know what I want to do yet, and all these calls and texts are totally bugging me. Stop it.'

He sounded all throaty. 'I want to put things right, Megs, that's all. Let's go back to being the way we were before.'

'That's not going to happen any time soon, Gabe. I'm collecting my last things from Seth's now, then I'll be at Holly's all summer and I'm working, too, so please leave me alone. I'll see you around in Linton Keynes on my days off.' She ended the call without waiting for his response. Hopefully that would get the message across.

Megan stuffed her phone back into her pocket, then biked

the last mile to Linton Keynes. She turned into Seth's street a few minutes later and nearly fell off her bike. Gabe was sitting on the garden wall, his bike leaning on the gatepost, and presumably he'd come to see her. What an idiot she'd been, telling him she was coming here. Send him on his way, Megs. On his bike. She grinned, though it was more a hysterical grin because it wasn't a bit funny.

Gabe gave her a kind of apologetic-but-determined grin, and Megan dismounted and gave him a hard stare. Miss Coulter couldn't have done a better one.

'Why are you here, Gabe?'

He screwed his face up. 'We can't leave things like this. I thought we were okay, Megs.'

Megan gripped her handlebars. 'We're still perfectly okay – as friends. Going on and on and on about it isn't the way.'

'I've said I'm sorry. We can take things slowly.'

Megan swallowed determinedly. This was never going to work; he wasn't getting the message and she mustn't start howling here or she might never stop. She gripped her handlebars and made her voice as firm as she possibly could.

'No. We both want different things and there's so much bad stuff going on in my life. I can't forget how you tried to snog me at my grandma's funeral, for God's sake. Scram, Gabe. Leave me alone.'

He tried to grab her hand, and Megan yanked it away. This was the worst convo ever. 'Don't you dare follow me.'

She remounted and pedalled furiously up the drive, ignoring his shout of 'Meg!' and sweeping round to the back of the house so he couldn't watch her go in. Had she been too hard on him? But he was impossible. It was all impossible.

She didn't have a key for the back door, but it was unlocked. Megan went in and was greeted by loud snores coming from the living room. Help. Seth was home and asleep – should she wake him up to say she was here? A toilet flushed above; good, Laura was at home too. Megan ran upstairs.

'Laura? It's me – I've come for my charger.'

Laura came out of the master bedroom, pulling a black and expensive-looking bathrobe that might have been silk around her.

'Oh, Megan. I'm about to jump into the shower. Seth's going to work, so I'm heading off for a night out with the girls later. D'you mind seeing yourself out again?'

'No problem. See you soon.'

Laura vanished back into her room, closing the door behind her, and Megan went into the spare room. The sooner she was out of here, the better. She unplugged her charger and stuffed it into her rucksack, and was back on the landing when Seth appeared at the top of the stairs.

He jerked, then came towards her, leering. 'Holy cow. What's our Meggie doing here?'

Bloody hell, was he drunk? He was in front of her, stumbling along, filling the space so she couldn't get past to the stairs, and this was so gross, the absolute last thing she needed today. He burped, and the smell of whisky wafted across to her. Megan ducked past, accidentally clunking him one with her elbow on the way, and made a dive for the stairs.

'Ouch! What the—?' He spun round and staggered after her.

Megan took the stairs two at a time, then grabbed the banister as she went over on one ankle, thudded down the last two stairs on her bum and landed on her side across the bottom step. *Hell!* Her ribs... Talk about having the stuffing knocked out of you. She stood up, breathing carefully and flexing her ankle. Bashed but not sprained, thankfully. She tried a few cautious steps.

Seth thundered downstairs, a plastic folder in one hand. 'You okay, poppet? Want a lift back?'

No way was she getting in a car with him in that state. 'It's fine. I have my bike.'

He grabbed his jacket from the coatstand. 'Sure? I'm off to work now, but I could easily swing by big brother's.'

'I'm sure.' Megan stood aside as he lifted his car key from the hall table. Should she try to stop him? Suppose he'd had more than one drink? But moaning at him would only make things worse, and anyway, that was Laura's job. Seth blew her a kiss, then opened the front door and sauntered out, and bloody hell, there was Gabe's head still sticking up above the hedge at the end of the garden. This was getting better and better, but if she was quick, she could just zip past him on her bike. Nursing her ribs, which were hurting like hell, and that was down to Seth, Megan went out through the back door to get her bike, and pushed it round the side of the house. Seth's van went down the driveway in front of her, and oh, no, he was stopping at the gate. Megan squeezed close to the side wall so that Gabe wouldn't see her, and peeked round as he and Seth had an animated conversation – animated on Gabe's part, anyway; he was waving his arms around like a windmill. Nausea rolled through Megan's stomach as Seth reached through the window and patted Gabe's arm. They were talking about her, that was clear. However, Seth did her a favour in the end, because Gabe got on his bike and followed Seth's van towards the village.

Megan's ribs twinged as she mounted her own bike. She was going to be stiff as a board tomorrow. She whizzed round into the lane with a quick glance in the direction Gabe and Seth had gone off in, but there was no sign of either of them now. Megan took the other direction and pedalled hard for Market Basing, thunder growling in the distance all the time.

CHAPTER 26

HOLLY ARRIVED HOME FROM HER LADIES' LUNCH AND PULLED UP IN the empty carport. This was another day when she'd see virtually nothing of her husband, what with the wildlife centre followed by lunch with the girls for her, and his boys' night out with the guys in his company. Happy families, but this time she was as much to blame as he was.

Holly's shoulders sagged. She still hadn't tackled Dylan about the condoms. There was giving someone enough time and space to settle back into daily life after their mother's funeral, and there was being a wimp about not tackling something that could mean the end of her marriage, and there, she'd said it. Talking about those ghastly condoms would be first on the list the moment she and Dylan had the place to themselves. Megan wouldn't be around all the time, and actually, where was Meg? She couldn't still be up at the wildlife centre, surely. Adam was generally good about not letting the kids stay on longer than they should. And while she was worrying about her family, what was going on with Seth? They hadn't heard from him for a day or two.

She tapped on her phone, but Seth didn't pick up. A quick message? *Hope you're okay? Take care x* It wasn't the tone she usually used with Seth, but heck, the guy was in bits. A thumbs up pinged into her phone a moment later, and Holly relaxed.

She slotted a stray plate into the dishwasher, the sound of Megan's bike going round to the back of the house solving another of today's problems. Time for a coffee – or should she make hot choc with marshmallows and all the comfort trimmings? They didn't need to eat until they felt like it.

Megan was taking her time about coming in, so Holly opened the back door. Fred shot in from the garden – talk about cupboard love.

'It's not grub time yet, Freddo. Meg? You there?' Holly stepped outside.

Megan was sitting on the iron bench under the kitchen window, her head leaning against the wall and eyes closed, and oh, Lord, no sixteen-year-old should be wearing such a care-worn expression.

Holly touched the thin shoulder. 'Megs? What's up?'

Megan gave a jerk. 'Ouch. I bashed my ribs at Seth's and the bike ride home nearly killed me. Got any paracetamols?'

Holly slid onto the bench beside Megan. 'Let me see.'

Megan pulled her T-shirt up, and it was Holly's turn to wince. Golly, no wonder poor Megs was down. An ugly reddish blotch was spread over most of Megan's right side, and it was going to get worse before it got better, too.

'That's shaping up to be the best bruise I've seen for a while. What happened?'

'Slipped and fell on the stairs when I was fetching my charger.'

Megan's face paled visibly as she leaned forward, and Holly

stood up. 'Come on. It's A&E for you. That needs an X-ray, and something that works better than paracetamol.'

'Nah, I'll be fine. Mum broke some ribs once and she could hardly move. I can take deep breaths okay so they can't be broken.'

Holly held out a hand. It was down to her to be the adult in the conversation. 'No arguments. Come on. Did Laura or Seth see you fall?'

Megan eased up from the bench. 'Laura didn't. Seth was around – he might have, I don't know. It wasn't so sore at the time.'

Anger rose in Holly. Dear God, if Seth had seen Megan fall then left her to bike all the way home, she would strangle him. But that could wait for now.

A&E was busy, but they arrived before the Saturday night rush started and only had to wait an hour. Megan was prodded and X-rayed, then given the all-clear. The ribs were bruised but not broken, and they walked out with an advice leaflet and a packet of strong painkillers, which the doctor thought Meg might need for several days. The storm that had threatened all day had broken while they were inside, and Holly drove home though torrential rain accompanied by thunder and lightning. It was all a bit apocalyptic.

Back at Market Basing, Holly settled Megan down on the sofa with her feet up and Fred for company. A bit of spoiling wouldn't go amiss. She went to make a cup of tea, and when she came back with it, Megan was asleep. Pity pierced through Holly as she watched the thin chest rise and fall, then she covered Megan with a light blanket.

It was after eight before the girl woke. Holly was in an armchair with her library book, and she smiled at the bleary-eyed face on the sofa.

'How're you feeling? Don't answer that. You always feel like death when you wake up after sleeping in the day, don't you? I'll get you something to eat in a moment.'

'Thanks. I don't feel too bad.' Megan sat up cautiously and touched her side. 'It's less painful now.'

Her phone buzzed on the coffee table, and Holly sat back while Megan took the call, her face glum.

'Hi, Sonya … No, not since this afternoon … Must have been about four … No … Okay. Bye.' She laid the phone on the arm of the sofa, frowning. 'That was Gabe's mum. He didn't go home for his tea.'

Holly put her book to the side. 'Oh? Was he with you at Seth's?'

Megan's lips trembled. 'Not really. He went there, but I – I sort of dumped him. I guess he's gone somewhere to lick his wounds.'

'What happened? If you want to talk about it, I mean.'

Megan hesitated, and Holly waited.

'He's been a bit – too keen lately.'

Holly winced. Oops. This might be where Meg needed some motherly advice. Would she be up to that? She'd have to be – and she'd been sixteen too, back in the day.

'Too keen as in—?'

Megan looked away, her face reddening. 'Sort of. He tried to kiss me at Grandma's funeral, even. He's a nice guy, Holly, but that was too much. And now he's swinging between being sorry and wanting more of the same.'

Holly leaned forward. 'I can see how it would upset you. I'm sure he's regretting what he did now. Teenage boys can have too many hormones to be subtle about stuff like that.' Heck – was this the time to mention contraception etcetera? Megan was sixteen; loads of kids were sexually active at that age.

'I guess. I might text him sometime.'

Holly stood up. A heavier chat in a day or two when she'd

had time to think about it would be better. 'Sounds like a plan. Let him stew for a bit first, though. He was in the wrong.'

Megan settled down with one of Bryony's books, and Holly went to make some salmon burgers for a light evening meal.

They ate on their knees in the living area, then sat chatting about life and ambitions and friends and family and – hell, Megan was such a lovely kid. It was almost eleven when Holly ushered her patient upstairs, administered another painkiller and tucked Megan into bed with a mug of hot choc. She sat in the kitchen afterwards, finishing her glass of Chablis, realisation dawning slowly.

She'd always been fond of Megan. But now, she loved the girl in much the same way as she loved her sister. That was good, wasn't it? A lifetime relationship, but oh, dear, it would be a complicated one if she and Dylan didn't manage to patch things up.

PART III
TILL DEATH US DO PART

CHAPTER 27

DYLAN AND SETH: THE MURDER DAYS

HERE HE WAS AT LAST, AND IT WAS THE ONLY PLACE IN THE WORLD he wanted to be right now. Linton Keynes. With Laura. He hadn't known what love was until she arrived in his world, full of fun and ideas about how to build the best possible life they could – together.

The village street was busy, with people zipping into the minimarket to buy something for dinner, collecting their meds at the chemist, or chilling in a café on a hot and sultry summer afternoon. It would rain soon, though; the sky to the west was darkening by the minute.

He went round the back way to avoid the lights and turned into Ash Lane, swerving immediately and violently to pull up behind a black van about fifty yards from Seth's house. *Holy* shit – Seth was there in his van; he'd stopped at the end of his driveway and was yakking away to Gabe. Even at this distance, it was plain Gabe was upset. The conversation continued for a few minutes, then Seth drove off in the opposite direction and Gabe followed. Dylan heaved a sigh that came from his boots.

That had been a close one; Seth should have been long gone by now.

No sooner had he put the car back in gear than Megan emerged from Seth's driveway on her bike, pedalling furiously and heading straight for him. He ducked right down, his head practically on the floor in front of the passenger seat, squinting out as she whizzed past, but she didn't spare him a glance. Good.

Thunder was rumbling in the distance as he turned into Seth's driveway and parked beside Laura's Toyota. Let the good time begin... Inside, he stood in the silence of the hallway, absorbing the atmosphere. Mm, Laura's perfume was seeping through the whole house; it was wonderful. And now, at last they had the place to themselves. This was his favourite time of all, the start of a lovely long evening together. It didn't happen often enough.

'That you, Dyl? I'm upstairs.'

Laura was absolutely the best thing in his life. She was – amazing. He'd thought he'd found love with Holly, but that was a mere shadow compared to what he had with Laura. They'd met, and – bam! They'd known straightaway. Laura was all about making the most of what you had, and her indignation about how Mum and Seth had treated him all those years was far more pronounced than Holly's had ever been. Hell, Holly even liked Seth. Laura was on his side, coming up with the plan to get the most out of their situation and show Seth how little he mattered. It was going well, too, even if this was the tough bit, not having her to himself. It would be worth it in the end. Dylan smiled. Darling Seth had no idea how humiliated he was going to be. Tit for tat.

He took the stairs two at a time, ran into the master bedroom and leapt onto the bed beside her.

'Mm, come here.'

She rolled on top of him and yanked at his belt while he unbuttoned his shirt. It was always like this between them. She was perfect, and oh, he could never have enough of her. Dylan reached up and pulled her down, kissing her neck, moving along to her ear, hands sliding – but take it slowly, Dylan, make it last.

They were lying panting afterwards when a creak came from downstairs, and they both froze. Then the click of the front door closing, and footsteps crossing the wooden floor of the hallway, and Dylan sat up slowly. God no, had Megan come back for something? Or shit, he hadn't locked the front door, had he? The intruder could be anyone, and whoever this was, they were coming up the stairs now. Dylan put a finger over Laura's mouth and looked into her aghast eyes. He slid off the bed and pulled on his trousers.

A familiar voice, sounding unsure. 'Meg? You there?'

Jesus, it was Gabe. Idiotic kid that he was. Didn't he know you weren't supposed to march uninvited into someone else's house?

'Wait here.' Dylan mouthed at Laura, and she nodded.

He shrugged into his shirt and marched out of the master bedroom to see Gabe appearing at the top of the stairs, spots of rain on his jacket and a bunch of supermarket flowers clutched in one hand. Don't think, Dylan, act.

'What do you think you're doing?'

'Oh! I did knock… I thought Meg was at home. We had an argument earlier and I've brought her some flowers.' A slow frown gathered between Gabe's eyes.

Dylan gave him a little push backwards. 'You thought wrong. Megan's not here, and you're trespassing. Now get out before I call the police.' Another push.

'Stop shoving me!'

This stupid little turd was destroying his precious time with Laura. 'You think that was a shove? Get out!' Dylan grabbed hold of Gabe to march him downstairs and out.

'Lemme go!'

Gabe wrestled himself free, whacking Dylan's stomach with

one elbow. Dylan fought back; the kid was stronger than he looked, but he had the advantage of height. A twist and a punch in the gut had Gabe bent double, then Dylan thrust him towards the stairs as hard as he could.

'Scram!'

Gabe stumbled and thudded to the floor, his head cracking on the wooden post at the top of the stairs. Silence fell, and Dylan clapped both hands to his mouth. The boy was motionless, his breath rasping and blood soaking through black hair.

Jesus, stupid kid. He had to fix this. Dylan wheeled round and flew back to the bedroom.

'It's Gabe. He knocked his head and he's – he was out cold for a moment. I'll have to take him home and make up some story about him being here. Go up to London, love, and I'll join you there as soon as I can. We'll work something out.'

'God, just when we had a bit of time to ourselves.' Laura got up and reached for her clothes.

Dylan grabbed a towel for Gabe's head and went back to the landing. He dropped to his knees beside the boy and – oh, Christ, oh no, no no no.

Gabe's eyes were half-open and empty, staring at the leg of the table on the landing and seeing nothing.

Dylan reeled. He bent over the body, and oh, how macabre, it still smelled of teenage boy. But a dead boy had no place here; think, think, what could he do?

He gathered Gabe in his arms, the boy's head rolling quite horribly over his shoulder, and took it into the family bathroom. Should he tell Laura? No – he had to fix this first. He couldn't risk losing her. But you couldn't fix death, could you? Dylan fought for control, nightmare thoughts of being locked away from everything he needed to feel alive whirling through his head.

'Where is he?' Laura appeared on the landing with her bag.

Dylan closed the bathroom door on the body. 'In the loo. I'll take him home now. Drive safely.'

She held out her hand. 'Can I take your credit card? I need fuel and I'm still transferring money around.'

Anything to get her away from what he'd done. Dylan handed over the card and stood at the front door waving like the dutiful husband he was desperate to be, then raced back to the body in the bathroom. It was as if he was on automatic pilot, the same as all those years when he'd been hiding the hurt, or trying to. Okay, all he had to do was get Gabe out to the car and away. Somewhere. He hovered over the body, flat on its back on the floor, one leg bent up grotesquely, and those eyes... But don't think, man, get it downstairs. This was dire; a massive complication just when he'd thought his life was back on track, or would be, once he got rid of Holly. Dylan grasped Gabe in the worst embrace in the world, and started down the stairs. Careful, now.

You don't need to be careful, his brain shrieked. He's dead, isn't he? Dylan arrived at the bottom and almost fell over the rucksack leaning against the stair post. Was this Meg's or Gabe's? He hadn't noticed it on the way up, but he'd been hurrying to get to Laura.

He sat down on the bottom stair with the body and rummaged in the rucksack. Yes, look – a travel card with Gabe's photo. This would have to be disposed of too.

He was still sitting there, gathering strength to stand up, when tyres crunched over the gravel and stopped outside the house.

———

STEADY RAIN WAS DRUMMING down on the van as Seth turned into his gate, thanking his stars he'd only been a few miles up the road when he remembered the box of equipment he'd left in the garage, and not almost in Chichester, where tonight's event was. He pulled up outside the house, gaping at the Audi parked in front of the living room window. That was odd. Laura's Toyota was gone, so she must be on her way to meet her friends. Why was Dylan's car here? Had the Toyota broken down and Laura'd called Dyl to bring her home? Hell, hopefully he hadn't missed a call from her. Seth fumbled his phone out, but nothing at all from Laura had come in that afternoon.

He jogged up to the front door fumbling for his key, but it was unlocked. Seth stepped inside and fell back in horror.

'Holy *shit*, Dyl, what's going on?' His legs gave way and he slid to the floor, landing two metres away from his brother, who was sitting there with scary eyes clutching Gabe, whose eyes would never see again. Blood was edging round the boy's hairline, smudging onto one cheek. Seth retched, then dived for the downstairs loo, Dylan yelling after him.

'It was an accident! He startled me and I shoved him. He lost his balance and hit his head, that's all.'

All? The kid was dead. Seth wiped his mouth on the towel and stumbled back to the hall.

'Jeez, Dyl… We have to… Have you…? Christ, man, the kid's dead! Did you call an ambulance?'

'What would they do? You said it – he's dead.'

Seth's legs gave way again and he crashed to his knees on the wooden floor, his brother's eyes shining down at him while he concentrated on not throwing up again. A long moment passed when neither spoke. Dylan looked very odd now, his face a mixture of gutted and vulnerable and somehow gleeful all at once, and Seth's mouth went dry. Dyl had lost it; he must have. They needed help here. Seth patted his pocket, but his phone was in the van.

He clenched both fists and forced himself to speak calmly. Gabe was beyond help; his job now was to get someone here who knew what to do next ASAP. 'Dyl, we have to call the police.'

Dylan propped Gabe semi-upright against the stair post, and stood up. He still looked odd. 'Oh, I don't think so, Seth. Why would I do that and ruin my life? We'll get rid of him ourselves.'

He was staring intently, and there was something just so scary about this. Dylan was smiling now, a crooked little smile that Seth had never seen before. His stomach lurched again.

'You don't just get rid of bodies, even if it was an accident.'

Fury flashed across Dylan's face and Seth stepped back. He was doing this the wrong way; he had to humour Dylan until help arrived. He cleared his throat and managed, 'Huh, Dyl?' in the shakiest voice he'd ever heard leaving his own mouth.

Dylan stepped towards him, reaching out with one hand to grab the back of Seth's neck. 'You'll do what I say, you know. Or your secret will be out.'

Fear sliced through Seth's middle as fingers squeezed cruelly on his neck. Fuck... Dyl was strong, stronger than he was, and didn't madness give you extra strength? He swallowed painfully. As for his secret coming out, hiding a package of cocaine when he was a young teenager had nothing on what Dylan was proposing to do here, but could he physically stop the man doing whatever he wanted to? Not unless he knocked him out.

Dylan let go of the back of his neck, only to grab his chin, and Seth shuddered. His face was inches from Dylan's and – oh God, Dyl was *enjoying* this, look at the way he was grinning and nodding. WTF?

'The drugs don't matter, Dyl.'

'Don't they? Would you keep your job, if it came out you'd dealt drugs?'

Seth twisted away. 'I didn't deal—'

'Think of all those concerts you manage, those gigs. For kids. Underage, a lot of them, aren't they? Do you think their parents would be happy about letting them go to a festival run by someone like you?'

Seth hesitated. Saying that the drugs didn't matter now

would only infuriate Dylan. The vague feeling that something he didn't understand was playing a role here intensified.

Dylan wasn't finished. 'And what about Megan?'

'This has nothing to do with Megan.'

'Which is why we have to get her boyfriend well away. She and Gabe had an argument this afternoon, you know. She'd be crucified in the media.'

'Because you had an accident with Gabe? Dyl, think, man. This is crazy stuff you're talking. You don't have a choice about what to do when someone's dead.'

'Maybe it was Megan who pushed Gabe, though. He came to see her, didn't he? In your house. While I was driving to London to meet my friends, you know. Oh, you'll help, Seth, or you and Megan will be the only ones who suffer. Ha! Not so much fun when you're on the receiving end, is it? I know all about that, you know.' With surprising gentleness, Dylan moved Seth to the side and lifted the body.

Nausea surged again, and Seth forced back bile. Trembling, he stared from the dead boy to his brother. Dylan hadn't gone mad, had he? Or not in the sense he'd thought at first. No, Dylan had seized the moment to turn this nightmare into an exercise in getting his own back on his family, that was what. The perfect revenge for all the times he'd come out worst, and there'd been a few of these over the years, hadn't there? Dylan hated him, that was clear, and there was no knowing what he'd do if he was provoked. So maybe it was a kind of madness... And Laura, what would she do when she knew? Seth clutched at his jacket, his heartbeat pounding in his ears; oh God, he was panicking now. It might be best to go along with this for the moment. Gabe needed help no longer, and he could tell the police later.

Rain pelted down on them as they heaved the body into the boot of the Audi and slammed it shut. Seth had to hold his breath several times, or he'd have been sick again. He made a move towards his van to get his phone, but Dylan grabbed him, one hand on his neck and the other on his upper arm and fuck, Gabe's blood was all over his jacket, soaking in along with the rain.

'Get in.'

Seth dropped into the passenger seat. Every muscle in his body was aching. 'Where are we going?'

'To the river.' Dylan nodded at the bike leaning against the side of the house. 'I'll leave it to you to get rid of that.' He slammed the door on Seth and walked round to the driver's door.

Seth shrank away as Dylan started the engine, leering across the car. He'd missed his chance; he should have made a run for it there. God, what a wimp he was.

The roar of rushing water was everywhere as they pulled up by the river. Seth was shivering now, but he had to go on. Ever more hellish, disturbing thoughts were swirling in his head now. It wasn't only the blood on his jacket, was it? He'd touched Gabe when they were talking earlier on. He'd clapped the kid's shoulder, rubbed his bloody arm in an attempt to make him feel better about Meg. They'd find his DNA all over Gabe and maybe they would think he was a killer – Gabe had died in his house. Fuck. It would be his word against Dylan's about what had happened, and Dylan could say what he wanted. Gabe wouldn't contradict him.

The car park was tiny and unlit, normally only used by walkers and canoers. Dylan strode round to the boot and opened it, and Seth moaned. That bloody face – but this was hysteria, stop it, man.

Dylan grasped Gabe's slight body, and spoke in an almost conversational tone. 'Bring the rucksack, huh? We'll put him over the bridge.'

The river pathway was slick with mud and parts of it were half-submerged. Seth slithered along in Dylan's wake. Hell, this was the most dangerous walk he'd ever taken, in more ways than one. Rain was pelting down, thick fat drops, and the sky promised worse to come. On, and on. Seth moaned, then slipped, caught his balance and stopped. The river was over its banks here; this could *not* be more dangerous.

The footbridge was submerged, torrents of water tumbling over the wooden structure, pouring through the gaps between the bridge floor and the flimsy wooden handrail. Dylan splashed on regardless, but vibrations shook right through Seth the moment he placed a foot on the bridge. Cold water caught at his ankle and pulled, and he stopped where he was and yelled.

'Dylan!'

'Yes. Here's okay.' Dylan balanced the body over the handrail. 'Wind the rucksack over his arm.'

Seth didn't move, but Dylan grabbed the rucksack and twisted it around a dead elbow before heaving Gabe up and over the rail. Seth screamed as the body crashed into the middle of a swirling mass of wood carried by rushing water. A grotesque wave from a dead boy flashed against the sky and was gone.

Dylan turned back, and never had a man looked more triumphant, more gloating. 'Come on, brother dear. All you need to do is act normally, because if you don't… Revenge is sweet, you know.' He drew one index finger across his neck in a cut-throat gesture, and marched back along the riverbank.

Seth trailed after him. The entire episode had taken less than an hour. It was the worst afternoon's work he'd ever done. And he still had to go to work.

CHAPTER 28

SUNDAY, 27TH JUNE

THE SNORES COMING FROM THE STUDY WERE ENOUGH TO WAKEN the dead when Megan tiptoed along to the bathroom on Sunday morning. So either Dylan had come home smashed and didn't want Holly to see him, or he just wanted to sleep alone. Hm. She looked at the shower, then decided against it. She needed another pill inside her before doing anything athletic this morning. A quick wash would have to do.

Fred was tigering about in the kitchen, but he bounded up as soon as she went in. Megan pushed him away, wincing, and poured a glass of milk to swallow her pill with. That counted as 'not on an empty stomach', didn't it? Now to wait until it kicked in.

Holly arrived when the pain was starting to ease. 'How are your ribs?'

'Okay, as long as I keep still.'

'Don't stop moving completely, or you'll stiffen right up. Can I look?'

Megan pulled up her T-shirt and revealed a colourful chest wall. 'It was murder putting my bra on.'

'I'll bet. Let's do you an ice pack after breakfast. Egg on toast?'

Holly fed them both, then Megan lay on the sofa with a packet of frozen peas on her ribcage, listening to the rain drumming on the front windows. The peas were helping too, so maybe she'd get over this quite quickly. Her phone blared from the coffee table, and she reached for it cautiously. Ouch – and oh no, this was Gabe's mum again.

'Megan, Gabe didn't come home last night and I can't get hold of him. I'm reporting it to the police. I thought he was at Davey's because he wasn't answering his phone either, and Gabe does sometimes stay there. But he's not. I'm worried sick.'

Fear wormed its way into Megan's gut. Gabe wouldn't do this to his mum, he wouldn't. Something was wrong.

'Oh no. I haven't heard anything more – I'll let you know as soon as anyone tells me anything.'

'Thanks. I'll text you if he turns up.'

Holly came in while Megan was saying goodbye. 'Everything okay?'

Megan frowned. 'I don't know. That was Gabe's mum – Gabe didn't go home at all after I saw him yesterday. She's reporting it to the police.' She tapped to call Gabe, but nothing happened. Was his phone dead?

Something here didn't feel right.

―――

WATERY SUNSHINE WAS SLANTING through the living room window when Megan jerked awake on the sofa, and she suppressed a painful moan. Those pills were turning her into an old lady who snoozed off in the middle of the morning, and oh

God, had Gabe gone home yet? What time was it? Megan reached for her phone, wincing again, but no messages had come in and hell, it was after twelve. Something must have happened, unless Gabe had lost his phone down a drain or something.

There was neither sight nor sound of Holly or Dylan. Megan went through to the kitchen for another painkiller, then sat at the table tapping around her social media apps, but none of them had any activity from Gabe in the past twenty-four hours. This was getting spooky. Hot tears spilled over, and she wiped them away with the back of her hand. Everything was totally disgusting, and she should eat something because she'd just taken a pill on an empty stomach.

She compromised with another glass of milk, the worry about Gabe churning around in her stomach like she was on a permanent rollercoaster at Disneyland. Gabe would enjoy Disneyland – oh, hell.

She was still waiting for the pill to kick in when Dylan banged into the kitchen wearing a blue bathrobe. His eyebrows nearly hit the ceiling when he saw her, and Megan felt like crying. What lovely caring uncles she had. One of them practically shoved her downstairs and the other didn't care enough to remember she was here.

Dylan wasn't a morning person, even when it was lunchtime. He muttered something that might have been 'good morning' and crashed around the cupboard for a cup. Megan sat cradling her empty glass while he jabbed at the coffee machine then left, espresso in hand. He hadn't even noticed she was in pain. He was clueless about everything.

A few minutes later, Holly and Fred arrived in the back garden. They must have been for a walk, because Fred was the muddiest dog on the planet. Holly opened the door and grabbed Fred's towel to wipe him down on the doorstep.

'Oh, Megan, sweetie – did you have a good sleep? Any news

from Gabe? Are you hungry? I'll do some cheese toasties in a mo.'

She released Fred and he shook himself, then came and put his head on Megan's knee. She stroked the damp fur, bending painfully to give him a hug.

Holly rubbed her shoulder on the way to the fridge, and it was too much. Megan burst into tears. Just when you thought you had a grip of yourself and what was going on, someone was nice to you and you were back in floods again.

Holly abandoned the toasties and cuddled her, and Megan sniffed dolefully into her neck. Holly smelled of outdoors and shower gel and rain. But she cared. Ten minutes later Megan was sitting with her feet up and a glass of elderflower syrup in front of her, watching as Holly fussed around comfortably making lunch, almost like Grandma had done when little Meg was sick.

'Would you like me to call Sonya for you?' Holly turned round from the worktop.

'I'll do it. But thanks.' She wasn't little Meg any longer; she had to deal with stuff for herself. 'I'll call after lunch.' Megan glanced at her phone. It was ten to one now.

Dylan came down to say he was going to Seth's to fill him in on what was going on with the lawyer, and would eat there. Holly looked pretty sick when she heard this; you could tell everything was wrong between her and Dylan.

Megan tried Gabe's number again as soon as they'd finished lunch, but it was as silent as it had been earlier. And now she had the same kind of worry-feeling that she'd had when Grandma was in hospital, and it went on and on getting heavier and heavier and there was nothing she could do to stop it.

She was about to connect to Sonya when her phone rang in her hand. Oh God, Sonya was calling her.

'Megan, the police have asked for contact details for Gabe's friends, so I gave them your number too. None of the kids have seen him. I don't understand it.'

'Oh no. Where can he be?'

'I wish I knew. Are you still at Seth's?'

'No, I'm with Dylan and Holly in Market Basing. Will you let me know the minute you find Gabe?'

Sonya promised and rang off, and Megan squeezed her phone so hard the case popped off. It was happening again. The bad stuff.

Rain was battering against the windows like the second flood all over again, but Holly made her go for a walk up and down the living room, because keeping active was important for your ribs. Megan walked, Fred at her side and one ear listening for her phone all the time. After twenty rounds of kitchen to front window, she settled down on the sofa with her laptop and opened a local news site. There was nothing about Gabe, though; all the recent stuff was about the flooding and road closures caused by the rain. Megan went into a chat group she had with Hope and Susie, but Sonya was right. None of the kids had seen anything of Gabe yesterday.

She was half-dozing at her laptop when the call from the police came, and Megan couldn't stop her voice shaking as she spoke to them. They wanted to talk to her straightaway, but they were coming here. Thank God she had Holly.

'The police are coming to ask me some questions about Gabe. They said it's routine, but Gabe going missing isn't routine, is it?' Megan eased up from the sofa and went to put some make-up on. Would she ever be able to run upstairs again?

She was barely back on the sofa when a police car pulled up outside. Two officers in uniform emerged, a young man and an older woman who introduced herself as Sergeant Anna Lee. They sat down in the two armchairs, refused Holly's offer of tea, assured Megan again that this was 'just routine', and asked about the last time she'd seen Gabe. Megan tried her best to sound grown-up and serious, but it was hard when your voice kept trembling and your ribs twinged every time your breath caught.

The woman officer was taking it all in. 'So Gabe left your uncle's house in Linton Keynes at around four yesterday afternoon, spoke to your uncle at the gate, and went on towards the village?'

'Yes. Gabe wasn't inside the house, though. He was waiting for me on the pavement and Seth stopped beside him as he drove away.'

'How did Gabe seem? Was he his normal self?'

This was what she'd been dreading. Megan licked dry lips. The truth, the whole truth and... 'He was upset because I wouldn't go out with him.'

The other officer spoke. 'He's not your boyfriend, then?'

'We're mates, that's all, but he wanted more and it was too—' Megan's voice choked up, and she shot Holly beside her a look.

Holly gripped her hand. 'Megan's grandma, who she lived with in Linton Keynes, died recently, and naturally she's very upset. Gabe wasn't quite able to cope with that.'

Both officers were nodding, and the woman gave Megan a kind look. Was it genuine, or were they playing Good Cop, Bad Cop? But why should they, when she'd done nothing wrong?

The woman spoke again. 'I'm sorry for your loss, Megan. Who would you say was Gabe's closest friend?'

She managed better with this one. 'Davey Burns, I think, but Gabe doesn't really do best friends. The kids at school are mean to him sometimes.'

'He gets picked on? Bullied?'

'Sometimes. He used to have braces on his teeth and he's a bit – enthusiastic about things. Do you know where he went? Have you found his bike?' Was she allowed to ask questions?

'We're looking for his bike too. Thank you, Megan. If you think of anything else, let us know.' Anna Lee handed Holly a card, and both officers stood up.

Holly stood up too. 'Do you have any idea what could have happened to him? Megan's really worried – we all are.'

Megan sat still because that was least painful, but the reply was reassuring, in a way.

'A couple of people have mentioned bullying. He could have gone off somewhere to be alone for a bit.'

Holly took the officers to the door, and came back as the police car drove off. 'I guess all we can do is wait until they find him.'

Megan picked at her sleeve. 'If he's just gone off in a hissy fit, I'll never speak to him again.'

Holly perched on the edge of the sofa. 'Let's wait and see, huh? Okay, what would you like for dinner? I could do spag bol, or lasagne?'

Megan relaxed back against the sofa. It was nice when someone was taking care of you.

CHAPTER 29

IT WAS ALL HOLLY COULD DO NOT TO POUR THE MILK OVER Dylan's head. He'd just uttered his first two words to her that morning: 'Milk, Holly', while sitting at the table like a pasha with a shedload of servants. She got that he was grieving, and stressed about all the complicated paperwork over Elaine's estate and a minor niece whose inheritance made it necessary to go through all the most official channels, but for pity's sake, he could at least be polite. He hadn't touched her all week, either, and she wasn't talking about sex. He literally hadn't laid a finger on her. As for the condoms, they'd turned into a gigantic elephant in the room, and she had no idea what to do. Odds-on if she mentioned them at all, it would be game over for her and Dylan, and she was almost at the stage where that would be a relief more than anything else. Unfortunately, things were more complicated now. She glanced at the teenager at the other side of the table.

Silently, Holly passed the carton and Dylan sloshed milk over his cornflakes without looking at her. Holly could feel Megan's discomfiture all the way across the table, but the best thing for now was to ignore his behaviour and concentrate on his niece. Meg's volunteer work at the centre was due to start today, but it would be near to impossible with her ribs the way they were. It didn't feel like a good idea for the kid to be home alone here until tonight, though. Megan herself solved that one by insisting on going to the wildlife centre anyway, so Holly made her call Adam, who – of course – agreed she could go and just chill out there.

Holly fixed her gaze on Megan. 'Sure this is what you want, sweetie? You could always come with me and spend the day in the staffroom. I'm at the practice all day.'

Megan shook her head. 'Adam says I can help Nadia with some light jobs in the treatment room, and rest when I need to. And it'll be good to have something to do.'

'Okay. I'll drive you there on my way to the practice, and we'll get someone to take you home after your shift, if I can't.'

Megan stood up. 'That's what Adam said.' She put her mug and plate in the dishwasher.

As soon as Megan was gone, Dylan stood up. 'Yes, I know you want to talk. But not now, not with Megan around, and not tonight, either. We need space, Holly, to think about what we want in this relationship.'

The ice-cold tone was enough to make her shiver. 'What do you mean? And if it's as serious as that, we should definitely talk tonight.'

He didn't look at her. 'I'm going to Seth's tonight, to talk about the will and the arrangements. Always supposing I get back from work on time, with all the bloody road closures with the flooding. Space, Holly. It's not rocket science.' He strode off, leaving his breakfast dishes on the table.

Holly took a deep, deliberate breath. Her suspicion was correct; he was being deliberately provocative. But why? For a wild moment she considered leaving his dishes where they were, but no, she wasn't going to rise to this. This wasn't the Dylan she'd fallen in love with, and maybe she was a fool, but she wasn't going to end her marriage until they'd at least discussed what was going on.

Megan came back wearing her wildlife centre sweatshirt. 'Holly, they've got Gabe's photo on the news and all over now.'

She held out her phone, open at the local news. *Missing teenager* was plastered over the top of the section, with Gabe's face grinning below and several paragraphs of no doubt lurid detail underneath again.

'Oh sweetheart – I don't know if it's a good idea to keep looking on news sites. Even when it's a serious site, it's not good to torture yourself like this.'

Megan's mouth was screwed up as she scrolled down the article. 'There are comments, too.'

Holly reached out and took the phone from Megan's hand. 'Meg – don't read them. You get trolls everywhere. Seriously – don't read comments.' Was saying that even any use? Megan could and would do as she liked about it. There was no way to protect her from what was going on.

'I – I'll try not to.'

Megan took her phone back, and Holly whistled for Fred. Time to go. Another thought sprang into her head, and she turned back to Megan.

'Did you know Dylan's going to Seth's tonight, to talk about Elaine's will?'

The girl frowned. 'No. Should I be there too? I wouldn't understand everything, though.'

'I don't know. We'll talk to Dylan before he leaves tonight.'

Megan nodded glumly and Holly gave her a quick hug. 'You should get in touch with Hope and the others, too, see what they're doing.' Megan wouldn't be the only worried kid; they could support each other. And after all this time, either Gabe must be staying away deliberately, or something had happened to stop him returning. Which meant there was precious little comfort anyone could offer poor Meg.

At the centre, Adam and Nadia were in the treatment room.

'Anything for me, while I'm here?' Holly stood in the doorway, watching as Nadia immediately involved Megan in weighing some very cute baby ducks. Bless her.

Adam joined her at the door. 'You could cast an eye on our latest bat. After seeing none for ages, we've had three within a week.' He followed her outside, allowing the door to bang shut behind them.

Holly started towards the sheds, but he was shaking his head. 'The bat's fine. I wanted to ask how Megan is. There's a lot of talk in Linton Keynes about that lad going missing and how he was being bullied. He's a friend of hers, isn't he?'

'Yes. No one's blaming Megan for anything, are they?'

'No, no. Or not that I've heard. They're going to start dredging the river today. I don't know if we need to be ready for bad news.'

Holly's heart thudded. 'Oh, I hope not. That would be too cruel, for Gabe, and his family, and for Megs. He's a nice boy, even if they had a falling-out.'

Holly drove the few miles back to Market Basing and the practice with her thoughts churning. Hopefully, Megan wouldn't hear about the river being dredged. They would face that one if anything ever came of it.

———

'WHY DO you think Megan should be at our meeting?'

Dylan glared across the dinner table, and Holly flinched. This was ridiculous. She couldn't live like this. Megan's mouth had all but fallen open at Dylan's attitude, but to Holly's surprise, the teenager answered the question for her.

'Because Grandma left everything to you, me and Seth

equally. I should have been there yesterday too. You can't decide anything without me.'

'You're underage.'

Holly remembered Elaine talking about all the complications after Bryony's death. Was Dylan allowed to organise things for his niece? If she said anything about it, he'd jump right down her throat, you could depend on that. But she'd say it anyway.

'Okay, she's underage, so shouldn't the guy who's in charge of Meg's trust fund be involved?' Holly held his gaze. The trustee was Elaine's bank manager.

Megan was nodding vehemently. 'I think so too. I'll come with you now, and I'll call Mr James tomorrow.'

Dylan was silent for a beat, then to Holly's surprise, he smiled at Megan. 'Good idea. We'll get these papers organised tonight, and we can make an appointment with Mr James as soon as he has time.'

He pushed his chair back and gave Holly the oddest look ever. 'I suppose you're coming too? We'll leave in twenty minutes.'

What was that supposed to mean?

It was Seth who opened the front door when they arrived. A nanosecond of surprise flitted over his face when he saw Holly and Megan with Dylan, then they all trooped into the living area. Holly looked around. Laura was good at putting her own stamp on a place. Seth's comfortable, shabby furniture had been zhooshed up with colourful cushions, and there was a bit of an African theme going on around the old fireplace, now flanked by large wooden elephants and a couple of long spears. Yet – somehow, the changes weren't as sweeping as you'd think they'd be, given that Seth was clueless about interior design and the house before he knew Laura had been a cross between a student flat and a junk shop. Holly remembered Megan's thought about the couple looking at other houses. That would fit in with the relatively minor changes made here.

'Where's Laura tonight, then?' Holly sat down in an armchair.

Seth was hovering over the papers Dylan had laid out on the coffee table. 'She went to her mum's in Cardiff for a few days.'

He fetched coffee and biscuits, and Dylan started talking about bank accounts and mortgages. It was all Holly could do to keep up with what he was saying, and Megan's eyes were wide. Definitely, Meg's trustee needed to be part of the arrangements. There was a lot of money involved here.

Holly glanced at Seth in the opposite armchair. He wasn't talking much, and he was paler than usual, one elbow on the arm of the chair and his head resting in his hand. He saw her look.

'Bit of a dodgy tum. Must have eaten something yesterday.'

Holly winced in sympathy. He'd been gutted about his mother, so this must be hard for him. She sat back as Dylan involved Megan in organising the paperwork into bank, house, insurance and diverse piles, while Seth added the odd comment. He was sitting suspiciously still; his gut was obviously uncomfortable and Holly wasn't surprised when he leapt up and ran from the room. He was still pale when he came back, though he joined in the discussion about Elaine's furniture. As did Megan. Holly smiled warmly at the girl – wow, Meg was being very grown-up here, insisting she wanted several pieces of furniture, and if no one had space to keep them for her she would ask Mr James to have them put into storage. Dylan was treating Megs like an adult, too, so in spite of Holly's misgivings, the evening was turning out pretty successfully.

The thought had barely crossed her mind when things took an abrupt downturn. Megan reached out to touch one of the wooden elephants, then gave Seth a tiny smile.

'I like what Laura's done with this room so far. Are you still thinking about moving away?'

Seth gawped at her as if she'd just beamed down from the moon. 'No – whatever gave you that idea?'

'Oh.' Megan squeezed back into the corner of the sofa. 'I saw Laura looking at a house advertisement, and I thought you might be, that's all.'

Dylan made a 'huh' sound in his throat. 'Your imagination runs away with you sometimes. Think before you open your mouth, Megan.' He sounded like everyone's least-favourite teacher, with an expression to match.

Holly gaped. That was harsh, even from someone who was organising his late mother's estate. Typical of what Dylan was turning into, though.

Seth was glaring at Megan. 'Laura looked at a lot of places to get ideas for this house, that's all.'

Dylan treated his brother to a very odd smirk and went on to talk about estate agents. The awkward moment passed, but Holly noticed that Megan didn't speak again until it was time to say goodbye.

CHAPTER 30

Bloody stupid Seth, and bloody effing stupid Dylan. Who did he think he was last night, talking to her as if she was some stupid giggly schoolgirl? And Seth could say what he liked – when someone ringed an advertisement it was a lot more likely they were thinking about moving than doing their own scabby place up. And even if she had been wrong, there was no need for them to have been quite so uptight about it. Anyone could make a mistake, couldn't they?

Megan pulled on her jeans, listening to Holly and Dylan having breakfast downstairs. All you could hear was the coffee machine, Holly talking to Fred, and chairs scraping on the tiled kitchen floor. Things weren't getting better with these two. Suppose Holly and Dylan did split up, like, next week? Who would move out? Dylan had used Mum and Grandma's money to buy this house, but Holly had paid into it too. Megan jerked a comb through her hair and tried to swallow the sick, scared feeling that was sitting like a ton of bricks in her stomach. Her life was getting shittier by the day, and Gabe still hadn't come home. Where had he gone, after he'd said goodbye to Seth at the gate? Had he said anything to Seth?

Megan hesitated, then lifted her mobile. Odds-on Seth was still asleep, but she'd keep on trying until she got him.

For a wonder he took her call, which wasn't really a good thing, because she hadn't worked out what she was going to say to him.

'Megan?'

'Oh, um, Gabe's still missing, and I'm worried. Did he – or the police say anything to you about where he went after talking to you at the gate on Saturday?'

'For God's sake, Meg, don't tell me you're turning into some kind of modern-day Miss Marple. Leave the investigating to the police, huh?'

Megan gripped the phone harder. She mustn't rise to the bait. 'Do you know if anyone saw him after he left you?'

'Why would I know that?'

He was being very defensive – after all, he lived in Linton Keynes. He could easily have heard people talking. But then, Seth lived on a different planet to most people even at the best of times. A picture of Seth in the car talking to Gabe floated into Megan's head. The two of them had gone off separately that afternoon; she'd seen that. And that convo had been – aggressive was the wrong word, but it hadn't been all fun and laughter, that was sure. God knows what they'd said about her. Seth could even have been warning Gabe off, telling him to stay away from her.

Megan gave up. 'Stomach still bothering you? I've heard that makes people bad-tempered.'

'It is, and you heard right.'

The connection broke, and Megan stuffed her phone into her pocket. There was something a bit off about Seth now, but for the life of her she couldn't see what.

THE ATMOSPHERE at the skatepark was weird that afternoon. None of the kids were on their boards, or kidding around like they usually did; everyone was huddled up in hushed little groups with their heads together. You didn't expect things to be normal when someone was missing, but this was worse than she'd expected. Megan trailed across to the little group of girls that Hope and Susie were part of.

Hope pounced on her. 'Where have you been? Is there any more news about Gabe?'

Megan felt like crying. How should she know that? 'I was at the wildlife centre until two. And I don't know anything new about Gabe. Doesn't anyone know why he went off? And who saw him last?'

Joelle, one of the girls in her tutor group, looked down her nose at Megan. 'Hope said you dumped him before he went missing. I reckon he was so gutted he couldn't stand it any longer. God knows what he's done.'

Hot misery swilled over Megan. She'd never forgive herself if she was the reason anything had happened to Gabe.

Susie spoke up for her. 'Shut the fuck up, Joelle. Gabe's big and ugly enough to take care of himself and he's not daft, is he? He wouldn't do anything stupid. Look at how he talks back to those morons that bully him. Gabe's tough.'

'Then why hasn't he turned up?' Joelle stuffed her hands into her pockets and sauntered off. Several other girls followed her, and Megan pressed cold fingers over her eyes. That was it exactly – why hadn't he turned up yet? She mustn't cry, not here. All the adults were saying was, we don't know anything yet, let's just wait for now and hope it all ends well. As if anyone was thinking that. Gabe had been missing since Saturday afternoon. Whatever had happened, a happy end was unlikely. Best case, he'd had some kind of breakdown and was holing up in the woods or something. Except the police would have checked that. Or maybe he'd run away to London. Or Brighton. Oh God, she had to get out of here. Quarter to four... there was a bus in twenty minutes; she'd get that. Holly would be back soon after five – that was only another hour or so to wait.

Back at Holly's, the house was deadly quiet. Megan made tea, and sat at the kitchen table scrolling through her phone. There was nothing new about Gabe anywhere. Eventually, she gave up and took her mug to the dishwasher. Several other things were waiting to go in there too; the kitchen could do with a quick clear up, and that wouldn't hurt her ribs. Holly was being so lovely to her, and Dylan never seemed to be home to help with the cleaning. She should do her bit.

Megan fished out a cloth, then flipped the switch on the radio beside the kettle. An old nineties hit blared out, then a jingle led straight into the news bulletin.

'A body has been found in the search for the missing teenage boy from Linton Keynes. Two kayakers...'

Megan jabbed the radio off and stood frozen to the spot. No. *No.* She fumbled for her phone – no messages. Not Gabe not Gabe, please not Gabe. How could she find out what was going on?

Read the news, said her sensible half. Megan went back to her phone. And there it was. Early this morning, two unnamed kids had gone kayaking, which was a bloody stupid thing to do with the river the way it was, and found the body of a teenage boy. It was in Barnham, which was miles downstream, but still – a body, and they were talking about it in combination with the search for Gabe. *No.*

Megan forced back her shriek of protest. She stumbled through to the sofa to search for more info on the iPad. Tapping around news sources brought out a few more details, but the important question was still unanswered. Then the Market Basing Courier put out a longer report, and Megan read it, cold fear chilling through her. The boy had been found with a head injury and other unspecified injuries, and the police were saying it could be accident or suicide. The 'family of the missing boy' had been informed, and the body would be identified later today. That didn't sound as if anyone was thinking it wasn't Gabe. The police would know from his clothes. She couldn't stand this; she literally couldn't stand it. This was all her fault.

Without much hope, Megan tapped to connect to Holly at the wildlife centre, but for once, fate was on her side.

'I'm almost finished, Meg – are you okay?'

And this was where she could show she was grown up enough to do things the adult way, even when she was breaking up inside.

'I thought you should know they've found a body in the river. No ID yet, but it sounds like they think it's Gabe.'

'Hell no. Are you all right?'

'Not really. Oh Holly, it's the worst ever.'

'Hang on, sweetie. I'll be home as soon as I can.'

Holly's voice was tight, and Megan swallowed hard. She hadn't brought much joy to what was left of her family, had she?

'I'll be okay, don't worry. I'm not a kid.'

Now Holly sounded teary. 'You're not getting out of a cuddle that easily, you know.'

Megan disconnected and had a cry, then checked again to see if the body had been identified yet. It hadn't, but it was going to be Gabe, nothing was surer – how could she cope with this? She looked around for Mum's book to hold, but it was upstairs in her room. Megan abandoned the iPad on the coffee table and headed for the stairs, swerving painfully to the door to lift the pile of snail mail she'd walked across earlier. Adults didn't walk over snail mail. Most were flyers and local advertisements, but one was addressed to Dylan and had the logo of the bank that Mr James her trustee worked at.

Megan left the post on the hall table and went back to the

sofa with her phone. Being grown up was exhausting, but she was in charge of her own life now, and if she didn't call Mr James before five, she might have to wait until tomorrow. It took a bit of listening to stupid canned music, but at last she was connected to Mr James. Megan gripped her phone.

'I wondered if you knew I'm staying with my uncle in Market Basing at the moment? I'm sixteen now, and I'd like to be part of any discussion or arrangements made about my trust fund, and Grandma's will and – estate.'

She almost forgot the right word at the end, but it came to her in the nick of time.

Mr James sounded surprised. 'I don't see why not. It would be good preparation for you taking over your inheritance when you're eighteen. Your uncles will still be informed, of course, but I'll send anything I send them to you as well, and I'll keep you informed about any meetings I have about the trust. Well done, Megan.'

Megan put her phone down and buried her face in her hands. It didn't make the day any better, but it made her feel more in control. You can do this, Megan.

But could she?

CHAPTER 31

HOLLY CHECKED HER PHONE AS SOON AS SHE'D FINISHED WORK, but there was nothing more about the identity of the body. If it was Gabe, Megan would need a lot of support, and the sooner she was home, the better. It was heartbreaking, seeing Megan trying to be grown up and not cause them grief while all the time the poor kid was breaking up inside. How on earth could a teenager cope with the death of her friend after losing her grandmother so recently?

Almost running, she collected her things from the staffroom. She'd taken longer than she liked after Megan called. A swan had been brought in with a load of paint on its left wing and chest, and Adam and Nadia's attempts to clean it off had completely stressed the bird. In the end, they'd had to anaesthetise it. Either the swan had fallen sideways into a pool of paint and then flown off again, or someone had sprayed it deliberately, and Holly knew which she'd put money on. People could be sick, they really could. Adam's lips were a thin slash in his face.

Nadia cornered her on the way out. 'Some of us are going for a drink in Market Basing tonight – want to come?'

Any other time, she'd have been thrilled to go. 'Next time, hopefully. I've still got Meg with her bashed ribs at home, and she's upset because her boyfriend's gone AWOL, too.'

And now to get home to her poor – to *Dylan*'s poor niece. And Seth's. It might be an idea to warn the brothers about what was happening with the body, especially as Seth wasn't well. Holly plumped into the driving seat and sat tapping. And send. Well, now they'd know a body had been found – if they opened the message, and that wasn't down to her.

Dylan's car was in the carport when she arrived back at the house, and Holly parked behind it. Had he come early to support her and Meg? It didn't sound likely, but you never knew. She grimaced. Hope dies last, they said. She left Fred in the garden and went inside. Megan was lying on the sofa, earbuds in and eyes closed, and judging by the slackness of her mouth, she was dozing. Good.

Dylan was folding shirts in the master bedroom, a suitcase open on the bed. Holly dumped her bag on the chair.

'Are you going somewhere?' Now there was a stupid question if ever she'd heard one.

His face was set. 'We have a big project on at work this week – I'm going to stay up in London from tomorrow until Friday. All the drama here is killing my concentration, and nothing more will happen about Mum's estate until next week.'

Holly watched as he squeezed socks in round the edges. 'Have you heard anything from Seth? Being home alone must be tough for him, when he's ill.'

Dylan made a 'hah' sound in his throat. 'You need to back off, Holly. Seth's fine, and if he's not, I'll be the one to do something. Okay?'

Holly gave up. Obviously, her opinion counted for nothing, and as he hadn't mentioned Gabe it seemed her messages weren't worth opening, either. And as Dylan wasn't making any effort to improve things between them, why should she? Not that an attitude like that would help them, but it was how she felt.

———

THE FOLLOWING morning there was still no news about the identity of the body, and Megan was back to being sheet-white and listless at the breakfast table. She didn't have a shift at the wildlife centre that day and was planning to go to Linton Keynes, and Holly made a decision.

'Meg, lovey, I think you need a quiet day. Hanging out with your friends when you have all this with your ribs and painkillers on top of Gabe disappearing is too much. You could rest here at home or come to the centre with me, maybe?'

Megan didn't argue. 'I'll come with you. Thanks.'

Holly made a second coffee, listening as Dylan bumped his way downstairs with his suitcase and carried it out to the Audi. He came in to say goodbye.

'I'll be in touch about when I'm coming back. Probably Friday evening. Let me know if anything happens here that I should know about.' He patted Megan's shoulder, then handed over a handful of banknotes. 'That should keep you going for a bit. We'll get some kind of allowance sorted with Mr James at the bank. Good luck with the ribs, and try not to worry about Gabe.'

Guilt flooded through Holly. She'd never even considered pocket money. What a rotten aunt she was. But this parenting when you weren't one wasn't easy. She was learning on the job – and if her marriage went tits up, it might not even be her job in the end. Hell.

She stared ahead glumly as Dylan pecked the air beside her cheek. A moment later, the Audi crunched over the gravel.

Megan slumped over the table, her head in one hand. 'He has no idea. How can I not worry?'

'Hang on in there, Megs. We must hear something today.' Holly took her mug to the sink. Even if the body wasn't Gabe, that would mean the lad was still missing. Thank God all this hadn't happened when Megan was in the middle of her GCSEs.

They drove up to the centre with Fred panting enthusiastically in the back of the car. Adam was going into the main building, the swan with paint on its wing under one arm.

He glanced up when Holly and Megan went into the treatment room. 'Hey, Megs, want to give me a hand cleaning this guy? I'll hold him, and you can wield the sponge.'

Megan joined him at the sink, and Holly went to look at the bird. Yesterday's attempts at cleaning had barely touched the paint, but a friend of Adam's had come up with a grim-smelling solution that was helping. Megan sponged carefully while Adam struggled to keep the swan still. Unfortunately, some of its wing feathers were broken as well as paint-covered.

Holly spread the wing, and pulled a face at the damaged section. It wasn't looking great. 'Reckon you'll get it all off, then?'

Adam nodded stoutly. 'Sure. Another couple of baths like this, and he can go to the swan sanctuary to give his feathers time to recover. We can't release him – he can't fly yet, and I'm questioning if he ever will.'

So the swan wouldn't be going back to the river and his mate. And swans mated for life. Oh God, how sad. How could people do this to defenceless creatures? Holly left them to it, and started her round of the sheds.

Adam kept Megan occupied all morning, then pulled Holly to one side before lunchtime. He jerked his head towards Megan, who was watching Nadia take some skin scrapings from another fox that had come in with probable mange.

'Why don't you take the afternoon off? I'll call you if we're in dire straits, but it would be better for Megan if she had peace and quiet to rest in after lunch, and someone with her if bad news does come in.'

He wasn't expecting a happy end either, then.

'Thanks, Adam – I'll owe you the hours.'

He hugged her. 'We'll cash them in with interest another time.'

Why did it always make you feel weepy when you were down and someone was nice to you? Holly sniffed. 'Make sure you do.'

He stood there with one hand on her shoulder. 'Holly, this is only a suggestion, so please feel free to think about it and say "no" if you want to. I've been finding out about funding, and we'll soon be in a position to expand the centre and employ a full-time vet. If you're interested, you'd get first refusal. I'll go over the plans in more detail with you another time, but – keep it in mind, huh?'

Tears shot into Holly's eyes. She was in the middle of a nightmare, but talk about a dream come true. 'I'd be very interested. Thanks, Adam. Let me know when you're ready to talk about the new plans.'

He saluted, and Holly went to get Fred from the staffroom. Megan was there too, hunched over her phone, the picture of misery. Holly drove home in beautiful afternoon sunshine feeling more despondent than ever, in spite of the boost Adam's news had given her.

They were in the living room after lunch when a strangled moan came from Megan, who was sitting with the iPad.

'It's Gabe. It's on the news. Oh God, Holly. Gabe's really dead.'

She pressed a fist in her mouth, her body shaking. Holly sat down beside her, and put an arm round the trembling girl. There were no words for this, were there?

CHAPTER 32

DYLAN AND SETH: THE IMPOTENT DAYS

SETH SLOSHED ANOTHER TWO FINGERS OF WHISKY INTO A GLASS and knocked half of it back before pushing the rest away. They'd found Gabe yesterday and identified him this afternoon. Or at least, they'd made the ID public this afternoon. What did he know about police procedure? There would be a post-mortem; Gabe would be examined and scraped and dissected and examined and maybe they'd come out at the end of it all saying he died in Seth Martin's house in Ash Lane. What a godawful shitty mess he was in, and it was all his own fault. If he'd gone to the police straightaway, they might have believed him. Instead, he'd lied by omission, and by doing that, he'd played straight into Dylan's hands. Oh, he'd told the police the truth about what had happened when he'd last seen Gabe alive, on Saturday afternoon, and why, why, why hadn't he admitted everything then and dumped his brother in it? Dyl was laughing his head off now; he had a stupid smug smirk on his face every time he looked at his brother. He was enjoying his horrible little

216

triumph. Silly Sethy, scared to confess in case – in case they didn't believe him. Dylan was a proper, serious business-type person, while he was a bloody aging hippy who didn't give a toss about looking respectable. The authorities were ten times, a million times more likely to believe what Dylan said, and that was before you even thought about the photo Dyl had apparently taken of that drug parcel.

Seth leaned his head on the table and groaned. Was hiding a parcel of drugs for your sister when you were a kid a bigger crime than helping to conceal a – what? Accidental death? Manslaughter? Murder? And what if the police thought he was the guilty one? What a toad his brother was, and to make matters worse, Dylan wasn't answering his calls or replying to his messages. Laura was still away too, and for some reason his calls to her weren't getting through either. She'd been moaning about her mobile for weeks.

Seth heaved himself to his feet. Hard to say if Laura's absence was a blessing or a curse. And now he had to get rid of Gabe's bike, in case the police came back for a more detailed look. He should have done it before now. And when he'd done that, there would be nothing, nothing in this world more that he could do.

Except tell the police.

———

THE BIKE WAS HIDDEN under a mess of tarpaulins and junk in his van, Gabe's helmet hanging over the handlebars. He'd worn gloves to put it there, and he knew where he was going to take it, too, and he'd better do it now while it was still light enough not to look odd that he was going for a bike ride. Seth knocked back a glass of water and slid behind the wheel. If he was stopped now for drunk driving it would be a fitting end to the disaster his life had turned into.

He drove for twenty minutes before pulling up in a walkers' car park by the woods near Dean Park. Two other cars were here; he'd need to be careful. Seth pulled on his gloves, retrieved the bike and jammed Gabe's helmet onto his head. It was as good a disguise as any.

From here, the trail into the wood was blessedly flat, because his legs were back to being so much jelly. He biked in for about five hundred yards before a smaller track appeared on his left. Up here... and along... and off the bike; this was no biking path, in fact it was about to disappear into the undergrowth. Seth stepped gingerly through a mess of trees and plants he didn't know the names of, then shoved the bike into a mess of dead bush and thorns. Done.

A dog barked somewhere to the right. He froze, then unclipped the helmet and gaped at it, his blood running cold. What a fool he was to have worn it; it would be covered in his hair and DNA and God only knew what now. But if the bike was found, the helmet didn't matter. He chucked it over his shoulder and went back to the main path. Now he was just a regular guy, out for a little stroll of an evening. Was he hell. He was a coward and a criminal. All his life he'd taken the easy road – not bothering about school, living so long with Mum, making sure he was always one up on a brother who was only too easy to get one up on – or so he'd thought. Talk about the tables being turned.

Back home, he went straight to the tumbler on the kitchen worktop and swallowed the rest of his whisky, the amber fluid burning its way down his throat. And another, just to take the edge off. And now to see if by some miracle, his family would take his calls for a change. But they wouldn't, would they? He was nothing to Dylan, and Laura would be busy with her parents.

Dylan did take the call, though, and Seth staggered in shock.

He should sit down. Whisky plus reaction to what he'd just done was making him light-headed. Music was playing in the background at Dylan's end, and the clink of glasses and a murmur of people talking told Seth his brother wasn't at home.

'Hey Dyl. Havin' a nice evening?' Talking out loud was a challenge.

'You're drunk. What is it?'

'Jus' t' tell you I go' rid of the bike.'

A scraping sound, and footsteps. Wherever Dylan was, he wasn't going to talk about bikes, ha. A door closed, then Dylan's voice returned.

'What bike's that, Seth?'

Seth slammed his phone down on the table and burst into tears.

He drank two coffees and waited a good hour before trying Laura. She'd seen him in bits, when Mum died, but she'd never seen him as drunk as this; she'd be... what? Dismayed? Sorry? Loving? Whatever, she wasn't here and he wanted his mum and he wanted his wife and he wanted – he wanted all this to go away. He tapped on her number, and – nothing, and had he ever felt so alone? Seth scrolled down his list of contacts, but of course there was no one he could ring up and say, hey, I helped Dyl hide a body and now I've hidden a bike and I'm not telling the truth to the police. He came to Roz's name, and stopped. Roz with her dreadlocks and her kind eyes. But Laura was kind too, or she would be when she eventually got back to him. Roz had belonged to a different part of his life and that was finished now.

He reached for the whisky bottle and emptied it into his glass. He was alone now. Mum was gone. Dylan had hung him out to dry, and if Megan knew what he'd done, she would hate him. The problems and questions were stacking up and he was helpless as a babe in arms. Pathetic.

What would happen about the post-mortem on Gabe? What

if the police did find something to connect the death to this house? What if Dylan managed to turn the whole thing round and convince the police that poor old drunk Seth was a killer?

What if they got away with it?

CHAPTER 33

THURSDAY, 1ST JULY

IT WAS FIVE A.M. AND SHE HADN'T SLEPT A WINK. MEGAN ROLLED on her side – ouch – and checked her phone for the millionth time, but there was still nothing. No messages, no emails, nothing, and she didn't dare go into any of her chat groups. Suppose they were 'chatting' about her? Megan, the sole cause of Gabe being dead and cold on a slab somewhere. Where did they take dead bodies? The mortuary? Imagine Sonya having to go and identify Gabe. Poor Sonya only had one child, and now she didn't have any and it was all, all her fault. She'd been horrible to Gabe and he'd gone and, oh, *God*, what had he done? Megan dropped the phone onto the bedside table. It clattered down harder than it should have, and she grabbed it again. It was okay, thankfully, her lifeline to the world that was ignoring her. What were the other kids saying?

A tap came on the door, and Holly slid into the room with a mug in each hand.

'Tea. I heard you were awake.' She put the mugs down beside Megan's phone, shifted a bundle of clothes from the chair and pulled it closer to the bed. 'Oh, Meg, look at you. Did you sleep at all?'

Megan shook her head, hot tears welling up, but she didn't let them escape. Her ribs were giving her gyp, but in a masochistic kind of way it felt good. She had nothing to cry about – she was alive.

Holly handed over a mug and one of Megan's painkillers. 'Sit up, lovey, and take this. I know it won't change anything, but it'll help you get through the day.'

Megan took the mug. She sipped, and yes, it was comforting, though she didn't deserve comfort. And with Holly sitting there waiting, she had to take the painkiller too.

Holly patted her leg under the duvet. 'Good. Have you heard from any of the others?'

'They're ignoring me. They know it's all my fault he's dead.' Her hand shook, and tea slopped over the rim of the mug onto the duvet.

'Megan, it is not your fault.'

Holly sounded almost angry, and Megan scowled. 'I don't know how you work that out. I was mean to him and he flung himself in the river.'

'I don't think you were mean. And if that is what happened, it was his decision. Nobody can make another person take their life by saying what you said to Gabe. And it could have been an accident. He could have gone to the river, out there in the middle of all that nature, because it's a good place to think, and then fallen in. The riverbank must be a sea of mud.'

Megan took another sip of tea. Gabe might have fallen in, but it was still her fault he'd gone to the river in the first place, wasn't it?

'Gabe wasn't like other people. He didn't care about the same stuff. He was brave.'

'It could still have been an accident. As for brave, you're one of the bravest people I know. Think of all that's happened to you, and you're still coping with your life – coping well, too.'

Megan pouted. 'That's different. I didn't have a choice. Gabe would just ignore stuff and not care. He put up with everything, but then – then he snapped and jumped in the river.'

'And if he did, it wasn't your fault.' Holly stood up. 'Look, it's nearly six. Why don't you get up and come down? I'll make breakfast, and you can see what the other kids are saying. I'm sure we'll hear more this morning.'

Megan put down her empty mug. 'S'pose. Can you send Fred up?' She hadn't wanted him here with her last night. She hadn't wanted any comfort; she still didn't, but Holly wasn't going to give up, was she? Megan lifted an armful of clothes and went into the bathroom. When she came back, Fred was sniffing around her room and the scent of bacon was floating through the house. She sat down and gave Fred the biggest hug ever. He smelled of outside and dog, and while nothing today was going to make her feel properly better, cuddling Fred was making her feel a very tiny bit less black.

She was at the kitchen table, chewing her way through her bacon roll and tasting nothing, when her phone pinged. Megan froze. It was Hope: *U ok, babes?* And a kiss. Oh God, a kiss. Megan tapped: *No. U? What are the others doing?* There was a short pause, then Hope's reply came: *All in bits. Waiting for more news. Are u coming to the skatepark today?*

Megan hesitated. 'She said, am I going to the skatepark.'

Holly turned round. 'I think you should stay right here today, sweetie. You're in no state to go anywhere.'

'I guess.' Megan swiped to call Hope. It was quicker to talk about this.

Hope sounded gutted too. 'It's awful. Nobody knows what to think.'

'I'm staying home today. I bet they're all blaming me.'

'Some of them are, but most of them think it was an accident.

Stu saw Gabe going into the minimarket not long after four on Saturday afternoon. He said he was walking all hunched up and not talking to anyone, but he wasn't heading for the river.'

Oh. Megan swallowed. That was after Gabe had talked to Seth and left Ash Lane, and in a way, it was good to know he hadn't gone straight to the river and jumped in. She ended the call and was about to tap into the news when Holly stopped her.

'There won't be anything new this early apart from gossip and sensationalism. We need to wait for proper news. I'll stay with you today, Meggie. They'll understand at the practice. Okay?'

'Okay. Sorry.'

Holly shot her a wry look. 'Do I have to say it again?'

'Not my fault. Okay.'

If she said it often enough, she might believe it.

———

HOLLY CLEARED THE KITCHEN, keeping one eye on Megan, who was throwing balls for Fred outside. It wasn't easy to know how best to help the girl, but being available must be a good start. Thank God Megan didn't have school to complicate things; life was difficult enough as it was. Holly tapped into her phone. Nothing had come in from either Dylan or Seth, which was pretty much what you'd expect from these two. She sent a bald message to them both.

The sound of tyres on the gravel in front of the house had her striding to the front window. The police had arrived. Megan had seen them too; she was back in the kitchen with Fred, her eyes huge and her face several shades paler than it had been ten minutes ago. Holly went to let the officers – the same two as before – in, wishing she had the chance to talk to them alone. Hassle wasn't what Megan needed.

The two officers took the same armchairs they'd occupied

last time. Megan sat down beside Holly on the sofa, and Fred flopped down on the floor at their feet, bless him.

Sergeant Anna Lee frowned. 'You don't look well, Megan.'

Megan pressed her lips together. Holly answered for her.

'The rib injury is still painful, and of course the news about Gabe is upsetting.'

The younger officer answered. 'Bruised ribs take a while to heal. I had that once.'

Sergeant Lee was nodding, and Holly relaxed. It didn't look as if they thought this was Meg's fault. She cleared her throat.

'This is dreadful for the kids. Do you know more about what happened yet?'

'The post-mortem is today, so we may know more after that. Gabe showed some injuries, but no, we don't know what happened. We're trying to fill out details of his last hours on Saturday. Have you thought of anything else that might be useful, Megan? Tell us again about the last time you saw him.'

Her voice shaking, Megan repeated what she'd said about arguing with Gabe, and added that one of the boys saw him after he'd left Ash Lane.

'So you biked back here from Linton Keynes, and arrived at—?'

Megan was looking at Holly. 'I think it was a bit before five?'

Holly thought back. 'Yes. I'd been out to lunch and arrived back sometime after four. My husband had already left to meet friends, and I hadn't been home more than a few minutes when Megan arrived.' Surely this had nothing to do with Gabe's death?

'Where was your husband going?'

What did that have to do with anything? 'Um – it was a night out with work friends. The company's in Croydon so I suppose they went somewhere there, or in London. He said afterwards the roads were bad with flooding.'

Anna Lee was noting all this irrelevant detail down, but made no comment.

The other officer was nodding away. 'Some of the roads are still closed. It was a real—' His boss glared at him, and he subsided.

Megan was twisting her hands together. 'When will we know what happened to Gabe? Will you tell us?'

Anna Lee spoke kindly. 'There'll be a press conference later today, so you'll see then what's been released to the public.

'Was it an accident?' Megan's voice was little more than a whisper.

Holly held her breath.

'That's one possibility. We'll know more soon. If you think of anything else, please get in touch.'

The two officers left, and Holly closed the door after them and leaned her forehead on it. Why on earth had they come? Apart from a few details that had nothing to do with Gabe, she and Megan had given them no information, apart from the bit about Stu seeing Gabe, and presumably they'd known that already.

Megan had gone upstairs, so Holly lifted her laptop. She'd barely opened it when one possible answer slithered uncomfortably into her head.

Maybe the police knew something about Gabe's death that they hadn't told them. Oh hell.

She was catching up with paperwork an hour or so later when her phone rang. 'Dylan?'

'How are things at your end? How's Meg?'

'We're okay. The police came again. They wanted to confirm what Megan told them on Monday. They said the post-mortem's today.'

'Have they spoken to Seth again?'

'I don't know. You'll have to ask him, but if they spoke to Megan again I expect they'll go back to see him too.'

'Right. Speak soon.'

Holly put her phone on the arm of the sofa. 'That was Dylan, asking how we were getting on.'

Megan was leafing through one of Bryony's books. 'I guessed that. Do you think we should call Seth? He was a bit – weird – when I spoke to him yesterday.'

Holly closed her laptop. 'Weird in what way?'

It was hard to describe. 'I asked him about talking to Gabe on Saturday afternoon, and he was pretty uptight.'

'Oh. It's a rotten situation, but Seth doesn't know Gabe well, does he?'

'No. I guess he's still stressed out about Grandma. I think they were closer than I knew.'

'Mm. We could go by after lunch and see what he's doing, if you like.'

Megan looked at her, her forehead creased. 'Okay. I want to talk to him about it. About Gabe, I mean.'

————

SETH'S VAN was in the driveway when they arrived at Linton Keynes, but there was no sign of the Toyota, so Laura was either out or not back yet. Holly clipped on Fred's lead in case he jumped up on Seth's dodgy tum, and Megan rang the bell.

They were about to give up when the door opened. Seth was unshaven and even paler than he'd been on Monday night when they'd come to talk about Elaine's estate. Was this still his stomach, or a hangover?

Holly stretched a hand out to him, then lowered it as he moved back. 'You don't look too hot, Seth. Is your stomach still bothering you?'

He leaned on the door. 'Hello to you too. I'll live. Didn't get much sleep last night. Are you coming in? It's a bit of a mess.'

Holly followed him into the kitchen, Megan silent behind her. Mess was an understatement. By the look of the place, Seth had been ignoring the dishwasher all week. He opened a packet of digestives and handed them round, but made no offer of tea or coffee.

Holly leaned on the worktop behind her. 'The police came to see us again this morning. Did they come here too?'

Seth wiped one hand over his face. 'Yeah. And I told them again I talked to the kid, then he got on his bike and I drove to work and that's all I know.'

Megan stirred beside Holly. 'What did you talk to him about?'

Seth pulled a can of beer from the fridge and popped it. 'You, if you must know. He wanted to know how to get you back. I told him to give you some space.'

He gave Megan a pointed look, and Holly held her breath. A drunk Seth was perfectly capable of adding 'and he's certainly done that, hasn't he?' He left it at the look, though, and Megan said nothing more either. Holly searched for something to break the silence.

'I guess Laura isn't back yet?'

Seth slumped down on a chair. 'I can't get hold of her. I think something must have happened to her phone – I haven't heard anything since Sunday. She doesn't even know about Gabe.'

Holly lurched upright. That was odd; four days was a long time not to be in contact with your newly married husband. If Laura's phone was dead, wouldn't she have got in touch with Seth some other way?

'Don't you know her parents' numbers? Or they might have a landline?'

He slammed a hand on the table. 'Don't you think I've tried that? I don't even know their address. If she's not back soon, I'm going to Cardiff to look for her.'

'Cardiff's a big place.' Megan shoved both hands into her jeans pockets, not looking at Seth.

Holly put a hand on the girl's shoulder. They weren't doing

any good here, and watching Seth drink his beer was – insulting, in a word. 'Keep us posted, then. Dylan will be back on Friday. And Seth – if you're driving to Cardiff tomorrow, lay off the booze tonight, huh?'

She bundled Megan back down the hallway, but Seth didn't answer.

CHAPTER 34

MEGAN DROPPED ONTO A CONCRETE PLINTH AT THE SKATEPARK, regretting the action before she'd even landed. Her ribs were much better, but she still shouldn't do violent things like that. She closed her eyes, massaging her poor side. Everything was wrong. There hadn't been anything real about Gabe on the news yesterday, in spite of what that policewoman had said. The one new thing was that some of their year at school were planning a memorial for him, down by the river after lunch today. Most of the kids and a couple of the teachers were going, and so were Gabe's mum and some of her friends. The funeral wouldn't be for ages, because of the police investigation, and this was a good way to say goodbye. Megan's breath caught in her throat. The image of Gabe in a coffin, his skin all pasty and dead, eyes closed and wearing make-up and his good clothes and – stop, stop. Picturing the body made it all so horribly real and it was the worst thought ever, that she could have been part of Gabe's decision to end his life. No no no no no. That hadn't happened. Gabe wouldn't have done that to her.

The sun came out at lunchtime, which made the memorial half a per cent better than it would have been in the rain. Megan trailed along in the crowd of kids from their class, Hope hanging onto her left arm. Susie had organised most of the memorial with Kev and Davey along with Mrs Sweeny the music teacher, who they'd gone to for help.

Everyone gathered on the river pathway at the bit where the meadow went right down to the riverbank. Megan had to clasp her hands together to stop them shaking. Two policemen were here too; what did that mean? Most of the adults gathered together at the side, with Gabe's mum and his auntie at the front, but it was the kids who led the memorial. They played 'Forever Young' on Hope's mum's CD player, then Hope read out a poem Gabe'd had in the school mag last year. Then Gabe's mum said a few words, mostly about how he enjoyed school, which was probably true but it wasn't easy to listen to, and a few of the boys especially looked a bit red at that. In between the talking parts they played some of Gabe's favourite songs from the charts, which was better because they could sing along, except it made nearly all the girls cry, and at the end, they all said why they'd remember Gabe. Mostly it was things like 'he was always kind' or helpful or whatever. Megan said, 'he was fun to be with', and Sonya wiped her eyes at that. To finish off, they all lit a little candle, and arranged them on the river-bank to spell out 'GABE'. Sonya was pretty choked up about that too; most people were. The first idea had been to put the candles on paper boats and float them downstream, but the river was much too high for that, and this way, they could leave Gabe's name burning brightly for an hour or two. Kev and Davey were going to go back later to collect the candles, which was good. The water might rise again, and Adam would go ballistic if he found thirty-odd tea light candles polluting the river.

Afterwards, most of the kids gathered into little groups that somehow didn't include Megan, and she blinked around as the kids moved away. What was happening?

Sonya came to hug her goodbye. 'We'll stay in touch, Megan. I'll let you know about the funeral.' She put an arm around Gabe's aunt on the way back up the river pathway, and Megan swallowed the lump that felt as if it would never go away.

Susie and Hope came over with serious faces, and Susie took Megan's arm.

'Kev says the police think it was suicide. He thinks it was all your fault, too.'

Megan's breath caught in her throat. 'No. It wasn't.'

Susie rolled her eyes. 'Kev's an idiot. Ignore it, Megs. Anyone would know it's not true, but we thought you should know.'

Hope was nodding. 'Yeah. The police would ask you again and again if they thought it was anything to do with you.' The girls led the way up the path, and Megan followed, her thoughts flitting back and forth. The police had asked again already, but they'd seemed quite satisfied with what she'd told them. But if Kev was thinking rubbish like that, other people would be too. Megan thrust her hands into the pockets. More angst and aggro, and Gabe wasn't here to help her see straight. Away, Meg, just get away from here.

She left Hope and Susie on the High Street and kicked a stone along the pavement. Holly was meeting her at Grandma's when she'd finished work, to sort through more things at the house. It was so weird, walking along here by herself, going 'home' again in Linton Keynes. Megan shivered as she walked up Grandma's path, blinking at the rose bush that was blooming away, huge yellow roses and a shedload of tight little buds. Grandma would have loved these.

She was still on Grandma's chair, face first in her phone reading what everyone had put on social media about the memorial, when the front door banged shut and Holly put her head into the living room.

'Okay, sweetie? How was the memorial?'

'It was fine. Shall I make tea? Except there's no milk.'

Holly fished in her bag. 'I brought some. I'll make it, and you can tell me about the memorial.' She vanished into the kitchen, coming back with two mugs, and Megan spoke before her brain engaged.

'I don't want to live with Seth and Laura. Ever.'

Holly put the mugs down and hugged her. 'I'm very happy to have you with us, Megs, and you're with us for the summer now at least. We can leave the definite plans until we know exactly what you're doing when school goes back in. Let's get your things packed, huh?'

Megan nodded, pressing her mouth shut. Seth and Dylan would say that school was in Linton Keynes and she should stay with Seth during the week at least. Maybe going back to school wasn't such a good idea, even if she got the grades.

There was no Grandma smell in her bedroom at all now. The house was turning into a museum. They set out boxes on the floor, and Holly helped her pack everything into them. It was after six before they were finished, and that was only the bedroom.

Holly looked at her watch. 'Dylan should be back soon. Come on, let's get these boxes into the car.'

And five minutes later Megan slid the final box onto the back seat and got into the front. Now Grandma really didn't live here any more.

Holly was answering her phone. 'Oh hell, poor thing. I'll be right with you.' She ended the call and turned to Megan. 'That was Adam. They've rescued a deer with a bad head wound and a shedload of airgun pellets in its skin, and he's not sure if it's saveable or not. I'm going there now. What do you want to do?'

Megan pressed a hand to her chest. A horribly injured animal wasn't what she wanted to think about tonight.

'Can you drop me off at Seth's, if he's here?' Seeing him again might help her decide about living there in term time if she got into sixth form, and she could ask him again about what he and Gabe had been saying about her that last afternoon.

Holly's eyebrows rose. 'Sure? I might be a while, if it's a big job. Pellets are ghastly.'

'I know. Worst case, I can get him to drive me home.' Megan called Seth's number in case he wasn't there, but he was, and he sounded sober today.

Holly dropped her and Fred off at Seth's gate, and Megan hurried on up the driveway, trying not to think about how Gabe had been standing right here waiting for her, that day. Jeez, the front door wasn't closed properly – didn't they worry about burglars here? Megan pushed it open, silence all around her.

'Hello?'

A thud from the living room. 'Oh – Meg! I didn't expect you so soon.'

She stepped inside, meeting Seth in the living room doorway. He still didn't look well, and he was leaning on the door frame as if he'd fall over without it. Oh hell – hopefully Holly wouldn't be long, because Seth didn't look as if he was in a fit state to drive anyone anywhere.

'Is Laura back yet?'

'No. She called yesterday, though. She's busy at work so she went from Cardiff to her old flat for a day or two, to catch up.'

Megan waited, but he didn't say more, so she ventured, 'I guess she'll be selling it soon, then?'

He stamped off to the kitchen. 'It's useful for her when she needs to work late. Most of her work's in London. Not that it's any of your business what Laura does with her flat.'

Megan twisted her fingers together. This was sounding a bit like Laura was avoiding Seth, which would be totally weird considering they'd only been married five minutes. Seth was looking as miserable as sin, too. Coming here hadn't been a good idea.

'Seth, about Gabe.'

'Christ, Meg, let it go, huh?' He flipped the kettle on. 'Tea?'

Let what go? Why wouldn't he tell her? Had they been so insulting about her? Megan stared round the messy kitchen. 'Do you have cola? I'll just go...' She started towards the downstairs loo, but Seth shook his head.

'That's full of sound equipment. Go upstairs.'

He turned back to the kitchen, and now he was walking in the same way Sonya had, all stooped, the weight of the world on his shoulders. Because of Laura? Megan stopped Fred following her, and went upstairs. Yuck, you could tell Laura was away by the state of the bathroom. Megan used the loo and washed her hands, and was heading back across the landing when a glint on the floor caught her eye. Something was lying under the little table at the top of the stairs, pretty much the same colour as the blue carpet but illuminated now by a stray blink of sun from the landing window. She bent to lift it – a green and blue badge, a metal one with 'ROADBLOCK' in a kind of petrol blue across a darker background. For long seconds, she stood there staring at it, tears burning in her eyes.

This was Gabe's, the badge he had pinned to his denim jacket. Gabe was a huge Roadblock fan; in fact, his biggest ambition was – had been – to see the group live. And this was definitely his badge, because it had the same little scratch across the first 'O' from the time he'd fallen off his skateboard on the way to the park last spring.

Megan sat back on her heels. How weird was this? What was Gabe's badge doing under Seth's landing table? Her mind whirled. Gabe had never been with her to Seth's place, had he? Or... The memory of that Saturday afternoon when she'd biked up here and found Gabe hanging around waiting for her flashed into Megan's head. Had Gabe been on his way out, that day? He could have gone to see if she was there yet. The front door was often unlocked, and she'd gone straight round the back when she arrived, so she hadn't tried it. Had Gabe been inside and come up here to leave a note in her room, or something? But surely not; it would be the most monumental cheek, with Seth snoring in the living room and Laura faffing around in her bathrobe getting ready to go out. But how else could the badge have got here? Maybe he'd come upstairs, then realised Laura was here and scarpered again to wait outside. That was possible. But it was still a bit rich, even for Gabe. Oh God. Something was off here.

Megan stood up slowly, the badge in her hand, then she slid it into her pocket and ran downstairs.

Seth was standing at the breakfast bar, two glasses of cola in front of him. Megan perched on a stool and sipped. 'We had a memorial for Gabe this afternoon. Have you remembered anything more about that afternoon?'

His face went brick red, then white. 'I spoke to the kid for thirty seconds, Meg, and told him no girl was worth breaking his heart over. Stop making it sound like you think I had anything to do with what happened to him.'

Megan pushed her glass away. 'No one knows what happened to him, that's the problem.' She pulled out the Road-block badge and held it up. 'Do you know how this ended up on the floor upstairs? It belonged to Gabe.' Seth stepped towards her, and she shoved the badge back into her pocket in case he snatched it.

He choked violently, then grabbed a piece of kitchen paper.

A car crunched up the driveway outside. Was Holly back already? Bad news for the deer if she was. Megan slid off her stool and started down the room, ignoring Seth. He was—

She fell straight into darkness.

CHAPTER 35

DYLAN AND SETH: THE PANIC DAYS

DYLAN DROPPED HIS BRIEFCASE AT THE FOOT OF THE STAIRS AND went on through to the kitchen with his case. Thankfully, the house was empty. Holly would still be doing something malodorous with an animal, and Megan would be hanging around some street corner with her mates. It was more than a bit of a come down after his lovely few days in town with Laura. That was how his life was meant to be – work during the day, then home for a perfect evening with the woman he adored. Hopefully, they'd get the house in Sevenoaks and he could start the next part of the plan – freeing himself of Holly. All these wretched complications with Gabe were tiresome, though it was liberating to have got the better of Seth. That had been a long time coming.

He stuffed clothes into the washing machine and was wheeling his case back to the hallway when his phone rang. Talk of the devil…

'She's out cold, Dyl!'

Seth's voice was high-pitched and squeaky, and Dylan rolled his eyes. Drunk as usual.

'Who is?'

'Megan! I – it was only a tap, I—'

What the shit had he done? 'What do you mean, it was only a tap? You hit her?'

'She found Gabe's badge upstairs. She's on the floor. Dyl, we have to stop this! It's all going wrong.'

The connection broke. Dylan swore, but Seth was right about one thing. This had to be stopped, or the stupid sod would end up confessing everything. He abandoned his case and ran back out to the car, reconnecting to Seth as soon as he had the phone on hands-free.

'I'm coming over. What's happened to Meg? Tell me there isn't another body to get rid of.'

'Jeez, when did you get like this? She's coming round a bit, but she's still only semi-conscious. We can take her to the doctor.'

Like hell they would. 'Nearly with you.'

He ran straight in at Seth's. His brother was kneeling on the kitchen floor beside Megan, whose eyelids were fluttering. Dylan reached out and felt her pulse. Fast, but strong and regular. He slapped her cheeks, and she made a little 'ha?' sound. She'd live. Dylan pulled her into the recovery position and shoved Seth out to the hall.

'Fucking idiot you are. What was that about Gabe's badge?'

Seth reached into his pocket. 'Here. She found it upstairs. He must have lost it when you…' He swallowed loudly. 'What are we going to do?'

Dylan snatched the badge and shoved it into his pocket. That was the million-dollar question, and they were going to need a bloody good answer to it. He needed time to think.

'I'll take Megan somewhere safe to recover, don't worry. Meantime, you stay here, and for Christ's sake try to get your head straight. And keep your mouth shut about this, you hear? Not a word to Holly, not to anyone.' An idea glimmered in his head, and Dylan wheeled round and went back to Megan. She had rolled on her back and was blinking up at the ceiling now. He hissed at Seth. 'Got any sleeping pills?'

'What for?'

'To make sure she has a good night's sleep, dummy, what do you think? Get them.'

Seth vanished, and returned with a white box. 'They're powders.'

'All the better.' Dylan dissolved one in a glass of water, propped Megan up and swilled most of it inside her. Hopefully that would do the trick, because they had a long drive in front of them.

He waited until she was asleep, breathing regularly, in and out, a nice little flush on her face. She'd be fine.

Dylan grinned at Seth. 'Ready to carry another body to the car?'

Seth retched, then leaned over the sink, spitting. Dylan heaved Megan up and carried her out himself. That was a risk, but no one passed the end of the driveway while he was doing it, and half a minute later she was sleeping soundly in the back of the car, covered with the tartan rug he kept there. If anyone stopped him now, he was taking his niece, who'd had a bit too much to drink, home to her mother. In a parallel universe, maybe he'd have been able to do exactly that. Tough luck, Megan.

Dylan got into the car, grinning. He waved to Seth, who was gibbering something about doctors now, and drove off. The upside was, once he'd sorted Megan, he could go straight back to Laura. Win-win.

CHAPTER 36

ADAM AND NADIA HAD THE DEER SEDATED AND X-RAYED WHEN Holly arrived at the centre, and were digging out the more superficial pellets. Holly went over to the X-ray box. Glory. About twenty pellets were scattered over this poor creature's front end, and the one at the corner of its eye had gone deep. Removing that could damage the eye permanently – was it fair to release a deer with only one eye? She turned round to find Adam glaring at her.

'I want this one saved, Holly. We'll find a place for it some-where safe, don't worry.'

He cared too much, sometimes. Holly bent over the deer's face. What a bloody mess, and its flank was no better. Most likely it had been shot at, then ran off in a panic and got entan-gled in barbed wire. She started to work on the long tear on the creature's neck, cleaning and stitching while the other two carried on with the pellet removal.

It took well over three hours, but at the end of it they had removed all the pellets visible on the X-ray, and Holly had repaired the eye socket as well as she could. It might be an idea to get Jim, the boss at the surgery, to have a look, if the animal survived the night. For now, they had done all they could. Holly helped Adam and Nadia transfer the deer to a shed, where they left it on a drip and under an infra-red lamp. It was up to nature, now.

Holly went back to the treatment room to clean her equipment and then herself; she had blood literally up to her elbows. Glamorous job, a vet's. She dried her arms, then winced as she saw the time. But Megan would have gone home by now, whether by car or by bus. Holly checked her phone, but no new messages had come in. She would call Meg in a moment – and Dylan must be back by now too. She should have texted him.

Adam joined her at the sink. 'I just hope it gets through the night.'

'Yes. I'll come back first thing, huh?'

'I'll be here.'

Holly patted his back as she passed to collect her jacket and bag. He'd be here, because he wouldn't go home, would he? He'd be sitting in front of the deer's CCTV camera all night, in case it needed help.

'Holly – I've been meaning to tell you something.'

He licked his lips, frowning, and Holly waited. He wasn't usually slow to say what he was thinking. She made a 'mmh?' sound.

He cleared his throat. 'That increased funding I mentioned before in combination with a full-time vet's job. It's definitely coming through, and as well as that, several schools have been asking about us doing talks. We could extend that into other educational and recreational areas. We're now in a position to offer you a definite full-time job here, employed by the Wildlife Centre Trust. Maybe one day, we'll make it to a wildlife hospital, not just a centre. What do you think?'

Wow. At long last, something was going right. Unexpected

tears flooded into Holly's eyes, and she blinked them back impatiently. 'I think it would be brilliant, and you know I love it here. Can we sit down together next week and go into the details?'

He grinned. 'Like how much we'd pay you, etcetera?'

Holly lifted her vet bag. 'Among other things.'

'Okay. Come and find me on Monday and we'll have a chat.'

Darkness was falling over the woods above the centre as Holly walked back to her car. Hallelujah, in fifteen minutes she'd be sitting in the garden at home, a glass of wine by her side, listening to whatever Megan wanted to talk about. Would Dylan be up for a talk? Not a deep one; that was as unlikely as rain was tonight, but any kind of chat would be an improvement on the past few weeks.

A few minutes later she was pulling up outside the house to find no Audi, and no lights in the house, either, heck. Meg was unlikely to be in bed already, so maybe Dylan had gone to fetch her from Seth's? Holly checked her phone, but there was nothing from either Dylan or Megan.

The house felt empty the moment she walked in the front door, though Dylan's briefcase was at the bottom of the stair beside his suitcase, so he'd been here at some point. Holly wandered through to the kitchen. There was a load of washing in the machine in the kitchen; Dylan must have arrived home, started to unpack, then taken a call from either Megan or Seth and gone to collect the girl? If that was the case, they'd be back soon. Holly pulled out her phone and sent a message to both Dylan and Megan: *Home again, where is everyone?* Her phone rang while she was waiting for the kettle to boil. Dylan.

'Holly, sorry. I was going to call you in a minute.'

His voice was fighting against a lot of background noise, people talking and rap music blasting out nearby.

'I've just arrived home. Meg would tell you we had an emergency at work? Where are you?'

'At a service station halfway up the M1. Megan's with me. I

nearly forgot it's Angela's birthday this weekend. We're going up to Leeds to surprise her.'

'*What?*' It was the last thing she'd expected. Holly sat still. 'And Megan's okay with that?'

'Why wouldn't she be? A weekend away from all the stress with Gabe and the police is exactly what she needs. We'll be back on Sunday night, don't worry. Though as she doesn't have school to go to, we might stay on for longer, if I can fix it with work. The poor kid's had way too much going on recently.'

That at least was true, and taking Megan away for the weekend wasn't the daftest idea. 'Fine, but can I speak to—?'

'Holly, you're breaking up, and we have to press on. Oh, we have Fred here too. Meg wouldn't leave him. Call you later, huh?'

The connection broke. How frustrating was this? Holly whacked off a quick message to Megan: *You okay with going to Angela? Call me when you've time.* She watched for a moment, but the little tick beside the message remained pale, showing Megan hadn't opened it yet. She was probably too busy looking after Fred. Or out of battery – that happened to Megan a lot.

And now she had two days me-time. Lucky her. Dylan must have remembered Angela's birthday while he was unpacking, and left as quickly as he could bundle Megan and Fred into the car. Holly poured a glass of wine and took it outside. So much for a good chat with Megan – if only she hadn't been so busy with the deer all evening. She flipped her phone open, but the messages she'd sent to Megan were still unread, so it looked like the no-battery idea was correct. Holly pursed her lips. The girl was fragile, dealing with a situation no kid that age should have to deal with. Having Megan out of reach didn't feel right.

CHAPTER 37

AFTER A NIGHT SPENT TOSSING AND TURNING, HOLLY WAS UP AT half seven and went down to an echoingly empty kitchen. Taking Fred to Angela's might not have been Dylan's best idea, but at least the dog would be there to comfort Megan if she needed it. Okay, she was due back at the wildlife centre this morning, and in the normal way, Meg would probably have come with her. Sudden longing to speak to the girl swept through Holly, and she flipped her phone open. Both messages she'd sent yesterday still had grey ticks beside them, so Megan hadn't seen them. Had she forgotten her charger? It might not be the kind of thing an eighty-something would have at home for Megan to borrow, and Dylan's wouldn't fit Meg's phone. Oh, well. Whatever had happened, Meg wouldn't tolerate being phone-free for long. She'd be in touch soon. Holly ate a solitary breakfast, then gathered her things together. She had a job to go to, weekend or not.

She drove up the track to the wildlife centre, mentally planning her morning's work – last night's deer first, of course, then a round of the sheds, then there was the cast on a badger's leg to remove. If the bone had mended, no problem. If not, it was bad news for the badger.

Adam was in the treatment room with Nadia and one of the older volunteers. He glanced up when Holly went in. 'How's Megan?'

'Okay, I think. She's gone to visit her great-aunt for a couple of days.'

'That's nice. A change of scenery after all she's been through will do her good.'

Holly headed for the sheds to check the deer. The bad stuff wasn't over for Megan. The public information about Gabe's death hadn't been added to, but the inquest was still to come, and there'd be a funeral to get through too. Megan would need strength and help for all of these.

The next few hours passed uneventfully, and Holly's conviction that working here full time was what she wanted grew stronger. It was all just so satisfying. Last night's deer was still sedated, fever-free and breathing well, and the badger's leg had healed beautifully. He'd be kept in the centre's own badger sett for another week or so, then he could go back to the wild. Another deer and a heron were well enough to be released, so Adam and the team would do that later today. And the ferret someone in Market Basing had brought in this morning after finding it in their garden shed was a joy, a lovely tame bundle of fun. He must have been a pet, and if no owner claimed him Holly could see the centre staff would be fighting to give him a new home. Megs would have loved him.

Holly washed her hands, then opened her phone to send a photo of the ferret to Megan. The messages were still grey-ticked, but Meg would need time to wish Angela happy birthday, go to buy a charger and revive her phone. She sent the photo and another message, hoping they were all having a good time and sending love to the birthday girl. Angela's number wasn't in her phone, but she'd call at home after work and pass on her good wishes in person – and have a word with Megan, too, if there was still no word from the girl.

Holly wrote up her treatment notes then drove home at twelve, the rest of the day stretching in front of her, waiting to be filled. Shopping trip down to Brighton? Nah, she wasn't in the mood, but she could see if John and Ella next door would like to go for a pub lunch. She pulled up in the carport and flipped her phone open to text Ella. Heck, those ticks by Megan's name were still grey, and this was beginning to feel wrong. She should catch up with her family before she did anything else. Holly jabbed her phone to connect to Dylan's as she went inside, worry squirming inside her. And what did you know; it went to voicemail.

Pub lunch forgotten, Holly went through to the living room and plumped down on the armchair beside the landline. Thank goodness they had one, but even nowadays it was important for a vet to be reachable by landline phone as well as mobile. She lifted the receiver and pressed to enter the address book, the nagging feeling that something wasn't right increasing tenfold when she saw that Angela's number wasn't there. Holly tapped in and out of the phone's address book, looking under A for Angela then D for Davies, in case the number was listed under Angela's surname. Nothing. Surely it had been here? It couldn't be under Uncle Mick's name; he'd died fifteen years ago, well before Holly had met Dylan and before this phone had been set up, too. She checked M anyway, but of course he wasn't there.

Holly took a deep breath. She was being irrational. This need to touch base with Megan, it wasn't logical, but with the memorial and all the uncertainty about Gabe's death… She whirled round and grabbed her car key again. The one place she would definitely find Angela's number was Elaine's landline phone. And as she'd be passing Seth's place on the way, she could call in there and see what was happening with him. He'd have the number too, actually. Or was he at Aunt Angela's birthday bash too? Holly's steps slowed as she walked across the driveway to her Corsa. Come to think of it, why hadn't Dylan included her in the invitation? It was the weekend; she could have arranged cover at work. Oh God, more uncertainty. The bad feeling was getting darker. Go, Holly.

Linton Keynes was bathed in glorious summer sunshine when she arrived. Everyone and their dogs were driving up and down the main street, or criss-crossing the road, holding up the traffic. Holly's fingers tapped on the wheel as she waited for the ninetieth person to nip across the zebra crossing. She was halfway along the High Street when her phone rang, and oh, thank God – it was Dylan. She swung into a space outside the library to take the call. Keep calm, Holly.

'Hi Holly, just to let you know we're staying on for a day or two.' He sounded pretty bushy-tailed.

'Oh. I'm not getting through to Megan, Dylan, and I'm worried about her. I want to speak to her, please.'

'She's fine, Holly, why wouldn't she be? She's lost her phone, that's all. She thinks it must have been when she was getting back into the car when we stopped for petrol yesterday. Chances are someone's driven over it by this time, so I've given her money for a new one. She and Angela are out shopping for it now. I'll get her to call you when she's all set up again.'

Aunt Angela helping Megan buy a new phone was a startling picture. Holly bit her lip. She wouldn't be happy until she heard Meg's voice in her ear, and by the sound of things, that wouldn't happen for another hour at least.

'Make sure she does.' But she would, of course she would. 'I tried to call you at Angela's earlier, but I can't find the number. Do you—?'

'Holly? Are you still there? Hallo?'

The call disconnected.

Holly punched her thigh. Call it neurotic, but it was beginning to feel as if he didn't want her talking to his niece. She put the car back into gear, and swung round the corner of Ash Lane and into the driveway to park beside Seth's van.

The front door and the back of the van were wide open, and Holly looked into the van. A rucksack was sitting on top of a box of some kind of electric equipment. She arrived at the front door to see Seth coming downstairs, another box under one arm. She stepped back. He looked ghastly, his face so pale it had a greenish-yellow sheen about it, as if he was jaundiced. He was sweating, too; his hairline was damp. Red, sunken eyes completed the horror picture.

'Seth, for God's sake, what's wrong? Do you need a doctor?'

'No. I need my wife. I'm on my way out, Holly. Did you want something?' He thrust the box into the back of the van and banged the doors shut.

Holly put a hand on his arm. He looked like he should be in bed. 'Aunt Angela's phone number, but Seth – where are you going? Are you fit to drive? Because you don't look it.'

'Laura's in London. I have to talk to her.' He shook her hand off and opened the driver's door.

Holly tried again. 'Have you seen a doctor?'

'Holly, it's not a doctor I need. I'm worried about Laura, that's all. I didn't sleep well.'

If he'd slept at all. But short of wrestling the car key from his hand and kidnapping him to take to the doc, there was nothing she could do to stop him. Holly stood in the driveway as he reversed in a circle then sped off down Ash Lane. Jeez, he hadn't even shut the front door, but that was to her advantage now. She could go in and see if Aunt Angela's number was in the phone here – if he had a landline, which wasn't a given. A quick round of the living area and kitchen convinced her he didn't. Worry about Megan surfaced again, and Holly returned to her car and Saturday morning traffic in a small English village. Elaine's home, with Angela's number, here she comes.

CHAPTER 38

SATURDAY, 3RD JULY

SOMETHING WAS WRONG. HER HEAD WAS POUNDING, AND wherever she was it was dark, pitch black. Megan struggled to clear her head, but everything was foggy… and it was cold here, so cold. She was having a nightmare; she must be. Go back to sleep, Meg. Things will be fine in the morning.

Dark, disturbing images of something she couldn't make out accompanied her in sleep, but when she woke again, it was daylight; she knew that while her eyes were still closed. Megan rolled onto her side and touched one hand to her face – her fingers were freezing and her head was still throbbing like it never had before. Was she ill? And where was her duvet?

She rubbed sticky eyes and forced them open, and slowly the blurriness cleared and she could look around her. What the…? She was on a single bed in a small, narrow room with a pine chest of drawers on the wall opposite the bed and a chair in the corner by the window, where a band of broad daylight was slashing through thick black curtains. Instead of a duvet she had one of those blankets made from knitted squares, and where the hell was this? She'd been – oh God, she'd been at Grandma's, yes, with Holly, and then she'd been at Seth's, but it was all swimmy and hazy in her head; she couldn't think straight. She needed a drink and she needed a loo, and pronto.

The room swayed as she lurched up to sit on the edge of the bed. Megan prodded tentatively around her scalp. She had a sore lump on the back of her head, and blimey, she was still dressed in her jeans and sweatshirt from – was it yesterday? What was going on? This was all wrong. Was Seth here too?

Her head swam, but a few deep breaths helped clear the dizziness, then she pulled herself up and staggered across the room to open the curtains properly. Sunlight flooded in, blinding her, and she turned and stared around the room. Her shoulder bag was nowhere to be seen, and nor was her jacket. Where the hell was this? She forced her legs to the door and opened it. A dim passageway stretched away from the room. A hotel?

'Seth?' One hand touching the wall for support, Megan stumbled on to the next door, which was half open. Another bedroom, with a bed that hadn't been slept in. A third door opened into a bathroom, and she went in. It was tiny, with a roll-top bath and an ancient toilet and basin. Everything was old-fashioned, but clean. She stood at the basin, and – oh no. Something shiny and – she touched her face – almost sticky was streaked down her chin from the corner of her mouth. Had she been dribbling? Or – *no*. Had someone given her something? Something to make her sleep? Or drugs? Arriving at Seth's was the last thing she remembered; she'd gone up to the bathroom there too, hadn't she? She hadn't been ill then. Seth must know what happened after that, though the silence all around was screaming at her that wherever this was, she was alone. It looked like some kind of holiday accommodation, but that couldn't be. She needed her bag and her phone.

Megan used the loo, splashed her face and drank some water,

but the boom-boom in her head was nauseating. She opened the bathroom cabinet – hallelujah, a packet of paracetamol. This was definitely a two-pill headache, so she pressed out a couple and swallowed them with another swig of water. That would help her aching ribs, too. Okay. Now to find out where she was.

The end of the passageway vanished round to the right, and she headed towards whatever it led to. The narrow passage turned the corner and widened out into a room, and *bloody* hell.

She stood still, gaping into a bright and airy open-plan kitchen-living area with a picture window at the far end. A picture window overlooking the sea. Jeez…

Walking slowly because this was just so weird, Megan crossed the room to the window and gazed out. It was a beautiful view, fifty yards or so of grass, then a gap that told her the land dropped away there before the deep blue sea beyond stretched into a hazy horizon. The sky above was pale blue with cotton wool clouds chasing in front of the wind – look, seagulls in flight and everything. Wherever this was, it wasn't Linton Keynes and it wasn't Market Basing either. Somewhere near Brighton?

She trailed back up the room, and oh, joy, her bag was on a chair at the kitchen end. She broke into a head-splitting jog across the room and rummaged for her phone. It wasn't in the section she usually stuffed it into, but she often did miss the pocket and the phone would end up floating around with the hundred and fifty other things in here. Megan gaped into the bag, then upturned it onto the table and scrabbled in the heap that landed there. No phone. She slapped frantically on all her pockets, then rushed back to the bedroom and hunted around the bed. Nothing. Her phone wasn't here. Megan sank down on the chair and buried her aching head in both hands.

Without her phone, she had no way to call Holly, or anyone else, for help. Panic rose, and Megan sat frozen, fighting to breath calmly. Okay. Think. Was there a landline? She went round the living area examining the walls for a phone socket, but phones were as scarce here as other human beings. But now she knew what, if not exactly where, this place was. Those pictures on the wall – unless she was way out here, Laura's brother had painted them. And – she opened the last door on the far side of the living area. An artist's studio. According to Laura, he – Chris – had a cottage on the east coast. But there was a lot of east coast, and without a phone she was pretty stuck. Seth must have brought her here – but *why*? Maybe there were neighbours she could ask for help? And oh, hell, no. Megan grabbed the back of a chair to steady herself. How could she have forgotten Fred? He'd been at Seth's with her. Was he here too? She barged round the cottage, going into every room and every cupboard, but wherever Fred was, he wasn't here. Unless he was outside.

Megan hurried out, but no amount of calling and whistling – which went right through her head – brought Fred running up. Seth must have left him at home. She stood outside the cottage, the sea breeze ruffling through her hair, then walked all the way round the building in a fruitless search for a neighbouring house, even a distant one. If isolation and peace had been what Laura's brother was after, he'd hit the jackpot here, because the only thing as far as you could see in every direction was nature. There wasn't even a barn or a shed in the distance. A low cliff meandered along the coastline behind the cottage, though it was still too high to scramble down, and grassland and meadows on the other side led to distant woods and hills. Like really distant, miles and miles away. What was she supposed to do now?

Megan went back inside and searched every corner of the cottage for a way to contact a person, but apart from a boiler, which she switched on because the water in both taps was stone cold, there was nothing technological here, not even a radio. All she could do was wait. What the hell was Seth playing at?

A hunt through the kitchen cupboards provided her with a

jar of instant coffee, a packet of peppermint tea bags, and a selection of tins and packets. Megan made tea, then drifted around the living area with her mug, looking at Laura's brother's paintings and knick-knacks. He collected shells, which were lovely, and birds' nests and things, which were spooky. His paintings were incredible, seascapes in muted colours that merged to form pictures that were almost alive, not so much photo-type images as illustrations. The guy had talent, but this wasn't helping her. She sat down at the table to think.

What happened yesterday? Her headache was abating, but it was still hard to gather her thoughts sensibly. She'd gone to Seth's, yes, she'd gone upstairs, then…

Cold clarity swept through Megan. Then she'd found Gabe's badge under the table on Seth's landing, that was what happened then. Holy *shit*. She crammed her hands into her pockets, but the badge wasn't there, and it wasn't in her bag, either. She'd taken it downstairs to ask Seth, but what happened after that was fuzzy, and next thing she remembered was waking up here. And by the look of things, she had a choice now of waiting for Seth to return, or going to look for help. What time was it? The sea would be to the east, but the sun was on the other side of the cottage. Why didn't she know more about stuff like this? It felt more like afternoon. Megan sipped glumly. Peppermint tea was disgusting, but it was hot and that alone was comforting.

She went back to the window and stood there, trying to stay calm. The view was breathtaking, definitely what you'd imagine an artist would like in the place he came to for inspiration, but the feeling that something was very wrong was growing by the minute.

Seth. He'd left her here without as much as a note to say when he'd be back. She had a bump on her head, practically no food and a headache like a steam train thundering through a tunnel. Had he clunked her one? And *why*, for God's sake? Or had he given her some drug in a drink – or both? No, no. Why couldn't she remember? Panic swelled anew, and Megan clutched her head, forcing herself not to hyperventilate.

Okay. The only certain thing was that she felt totally Godawful. And she wasn't going to get away from here today; that was certain too. The best thing she could do was open a tin of something, take another paracetamol and try to sleep this headache away.

––––––

HOLLY LET herself into Elaine's house, went through to the living room and sank into Elaine's big squishy armchair. Still nothing from Megan. Her legs were aching; funny how tired worry made you. Oh Megs, please phone. Was she having problems setting up her new phone? Holly tried Dylan's number again, but no luck. Right. Elaine's landline phone. The handset was lying on the shelf beside the chair, but the battery was right down and the phone was dead. Holly shook it, but it needed to charge before it did anything else, and she clunked it down on the base station. Dear God, could nothing go right today? This was like one of those nightmares where you had to do something urgently, but never quite managed to and woke up in a cold sweat.

Anxiety pulling at her gut, Holly's gaze wandered along the shelf on her right, and landed on Elaine's address book. Oh, thank you, fate. She was sorted. Elaine would have her sister's details in here. The book was ancient and disintegrating; it obviously spanned a large chunk of Elaine's life, and odds were, Angela would have moved house a couple of times.

Holly lifted the book and leafed through it. How sad this was, an old lady's contacts over the years; all those names, a depressingly large number scored out. Had they moved house, or died? Elaine had added birthdays for some of these people, and dates of death, too. Holly turned a few pages and found Angela's name and address, and – oh no. God, no.

She dropped the address book onto her lap and buried her face in both hands. It was definitely Aunt Angela's name on the page, in Leeds, the third address in the book for her, and her date of birth was there too, printed in black ink. Holly gripped the book again with shaking hands.

Angela had been born in November. November the ninth, to be exact. Whatever Dylan and Megan were doing today, they weren't taking Angela out for her birthday. Oh. My. God.

This was far, far worse than anything she'd ever imagined. She couldn't believe anything Dylan had told her about the past few days. He could be anywhere, and so could Megan.

CHAPTER 39

GREY AND PINK DAWN WAS TINTING THE SKY WHEN SHE WOKE again, and Megan sat up cautiously. Good, her head was almost better. But she was still alone in this place, with no idea what had happened to her. She went to try the hot water; it was luke-warm, and a wash made her feel better, even with no clean clothes to put on. There was a deodorant in the bathroom, so she used that, and did her best with her face from her make up bag. Funny how stuff like that made you feel stronger. Breakfast was a mug of disgusting instant coffee without milk, and she opened a packet of biscuits from the cupboard and sat down to think. Her head was a lot clearer today. She would do this.

No Seth. So he'd left her here deliberately; he must have. Why? Because she'd found the badge? Megan pressed her hands to her cheeks. Why had Gabe been upstairs in Seth's house? That was what needed clearing up. And Gabe was dead, but Seth couldn't have anything to do with that, could he? Oh God, this was getting scary. She had to get in touch with poor Holly, who didn't have a clue where she was and was going to be worried sick. Megan took a deep, steadying breath. She had to act as if no one was going to help her. She would have a look around here and see if she could find a map, and when the sun was properly up, she would go and find help.

That was one thing. A much less palatable thought and another reason to leave ASAP was that Seth meant to come back here and harm her in some way. They were pretty close to a cliff, but again, why would he do that? He was her uncle and okay, they didn't always see eye to eye, but what family did? He couldn't have left her here because of anything to do with her, unless he was after her money, which was just so ridiculous she wasn't even going to think about it. Seth didn't do money; that was Dylan. So, she was back to the thought that Seth had something to do with Gabe's death. Megan took her mug to the sink, pushing the picture of Seth talking to Gabe at the end of the driveway to the back of her mind. None of it made sense. She'd seen them leave that day, and Stu had seen Gabe later in the afternoon, too.

A search of the cottage did turn up a map of the east coast, but as she didn't know where the cottage was likely to be, the map was no help after all. She could be anywhere north of Dover. Megan folded it up and put it in her bag anyway; she might find a signpost or road sign and be able to work out where she was. She packed the biscuits, too, and rootled around until she found an empty plastic bottle, and filled it with water. A bar of chocolate from the cupboard went into her bag too, and one of those see-through waterproof cape things you got at rock festivals. Seth... Megan's stomach lurched. The sooner she was out of this place, the sooner she'd be safe.

She made a note of what she'd taken on the pad in the kitchen, and left a tenner beside it. She didn't want to steal from Laura's brother. Okay. Go, Megan.

The sun was emerging from the sea as she left the cottage, and she stood gazing eastwards. This was a lovely place, but the wind would be against her all the way along that track. At least it wasn't raining.

Determinedly positive, she slung her bag over her head and pushed one arm through the strap. That was better, she didn't need to hold it now. Please let there be a village close by, please let her find someone who could help her. Where were all the policemen when you needed them?

The track was exactly that, a track. A dirt road. But Seth must have brought her here by car, so it would lead back into civilisation eventually. On, and on. She should have taken another paracetamol; her head was still aching and so were her ribs. Megan strode along breathing as deeply as she could. This was sea air; it would do her good. The countryside was pretty wild here, scrubby bushes and winding little pathways just begging to be explored. Surely she couldn't be far away from somewhere, not in Kent? Megan thought back to the map. This might not be Kent, she could be further north, on the Isle of Sheppey, for instance. That was much less populated, wasn't it? But no matter where it was, the way out was along this track, and that was where she was going.

HOLLY WAS UP BEFORE SIX, after a night spent mostly lying awake and worrying. What the hell did Dylan think he was doing? He'd lied to her face, gone off with Megan and wasn't letting her speak to the girl, who was having a really tough time. Okay, she and Dylan were having what you could comfortably call a rough patch in their marriage, but his behaviour was incomprehensible – and what she was going to do about it was still a mystery. She'd wondered about the police last night, but what would they say if she went there and told them her husband had taken his niece away for a day or two and lied about what they were doing? Oh, and their marriage was going tits up... It wasn't as if he'd abducted a small child. Megan wasn't stupid and she had a mouth on her; she wouldn't have gone with Dylan if she hadn't wanted to, and if she'd needed to get in touch, she'd have found a way even without her phone. So going to the police was a duff idea, but a careful call to Angela might be a good one. Just in case.

Holly grabbed her phone from the worktop where it was charging, then put it down again. She couldn't possibly phone Angela at twenty past six on Sunday morning. What she could do was try to think where Dylan and Meg could have gone. She wasn't at the stage of trying to break into his email account, but it wasn't impossible she'd find a clue lying around his things, was it? In the study, for instance. Hard to think what, but in the absence of a better idea, it was worth a look. And then she'd break into his email.

She made a coffee and toast and took them upstairs with her. The study was a box room and contained nothing more than a single bed and two small desks, one for each of them, though she rarely used hers. Dylan's was covered in neat piles of papers and notes; he was one of those people who worked with everything spread around him. Holly lifted a few papers, but they were all about work or the house. Dylan had been telling the truth about his work pressure, anyway. This all looked horrendously complicated; pages of print-outs with scribbled notes running up and down the margins. She lifted them carefully in piles to put back the way she'd found them, and deposited them on the bed while she had a sift through the non-work stuff on the desktop. Nothing came to light that would help find a destination for a spontaneous weekend trip. It had been spontaneous, hadn't it? Holly thought about this, but all she came up with was that it had been spontaneous for Megan, at least. And there was nothing helpful in here, unfortunately. The desk drawer was almost empty, and the bin held nothing but a chocolate bar wrapper and a dead pen.

She was putting the papers back where they'd been when a page with bright green notes in the margins caught her eye. That wasn't Dylan's writing, but it looked familiar. She leafed through the pile. The handwriting occurred on most pages, but more often in a less in-your-face black ink. Nearly all the notes were followed by: Lx. Roman numerals? Some technical shorthand? Holly's breath caught. Or an initial and a kiss? L for... Laura. This was – yes, it definitely was Laura's handwriting. Okay, she and Dylan had worked together pretty intensively for a week or two, so maybe signing off with your initial and a kiss wasn't too unusual, except...

Except the previous page, which was the first page of the same report, was dated in April, well before Laura had started working there. And the note in Laura's handwriting mentioned a meeting 'on Apr. 25th'. Holly's mouth went dry. This was beginning to feel like finding another bag of condoms. But... *Laura?*

Wild thoughts circled in Holly's head and she fought to make sense of them, scrabbling through more pages, finding Lx all over the place, and one page even had L with a tiny heart instead of an x. All the notes seemed work-related, but still – something was far from right here. And this was where she was going to break into his email. Just hopefully he hadn't changed his password.

He hadn't. Holly sat on the sofa with the laptop, scrolling guiltily through Dylan's inbox. Nothing from Laura... but of course most people would communicate on messenger, wouldn't they? She had another scroll through the bin folder, and was about to give up when she spotted it. One of the sub-folders in the 'business' section was named 'LL'. Laura... Love? Lovely? Loveable? Lascivious? Luscious, lusty, lithe – good God, the list was never-ending. Holly tapped, and bingo.

Darling Dyl, can't wait for the weekend... And the reply: *Six more hours. Counting the minutes...* Holly didn't read any more. There weren't many emails; the pair must have used email only when a message was impossible for some reason. White-hot anger flooded Holly's head and she sat there stupidly, sifting through the events of the past few months, the ball of lead in her middle getting heavier with every thought.

Looked at in the light of what she'd found, Dylan and Laura had fallen head over heels months ago. Okay, it happened, even to people like them. Marriages went wrong; nothing was risk-free and certain nowadays. Not everyone was upfront about it. But – and this was the unanswerable part – why had Dylan told her Laura had only started in the company a few weeks ago? Why had he kept up the pretence of a marriage? And the truly gobsmacking one – why the shit had he introduced Laura to Seth, who she'd then *married*? Holly's brain reeled. *Were* they properly married? And now Dylan had disappeared with Megan, and where was Laura? Seth seemed to think she was in London, but who knew where any of them were? There was something horribly, stinkingly wrong about all this.

Holly clattered the laptop down on the coffee table and curled up in a ball on the sofa as the implications thudded into her. Talk about being punched in the gut. All those times Dylan had been 'working late' because he'd been 'trying to sort things out' or 'the boss wanted to show me a couple of things to help me settle into the job'. Not to mention the 'meetings' he'd had after work. He'd have been out to dinner with Laura, and what she'd been showing him didn't bear thinking about. Worst of all, that weekend 'course' he'd been on a few weeks ago. He'd spent a whole bloody weekend with Laura, and fuck, she'd been sorry he wasn't at home; she'd wanted to get things sorted out between them. And all the time he'd been screwing Laura.

Holly scrambled up, ran into the downstairs loo and vomited coffee and toast into the pan.

CHAPTER 40

SUNDAY, 4TH JULY

A RUSTLE IN THE UNDERGROWTH. MEGAN JERKED AWAKE, HER back pressed uncomfortably against the trunk of the tree she was sheltering under. Having a sit down for a drink and some biscuits had seemed like a good idea after she'd walked for hours and was still in the middle of nowhere with the dawning realisation that a) she'd have to walk the same hours in the opposite direction if she wanted to get back to the cottage, and that would the worst idea ever because b) Seth might come back. And he hadn't dumped her there for anyone's good but his own. The only way was to go on until she found civilisation and help, and falling asleep on the job was doing nothing for her chances. It must be all the painkillers she'd been swallowing recently. Now she didn't have a clue what time it was, and here in the woods you couldn't see the sun. She craned her neck to see the sky. White, even cloud cover floated above the tree tops; the blue of before was gone. She took a slug of water and fished out another biscuit. Time she wasn't here.

At least she'd found where she was on the map – or she

hoped she had, and if she was right, this path through the woods was shorter than the track that wound round them. On the other side of the wood, quite a long way along a road, was a village called Marburn. She'd never heard of it, but that was where she was going.

The rustle came again. A fox? A badger, snuffling around looking for worms? No, they came out mostly at night, didn't they? Megan thought longingly of Adam's comforting voice as he told her all about badgers. They ate earthworms and slugs and things. And even rats or mice, which was a less comforting thought. Would a rat be rustling around in the woods? If only she knew what time it was. It was dim here amongst the trees, and it was perishing. And she was dead on her feet. Oh, for her nice warm bed at Grandma's. Hot tears threatened, and Megan took a shaky breath. Face it, Meg. You'll never sleep in that bed again.

Was Holly looking for her? But she could search for a long time and never think of looking here, and this was all too much and that bloody rustling was doing her head in.

Megan hauled herself to her feet, and the rustling stopped abruptly. Good. Go, Meg. The track was indistinct and the trees too close together to let in much light, but enough was tipping through the treetops to show her where to go. Thank you, trees.

On, and on. Megan stumbled at every second step, but the trees were further apart now, so it was lighter. Please let there be enough day left to let her get to Marburn. The track bent round a denser group of older trees and – yes! Oh joy, look, look – a wooden bench at the side of the track. And a bin. She was on the way to civilisation.

Megan arrived at the bench and collapsed onto it, swinging round to lie flat. Having her feet off the ground made all the difference; it didn't matter that the bench was as hard and uninviting a bed as she'd ever lain on. She closed her eyes. Five minutes, that was all.

The sun was out again when she woke up, and she lurched upright and had a drink from her bottle. She didn't have much left, but she'd reach Marburn eventually if she just kept going. Perhaps she'd meet a dog walker, too, someone to help.

The track continued straight for several hundred yards, then came another bend and another and – yes! Two more minutes and she was standing in a car park – empty, true, but there was a proper road heading uphill past the woods and down through sunny countryside, and where there was a road, there'd be a car, if she waited long enough. Hopefully just not Seth's. She had to go on, and she had the choice of left and uphill along the road, or right and downhill. Megan consulted the map before turning right and marching on.

The road was deserted, but hope made the journey so much easier. Bright sunshine was dappling across the fields to her left, and they were proper fields here, not scrubby grassland like she'd walked over to get into the woods. And oh, wow. Megan's heart lifted as if she'd won the EuroMillions – she was coming to a bus stop. Two bus stops, even, one on either side of the road, and bus stops meant buses. Thank God she still had her purse.

The bus stops were metal posts with a yellow logo attached near the top: Eastern Buses. Only one boasted a timetable, and Megan peered at the grubby page behind scratched and foggy plastic. Okay. This must be the stop in bold print, Renton. The timetable was complicated because it was for both directions, and she was so horrendously tired she could barely read, never mind make sense of numbers. Eventually she worked out that buses ran at thirty-five minutes past every hour to Renton Woods, and at quarter to the hour to Marburn. The buses came hourly on Sundays – it was Sunday, wasn't it? All she had to do was wait. Megan plumped down on the bench beside the stop. Hopefully she wouldn't fall asleep again.

In a way it was peaceful, sitting with nothing to do, but the thoughts scrambling around her head were scary. What was Holly thinking? Where was Seth? And the biggie: why was he doing this? And what was she going to do when she got to Marburn? A movement caught her eye, and Megan leapt to her feet. A bus was coming downhill.

The driver was a young guy and he gave her a very odd look as the doors opened, but Megan was past caring. She stepped into the bus, purse in hand. 'I need to get to Market Basing. Got split up from my friends.'

His eyebrows shot up. 'You okay, love?' Megan nodded, and he jabbed at the ticket machine. 'That'll be fifteen pounds twenty. You'll get a number forty bus at Marburn market place, and change again at Tunbridge Wells.'

He was wearing a watch, and Megan squinted at it. Ten past four, earlier than she'd thought. She handed over the money and went to sit down. Unsurprisingly, she was the only passenger, and she was half asleep before they'd gone ten metres, but she was on her way home, and the horrible, dragging feeling of not being in control of her life was gone. Going back to Holly and Dylan's might not be the best idea, though – suppose Seth was there? She needed to get Holly alone. Inspiration struck as the bus meandered through countryside with fields of cows and sheep. She would go to Grandma's. There was a phone there; she could call Holly and see what was going on.

Marburn looked even smaller than Linton Keynes. Megan got off at the market place, and the driver pointed out the stop for a number forty. It was a twenty-minute wait, so Megan went into a filling station shop and bought a bar of fruit and nut chocolate and a coffee. This was better, and she could use the loo at the other side of the market place before the bus left.

There was an old-fashioned public phone booth on the other side of the toilet block, and Megan went over to it. She'd never used one of these, but how hard could it be? She lifted the receiver, staring at the machine and – she couldn't remember

Holly's number. And she didn't have time to try things out, either.

It was over an hour to Tunbridge Wells, and Megan's tired head bobbed around helplessly as they drove across yet more countryside. Every so often she'd nod right off, then jerk awake again. It was stomach-churning; she'd end up being sick if she kept on doing this. Another few squares of chocolate and the rest of her water helped, and they arrived in Tunbridge Wells with time to spare for the bus to Market Basing. Megan bought another coffee and a fresh bottle of water. The next part of the journey was better; she was travelling through places she knew. Had Seth returned to the cottage yet? Megan smiled grimly. Guess what, Uncle Seth, I'm not there. What a slimeball he was – hopefully he was mad as hell. At Market Basing, she had to run for the bus to Linton Keynes, but at least she didn't see anyone she knew, and definitely no Seth, and a short time later she was getting off at the end of Grandma's street.

Megan kept her head down as she walked past the house next door. Was there any more news about Gabe? She'd have to find out, but first she needed to get inside, sit down and organise her head, as Grandma would say. And of course, first thing of all, she should phone Holly. Thank God they hadn't finished emptying the house yet and all the things like electricity and phones were still working. Megan dropped into Grandma's chair and lifted the landline phone. Holly's mobile number was there under H.

Megan's finger hovered over the call button, then she hesitated. Seth had taken her phone, and she couldn't trust him. Suppose for a moment that he'd taken Holly's too, somehow, and was sitting waiting for someone to call? And he'd see that this call was coming from Grandma's, so if she called Holly now, Seth could be round here in minutes.

Megan replaced the receiver and sat back to have a think about that. She wasn't as safe as she'd thought.

HOLLY SAT HUNCHED over the kitchen table, her head in her hands. Nothing in her life here was real. Dylan had put more money into the house than she had. Had he been planning on chucking her out and bringing Laura to live here? Heck... But it was Laura and Seth she couldn't get her head round. Holly pushed her hair back and stood up. One thing was clear – her marriage was over, finito and dead, but right now, the important thing was Megan. Everything else could wait. Was there anything in Meg's room to show where they could have gone? Presumably she'd grabbed a few things to take with her. She should have thought of that before.

She went up to Megan's room and stood in the doorway. It looked like any other teenager's bedroom, more insipid than many, perhaps, but then Megan had only just moved in. Bits and pieces of clothing were spread around the chair and bed, and the top of the chest of drawers was covered in a collection of coins, pieces of paper, a comb, some make-up, perfume – nothing you wouldn't expect, although you'd have thought Meg might have taken some of this with her. Holly opened the top drawer. She wasn't familiar enough with Megan's underwear to work out how many pairs of knickers she'd taken with her, but there was still a largish pile in here. Oh, Meg. She pulled out a tissue to wipe her eyes, then blew her nose and went back down to the kitchen, opening the bin to dump the tissue as she passed it. Bleah, this was stinking to high heaven.

She yanked the bag from the bin and put it down on the floor to tie shut before it went into the container outside. Something shiny and pink near the top of all the gunk caught the light, and oh, no, that pink was familiar. Holly grabbed a spoon, dug around in the bag and found herself looking at a phone case, the kind that clicked onto your mobile phone and provided you with a flip cover to protect the screen. A slim pink phone case like millions of others, but unlike the rest, this one had a green wildlife centre sticker on the back. And – she grabbed it and flipped it open – not just a phone case; this was Megan's phone. *No.*

Dread seared into Holly's gut, and she moaned. She had to get out of here, out of this house and this marriage, and as soon as she knew Megan was safe, she'd do just that. Dylan had said they'd be back on Sunday night. Was it stupid to hope that for once, he'd been telling the truth? Holly stood still, barely breathing. Yes, it was. Very stupid. She would call the police right now – where was that card Sergeant Lee had given them?

Her phone rang on the coffee table, and Holly ran across the room. Dylan? No, it was Adam. For a second, she considered not taking it, but oh, how she needed to talk to a friend.

'Holly, I've just had a very odd call from Megan. She's at her grandmother's house – she says she's all right, but clearly something isn't. She asked me to get you to call her there. Do you need help?'

Holly fell to her knees on the floor, relief making her weak all over. 'You're sure she's all right?'

'She said she was. What do you want me to do?'

'I'll call her now, then I'll go there. If we need help, I'll get back to you. Thanks, Adam.'

She ended the call and connected to Elaine's landline, unexpected tears running down her face.

'Meg, are you all right? What's going on? Where have you been?'

Megan was in tears. 'I'm okay, I'm at Grandma's. Where are you? Can you come and get me?'

'I'll be with you in a few minutes. Sit tight.' Holly ran for her car key. She drove the five miles to Linton Keynes as fast as she dared, and less than fifteen minutes later she was pulling up in front of Elaine's house and Megan was opening the front door.

Tears and explanations followed. Holly examined the back of

Megan's head where she'd been knocked unconscious, but nothing was broken. Megan's headache was gone, and she was alert and showing no signs of raised intracranial pressure, so Holly covered the exhausted girl on the sofa with a rug and left her to rest while she went into the kitchen with her phone. First up, she'd better let Adam know they were all right. It would be best not to go into too much detail until she knew what was going on, but a text to say Megan was fine and she'd be in touch later would be enough for the moment. A thumbs up came in reply, then *You know where I am.* Fresh tears came into Holly's eyes. She could depend on Adam. Okay. What were they going to do now? Going to the police was still an option. Megan's story beggared belief, and what Seth had done to the poor girl should definitely be reported. And then there was Dylan and the story about Aunt Angela's birthday. He'd lied, yes, he'd betrayed them both, but that might not be a crime. And where was he?

Megan was dozing, and Holly went back to sit on Elaine's armchair, going over and over what had happened. Could she get more info from Seth? Meg was convinced he'd taken her to the cottage, but it could have been either twin. Suppose whoever it was returned to the cottage today and found Megan gone – what would he do then? He'd search round about first, then he'd go home and oh, glory, at some point he'd come here too, wouldn't he? Suppose he appeared in the middle of the night? And oh, hell, what was happening to her dog? A fresh wave of misery swept through Holly. She glanced at the carriage clock on the bookshelf, but it had stopped. Elaine was gone, her home was dying and her family was disintegrating. Holly flipped her phone open – nine o'clock. Meg needed a good night's sleep, but not here. She would take the girl to the safety of the King and Garter for the night. They could go to the police in the morning.

Holly gave the girl's shoulder a gentle shake. 'Meggie? Change of plan. First of all, we'll go back home and you can pack a few things. Then we'll go to a hotel for the night, somewhere we'll be safe. We must be missing something here. Those guys are doing all this for a reason.'

And whatever the reason was, it was nothing right and nothing legal, she would bet on that. Going to the police would be top of the list for tomorrow morning.

CHAPTER 41

MONDAY, 5TH JULY

MEGAN JERKED AWAKE. THE RADIO ALARM ON THE BEDSIDE TABLE was in her field of vision – quarter to seven. She'd slept for over eight hours straight, thanks to the peace and quiet in the King and Garter, and most especially thanks to the knowledge that Seth and Dylan didn't know where they were. A jingly noise came again – that was what had wakened her, and it was Holly's phone on the other bedside table. The en suite shower was running, so Megan lifted the phone.

It was an unknown number. Was it a good idea to answer this, or not? But she could always disconnect if it was Dylan or Seth with an earful of abuse.

She swiped to take the call. 'Hello?'

'Hi, I'm Jill Hardy. We live just outside Linton Keynes and I think we might have your dog in our garden. He has this number on his disc. He's fine, but he's quite keen to stay, though we told him a couple of times to go home!'

'Oh my – thank you! He's been lost for a couple of days and

we've been worried sick. I'll get my aunt for you. This is her phone.'

Megan thumped on the en suite door, and Holly emerged wearing a towel. Megan dived in to get dressed. At least something was going right.

They had to drive right through Linton Keynes and out the other end before arriving at Jill's home, where Fred was deliriously happy to see them. He bounded between Holly and Megan, jumping up and trying to lick their faces, tail sweeping non-stop from right to left. Jill was right, though – he'd had breakfast along with Jill's dog and he was fine, though Holly examined him from head to toe. Megan gave him a big hug and rubbed his flank the way he liked. He went mad with joy.

Jill laughed. 'Nobody gives you a welcome like a dog, do they?'

With Fred panting loudly in the back seat, they drove back through the centre of Linton Keynes.

'Let's stop at the bakery and get something sticky for breakfast,' said Holly. 'Starting the day at a hundred miles an hour on an empty stomach isn't much fun. Then we'll go to the police, and decide what to do about the hotel.'

Megan turned to pat Fred again, and caught sight of a familiar dirty white van speeding across the junction behind them, heading down a side street. 'Look! It's Seth!'

'Where?'

'He went down Maple Drive. I'm sure it was him.'

'He could be going home. Right. Let's see what he has to say for himself.'

Holly pulled the car into an abrupt U-turn right in the middle of the High Street, and Megan held on to the dashboard, her heart beating uncomfortably fast. Holly was a lot braver than she was. They swung into Maple Drive, which led to Ash Lane, and took the corner in time to see the white van vanish into the driveway at Seth's. Megan's stomach twisted. Holly was mad as hell about what had happened to her and Fred, but confronting Seth like this didn't feel safe.

Laura's car was in the driveway too, so they had to park on the street. Megan swallowed as she got out of the car. Yet again she was standing in the exact same space Gabe had been in that day, when he was talking to Seth. She grasped Fred's lead and ran after Holly, who was charging up the driveway.

They caught up with Seth as he was going in the front door.

Holly was spitting with rage. 'What the hell did you think you were doing, dumping Meg like that? I hope you have a bloody good excuse because you're going to hear a lot more about that before you're much older.'

Megan joined in. 'Did you think I'd just stay there?'

Seth gawped from her to Holly and back again, his face blotchy red on top of a weird grey-yellow colour. 'I dumped you nowhere. Now get lost. Both of you.'

He stamped up the hall and into the kitchen, Holly at his heels, though Megan hung back in the kitchen doorway with Fred. He wasn't growling, but he'd picked up that something was wrong. He stood stiffly at her side, whining and giving the floor in front of him the odd scratch.

Laura had two large removal boxes on the table and work-top, and she didn't even look up from putting a collection of mugs into one of them. Seth's eyes were practically sticking out of his head.

'What are you doing? Laura?'

'I'm taking these back to my flat.'

Holly slammed a hand down on the table, and Fred growled. Megan shortened his lead. What was coming now? Holly was red and shaking all over, but her voice was low and calm. At least it sounded calm.

'You seem to have a bit of a domestic going on, Seth, so I'll ask you another question and once I have an answer, we'll leave you to sort yourselves out. Did you, or did Dylan, abandon Megan in the middle of nowhere on Saturday?'

Dylan? He hadn't even been here on Friday night. Had he? Megan strained to remember. She'd shown Seth the Roadblock badge, and then, oh God, had a car arrived outside? Jeez. Now she knew even less about what had happened to her.

'I said I dumped her nowhere. Now get out.' Seth stumbled over to Laura and pulled her arm. 'Laura? Stop, we need those—'

'Wrong, Seth. I need those. I'm out of here.'

'Laura.' He wiped snot and tears from his face, and Megan looked away. This could not get any worse.

Holly stepped forward and put a hand on Seth's arm. 'Dylan and Laura have been having an affair for weeks, Seth. Months. I don't know what the plan is here, but you might want to consider changing any joint bank arrangements you have.'

Megan's stomach plummeted and her knees started to shake. *Dylan* and Laura? This was much worse than she'd thought. She gaped as Seth shook Holly's hand away and stood there, panting. His eyes were wild. He made a sudden lunge at Laura, screaming soundlessly and shoving her back against the worktop, one hand around her throat – no, no, this wasn't happening. Megan sobbed aloud, and Fred barked, pressing his body against her legs.

'Money? You bitch – and that fucker of a—'

A hand from behind shoved Megan's shoulder and she staggered to the side. The scene in front of her was like a horror movie. Dylan strode in and seized Seth, trying to pull him away from Laura, who was red in the face and aiming ineffective punches at Seth as he whacked her around the head and oh no...

Dylan swung away from Seth, grabbed a knife from the block on the worktop and thrust it into his brother. Seth staggered back, falling onto the table top where he hung onto the edge, panting. Megan screamed as rich crimson seeped through Seth's grubby yellow T-shirt, and now Holly was pulling Dylan away and Laura was hanging onto his other arm and Dylan was still trying to get at Seth with the knife. All you could hear was gasps and heavy breathing and feet scuffling around on the floor.

'Dyl! Stop!' Laura's face was almost as blotchy as Seth's now.

Holly looked straight into Megan's eyes. 'Get help.'

Megan fled, hauling Fred after her. Outside, she tapped her phone three times. She'd never done this before. '4 Ash Lane, Linton Keynes. There's been a stabbing. Come quickly!' She disconnected and tapped again. Voicemail, shit. 'We're at Seth's, and Dylan has stabbed him, please come.' She dropped the phone in her pocket and grasped Fred's lead firmly. She had to go back in there. Holly needed her.

————

DYLAN'S FOREHEAD dropped onto Laura's, and Holly loosened her grip of his arm. Seth was still collapsed over the table; he needed help.

Dylan was crying now. 'Laura, oh baby, are you all right?' He still had the knife gripped firmly in one hand, but he'd stopped thrashing around.

Holly shoved a chair under Seth and supported him down, then grabbed a tea towel and pressed it against his side. He was losing blood; he was barely conscious. She dug her fingers into his neck, wincing as a weak and thready pulse flickered much too quickly under her fingers. This was the worst thing she'd ever lived through. Dear God, Dylan was standing there cuddling Laura as if nothing had happened. Laura was breathing heavily and he was saying, 'shh, shh', as if stabbing Seth was something completely inconsequential. He hadn't let go of the knife, and the alien glow in his eyes now was terrifying.

Laura evidently thought so too. She cleared her throat, then whispered, 'Dyl. You don't look right. What's going on? Why did you abandon Megan?'

'She found Gabe's badge. We couldn't let her tell anyone what happened.'

As matter-of-factly as if he was talking about the price of milk. Laura's eyes skewed round to Holly, but it was Dylan she was speaking to. 'What happened, Dyl?'

Holly held her breath.

'He saw me, you know that. That's why you had to leave. Seth and I took care of him.'

Holly tried desperately to catch Laura's eye again. Dear God in heaven – what had Dylan done? For whatever reasons, Laura didn't seem to know that Gabe was dead. The other woman was looking at Dylan, her brow creased.

'You took Gabe home, right?'

Dylan was shaking his head, back and forth, slowly, a frown growing between his eyes. Now Laura did look at Holly again, and she seized her chance.

He's dead, she mouthed, as clearly as she could. *Gabe's dead*.

Laura sprang away from Dylan. '*What*? You told me you took him home!'

Dylan was still shaking his head, still frowning, and the hand holding the knife was swaying from side to side.

Holly spoke in a low voice. 'He was found in the river, Laura. Didn't you see the news reports?'

Laura clenched both hands to her chest, still backing away from Dylan. 'What the fuck have you done? I'm out of here. This was never the plan.'

'No! It was all his bloody fault!'

Dylan sprang, and out of the corner of her eye Holly saw Megan cowering in the hallway with Fred. Dylan leapt towards Seth, the knife flashing as he thrust it forward. Holly made a grab for his wrist. No, no – but Laura was there too, trying to shove Dylan away from the table. He swung round, and Holly swung with him, her fingers clamped round his arm as he struggled to get at his brother. A scream from Laura, a grunt from Dylan as he lost his balance, and Holly strained to reach the knife; it was almost in her grasp now...

Deep voices came from the front door. 'Hello? Police. Do you need help?'

Holly and Dylan and Laura whirled round, and Holly made a final grab for the knife, losing her balance. Dylan fell against her, and this time it was Megan who screamed. Laura jerked away, and Dylan dropped to the floor like a stone.

Holly stared at the man lying by her feet. Her husband. Blood was gushing from a long wound on his neck.

And she was holding the knife.

CHAPTER 42

MONDAY, 5TH JULY

MEGAN'S GUT WOULDN'T STOP CHURNING. THE POLICE HAD taken her outside as soon as they arrived, and now she was sitting in the back of a police car with Fred squashed in by her feet and a woman officer beside her. An ambulance had arrived but it was blocking her view of the house; she couldn't even see if they'd put anyone into it. Dylan and Seth were both hurt, and Holly'd had the knife at the end, so – oh God, what had happened to Dylan? They'd all been thrashing their arms around...

'Please. I have to know what's happened to my – my family.'

The woman nodded. 'We'll tell you as soon as we know, don't worry. And we'll need you to tell us exactly what you saw, love.'

'Dylan stabbed Seth, and Holly and Laura tried to stop him and then Dylan collapsed. Is Holly all right?'

'We'll know very soon. So they're not your parents? How old are you, love?'

'Sixteen. Dylan and Seth are my uncles.' Megan pulled out her wildlife worker card and handed it over. Her date of birth was there. Had Adam got her voicemail yet? Not knowing what was happening to Holly was unbearable.

The officer returned the card, then got out of the car as another officer came out of Seth's driveway and approached them. Megan strained her ears, but she couldn't hear anything and this was just – she would be sick if she had to wait here much longer. At last they came back to the car, the male officer getting in behind the wheel.

Megan closed her eyes and answered their questions about parents and living arrangements. If she cooperated now, they'd tell her more, maybe.

'Okay, Megan. Your uncles are being taken to hospital. We'll know soon how they are, and your aunts are going to the police station to make statements. We'll drive you back home to Market Basing and take a statement from you there. Is there another family member you can call to be with you afterwards?'

'I – I've left a message for a family friend. He's the boss at the wildlife centre. I'm sure he'll help. I'll try him again now.' She tapped, and oh thank you, thank you – the call went through.

'Meg – I've just – what's going on? Is Holly all right?'

Megan explained in a few sentences. Adam didn't waste time either.

'I'll join you at home in ten minutes.'

Megan sat back. Just breathe, Meg.

Adam arrived at the house while she was getting out of the police car. He hugged her, then the four of them sat round the kitchen table while she answered all the questions, Fred running in and out and obviously glad to be back, and Adam strangely silent beside her. It was hard to sort out what she'd seen, those last few moments when the police arrived, but Megan did her best. The worst thought of all was – how had Dylan been injured? They made her go over that part three times, although she couldn't say exactly what had happened with the knife. Her head was pounding by the time they stopped.

'We'll be in touch as soon as we hear anything.' The male officer, the older one, stood up.

'Shouldn't I go to the hospital? When will Holly be home?'

'You could call the hospital and ask them. We'll let you know anything further.'

Megan nodded miserably. They weren't being unkind, but they weren't telling her anything either, were they? What did that mean?

Adam found the number for her, then made tea while she phoned the hospital and was told Dylan and Seth were both in surgery and she should call back later. They sat in the kitchen and Adam listened silently while Megan poured it all out all over again, everything that happened from finding the badge at Seth's to waking up in the cottage, to falling asleep in the woods and thinking about rats and badgers, to arriving back at Grandma's. The words kept coming and coming, then she ground to a halt and sniffed.

'I think I have the worst family in the world.' Dylan had stabbed Seth. She'd been there, she'd watched as one of her uncles stabbed the other and Seth went down. She'd seen blood, too, when Dylan went down. And all she could do was tell Adam all over again and it wouldn't change a thing.

'Hang on in there, Meg.' He handed her another mug of tea.

She'd be sick if she drank any more tea. Megan warmed her hands on it instead. Fred put his head on her knee, and it was all she could do not to cry into his warm and smelly fur, and all this was doing her head in.

It was nearly one o'clock when her phone buzzed on the table. Megan nearly jumped out of her skin, then she fumbled it to her ear. This was it – Holly. Oh God, what was happening?

'Holly – are you okay?'

'Yes. Is Adam still with you? The police said he was there.'

'Yes. What happened?'

Holly's sigh trembled into Megan's ear. 'I'm coming home now, Megs. We'll talk then.'

For long minutes Megan sat with her hands pressed between her knees, fighting not to hyperventilate, and then, oh, then Holly came running in and grabbed her as if she was about six and they were both crying and Fred was trying to get as close to Holly as he possibly could.

It took a moment before they could sit down while Adam made yet more tea. Megan waited, her eyes fixed on Holly's face. You could tell it wasn't good news. Did she want to hear it? No, but she had to cope with it, so she needed to.

Holly took her hand. 'You'll need to be brave, Meggie. Seth's hurt, but he'll be okay eventually. Dylan died at the hospital. He'd lost too much blood and they couldn't save him. It was Laura who slashed him. The police were able to work that out from what they saw when they arrived and what you told them about which side of Dylan Laura and I were on while… while it was happening.' She pressed her lips together. 'She's confessed now, and they arrested her. Oh, Meg. I didn't know at first if I'd killed him or not. It was all so quick and so muddled.'

She sat there, her mouth working and her eyes closed while tears trickled down her cheeks. Megan had no tears left. What a mess it all was, and nothing would put it right.

Adam stood up. 'I'll leave you two to be together. I'll call you later, and meanwhile, you know where I am.'

Megan took him to the door, then went back to the table. Holly was sitting there taking deep breaths, but she'd stopped crying.

Megan sat down. 'What do we do now?'

Holly cleared her throat. 'I think for the moment, we have two options. One, we stay here. Two, we go and stay at your grandma's place. Your choice. It's going to be complicated and nasty, Megan, getting everything sorted, but we'll get there, you and me.'

Tears welled up in Megan's eyes. Thank everything under the sun that Holly had come into her life.

'Holly – why did you marry Dylan?'

Holly wiped her eyes with her fingers. 'Oh Meg. It wasn't like this, at first. He was fun, and sweet, and we liked the same music and shows and things. He was easy to get along with, and we fell in love. I hope it was genuine for him too. I think it was, though I'm wondering now if he ever truly felt loved.'

Megan thought back to the first time she'd met Holly, at Grandma's birthday dinner at the restaurant. They'd come a long way since then.

'Why do you think Laura married Seth?' That was even harder to understand.

Holly slumped in her chair. 'We don't know if they were properly married. It could have been some kind of alternative unofficial joining together thing – Seth would be up for that. I think Laura was after money. We'll never know whether she really loved Dylan or whether she duped him too. I guess he thought she was the love of his life.'

Megan blinked. Now it was her turn to have tears running down her face. 'Is it okay, me staying with you?' Holly wasn't a real relation, and she didn't need to make her home with her husband's niece. There was Seth... but no way was she ever going to live with Seth again.

Holly reached across and took Megan's hand, swinging it gently in the space between their chairs. When she spoke, her voice was all choked up. 'You don't get rid of me that easily, you know. We're mates, you and me. Family.'

'Mates yes, but...' More tears.

Holly passed her the kitchen roll. 'Okay, we're not blood family. We can be – un-family, that's what we'll be.'

Megan wiped her eyes. Un-family would do just fine.

EPILOGUE

TWO YEARS LATER

Holly stood in Megan's bedroom doorway, watching as Megan pulled on the black stilettos they'd shopped for that afternoon. Meg looked ridiculously grown-up in her black-and-white dress, her hair piled loosely on top of her head. But then, she was grown up now, an independent eighteen-year-old woman with a handful of online courses in digital photography under her belt, about to leave home and start the next stage of her life, a BA in photography in London. Little Meg was gone for good.

'Hope I don't get blisters.' Megan teetered across the room.

'You won't need to walk far tonight. Look, here's Adam's car. Let's go.'

Holly collected her handbag from the kitchen and consoled Fred with a large-sized chew before they left the flat, a garden apartment in a new development in Linton Keynes. The house had been sold now, and so had Elaine's. Holly shivered. That part of her life was over, but Dylan's betrayal had taken a long time to digest. She was still learning to trust again, but fortunately Adam was the most patient bloke on the planet. He'd given her time. They'd been together for four months now, and one day – soon – they'd make a home together. She closed the front door behind her, and he got out to kiss her. Holly removed a swan bag from the front seat before sitting down. Animals were right up there with them both.

Megan got into the back and buckled up. 'Is it really okay with you that Seth and Roz are coming too?'

Holly shot her a grin. 'It's your dinner party, love. 'Course it's okay. I'm glad you and Seth are finding a way forward.'

That had taken a long time too, hadn't it? The arrival of Roz back in Linton Keynes had helped, and heck, now she thought about it, this dinner party was a weird and distorted image of the one they'd had with Elaine, the first time she'd met Megan and Seth. This time, though, they had Adam as well as Hope and Susie. The girls all had boyfriends from school, but none were coming tonight. Megan's goodbye dinner was in a very posh hotel in Market Basing and being funded from her trust, which she was now in charge of, with a lot of help from Mr James at the bank.

The others had gathered in the hotel car park. Seth greeted Megan quietly, touching her arm but not kissing her, which was the way it was now. They'd get there, though. One day. Maybe. For now, Megan seemed content to have him back on the fringe of her life.

Inside, the hotel host ushered them all to a table, and Holly took her place between Adam and Susie. Megan was at the top of the table, looking every bit the grown-up heiress that she was. Wow. Holly blinked hard. Her girl.

Family was a very odd thing.

ACKNOWLEDGMENTS

I can hardly believe that *The Un-Family* is my twelfth psychological suspense novel, and my third with Hobeck Books. First thanks go to Rebecca Collins and Adrian Hobart of Hobeck for their help, support, vision and sheer hard work as we continue through another difficult year of the pandemic and economic downturn.

Editing thank yous go to Rebecca Collins and Sue Davison, who helped me structure and polish the text of this book; thanks also to my early reading team, Mandy James, Helen Pryke, Diane Warburton and Matthias Huber for their help here; also to Josh Collins for information about GCSE exams in England, to Jayne Mapp for details on becoming a photographer and to Louise Mangos for information about kayaking.

The animal sections of the book came from visits to our own vet over the years and from a host of nature programmes on television; I hope I have most of it right.

Jayne Mapp Design has provided another amazing cover image, big thanks for that too!

Home thanks and love to my sons, Matthias and Pascal Huber, for help with all the day-to-day and technical aspects of being a writer. The usual big thanks go to Pascal for website management and for his patience.

My writing friends here in Switzerland have kept me going too, thank you Alison and Louise for your support and for all those glasses of fizz.

Last but by no means least, thanks to the book groups, bloggers, other writers on social media, and above all, thank you to all those readers who have read a book, left a review or sent me a message that they've enjoyed it. I really appreciate it.

LINDA HUBER

ABOUT THE AUTHOR

Linda grew up in Glasgow, Scotland, but went to work in Switzerland for a year aged twenty-two, and she has lived there ever since. Her day jobs have included working as a physiotherapist in hospitals and schools for handicapped children, teaching English in a medieval castle, and several extremely strenuous years as a full-time mum to two boys, a dog and a rapidly expanding number of guinea pigs, most of whom have now fortunately left home. After spending large chunks of the last few years moving house, she has now settled in a beautiful flat on the banks of Lake Constance in north-east Switzerland.

Her writing career began in the nineties, when she had over fifty short stories published in women's magazines before finding the love of her writing life, psychological suspense fiction. Her first book was published in 2013 and followed by a number of others, all standalone novels set in the UK.

Linda says she finds her plot ideas in little incidents and moments in daily life – talking to a fellow wedding guest about adoptions, a Swiss documentary about fraudsters, a BBC TV programme about family trees.

For Linda it is when you start to think 'what if…', that is when the story really starts.

DARIA'S DAUGHTER

Published in 2021 by Hobeck Books.

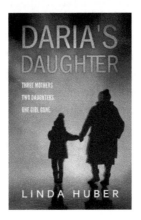

A mother and daughter torn apart
An explosive accident on the way to Glasgow airport leaves
Daria hurt, bereaved and confused. Her daughter has vanished
without a trace and nobody is telling her what happened. Evie's
gone. That's all. Gone. What does Daria have left to live for?

A mother and daughter reunited
Margie can't believe it. Bridie is hurt. Bridie needs her. They manage to escape the smoke, the noise and the confusion. They are together, that's all that matters. Everything will be better in the morning, Margie tells Bridie. And it will.

The bonds that never break
Will Daria ever be able to put the pieces of her tattered life back together after the loss of her daughter? Is it possible that things aren't quite as they seem? Can the unimaginable turn out to be the truth?

'A book I found so difficult to put down.' *****
'This gripping and emotional family drama kept me on tenterhooks from start to finish.' *****
'Brilliant, absolutely brilliant.' *****
'Kept me gripped for the entire story.' *****
'Linda Huber you are a gifted writer.' *****
'What a remarkable story.' *****
'The writing is flawless. Loved it to bits!' *****
'I was captivated from the beginning.' *****
'Can't wait for the next one!' *****

Daria's Daughter is available on Amazon as ebook or paperback.

PACT OF SILENCE

Published in 2021 by Hobeck Books.

'What an emotional rollercoaster! Darkly addictive and packed to the rafters with secrets, I was flipping those pages, desperate to see how it unravelled.'
Jane Isaac, psychological thriller author

A fresh start for a new life
Newly pregnant, Emma is startled when her husband Luke announces they're swapping homes with his parents, but the rural idyll where Luke grew up is a great place to start their family. Yet Luke's manner suggests something odd is afoot, something that Emma can't quite fathom.

Too many secrets, not enough truths
Emma works hard to settle into her new life in the Yorkshire countryside, but a chance discovery increases her suspicions. She decides to dig a little deeper…

Be careful what you uncover
Will Emma find out why the locals are behaving so oddly? Can she discover the truth behind Luke's disturbing behaviour? Will the pact of silence ever be broken?

'It's suspense with a capital 'S'.' *****
'A dark and gripping five star page turner.' *****
'A heart-in-the-mouth read – I couldn't put it down.' *****
'I stayed up all night to finish this real page turner of a novel.'
*****
'My first book by this author, but definitely won't be the last. From the first page, I was drawn in and couldn't put it down. Read it in less than a day.' *****
'I was absolutely gripped by this book..' *****
'Brilliant storytelling.' *****
'An undeniable page turner.' *****
'Her best book yet.' *****

HOBECK BOOKS – THE HOME OF GREAT STORIES

We hope you've enjoyed reading this novel by the brilliant Linda Huber. To find out more about Linda and her work please visit her website: **https://lindahuber.net**.

If you enjoyed this book, you may be interested to know that if you subscribe to Hobeck Books you can download a free novella *The Clarice Cliff Vase* by Linda, exclusive only to subscribers. There are many more short stories and novellas available for free too.

- *Echo Rock* by Robert Daws
- *Old Dogs, Old Tricks* by A B Morgan
- *The Silence of the Rabbit* by Wendy Turbin
- *Never Mind the Baubles: An Anthology of Twisted Winter Tales* by the Hobeck Team (including all the current Hobeck authors and Hobeck's two publishers)
- *Here She Lies* by Kerena Swan
- *The Macnab Principle* by R.D. Nixon
- *Fatal Beginnings* by Brian Price
- *You Can't Trust Anyone These Days* by Maureen Myant

Also please visit the Hobeck Books website for details of our other superb authors and their books, and if you would like to get in touch, we would love to hear from you.

Hobeck Books also presents a weekly podcast, the Hobcast, where founders Adrian Hobart and Rebecca Collins discuss all things book related, key issues from each week, including the ups and downs of running a creative business. Each episode includes an interview with one of the people who make Hobeck possible: the editors, the authors, the cover designers. These are the people who help Hobeck bring great stories to life. Without them, Hobeck wouldn't exist. The Hobcast can be listened to from all the usual platforms but it can also be found on the Hobeck website: **www.hobeck.net/hobcast**.

Finally, if you enjoyed this book, please also leave a review on the site you bought it from and spread the word. Reviews are hugely important to writers and they help other readers also.

ALSO BY LINDA HUBER

Published by Hobeck Books

Daria's Daughter

Pact of Silence

Published by Linda Huber

The Runaway

Stolen Sister

Death Wish

Baby Dear

Ward Zero

Chosen Child

The Attic Room

The Cold Cold Sea

The Paradise Trees

Lightning Source UK Ltd.
Milton Keynes UK
UKHW021957111022
410316UK00011B/769